JENNIFER HARLOW

MIND OVER MONSTERS

A
F.R.E.A.K.S.
SQUAD
INVESTIGATION

MIDNIGHT INK
WOODBURY, MINNESOTA

FIRST EDITION
First Printing, 2011

Book format by Bob Gaul
Cover design by Kevin R. Brown
Cover illustration by Carlos Lara Lopez
Editing by Nicole Edman

Midnight Ink, an imprint of Llewellyn Worldwide Ltd.

This is a work of fiction. Names, characters, places, and incidents are either the product of the author's imagination or are used fictitiously, and any resemblance to actual persons living or dead, business establishments, events, or locales is entirely coincidental.

Library of Congress Cataloging-in-Publication Data
Harlow, Jennifer, 1983–
  Mind over monsters : a F.R.E.A.K.S. Squad investigation / by Jennifer Harlow.
  —1st ed.
    p. cm.
  ISBN 978-0-7387-2667-0 (alk. paper)
 1. Women psychics—Fiction. 2. Occult crime investigation—Fiction. 3. Supernatural—Fiction. I. Title.
  PS3608.A7443M56 2011
  813'.6—dc22

                                    2011012687

Midnight Ink
Llewellyn Worldwide Ltd.
2143 Wooddale Drive
Woodbury, MN 55125-2989
www.midnightinkbooks.com

Printed in the United States of America

To Mom and Dad:
You told me I could do it, so I did.
Thanks.

With great power comes great responsibility.
—Stan Lee

Oh, fu … dgesicles!
—Beatrice Alexander

ACKNOWLEDGMENTS

First, thanks to my partner-in-crime Sandy Lu at the Lori Perkins Literary Agency who took a gamble on me in spite of my formally abysmal grammar skills. I hope I never let you down.

Thanks to Terri Bischoff, who also took a chance on a first-time author, and Nicole Edman, Steven Pomijie, and Courtney Colton at Midnight Ink, who helped bring my imaginary friends out to play with the world.

Thanks to my beta testers Susan Dowis, Jill Kardell, Ginny Dowis, and Theresa Friedrich for all their suggestions and hard work shaping the book. I promise to be less defensive and shouty from now on. (Yeah, right.)

Thanks to the fine people at Barnes & Noble in Charlottesville and Manassas, VA, Borders in Woodbridge, VA, and the Alberlmarle, Prince William, and Fairfax County Library systems for not kicking out the strange redhead who was there for hours scribbling away.

Thanks to Bill Fitz-Patrick for my author photos. At least I was prettier than Ronald Reagan, huh?

And last, but by no means least, to my family and friends, who never, not a single one of you, ever told me this wasn't possible. You all believed in me even when I didn't. You were right, I was wrong. There. I just made hell freeze over.

ONE

A CONVERSATION WITH
DR. GEORGE HERBERT BLACK, PH.D.

I WAS SURPRISED TO find that a man who wore a three-thousand-dollar suit was staying at the Comfort Inn. I thought for sure he'd be at the Hilton, not the hotel known as the best place in town to have a quickie. His choice in lodging does not inspire confidence.

I walk down the hall as slowly as I can. I'm good at delaying the inevitable. I'm not sure if it's the fact I have nothing in my stomach or the fact that I'm scared out of my mind that's making my legs wobble like two blobs of Jell-O. As I reach room 403, I take a deep, cleansing breath like I was taught at my one yoga class. Do I really want to do this? What if he's some crackpot waiting for me to come in so he can attack me and chop me up with a chain saw? Dang it, I should have left a note.

Dear Nana, went to meet some strange guy who came to my hospital room today and started talking about ghosts, goblins, and ghoulies. If I don't come back by morning, I'm probably floating in the Pacific being eaten by sharks. P.S. Sorry I almost killed Brian tonight.

Yeah, she'd finally throw me in the loony bin for sure.

The door swings open without warning, nearly giving me a heart attack. A small gasp escapes my throat. I'm not usually the jumpy type, but the last few days have really taken it out of me. Dr. Black, who towers a foot above my five foot four frame, is still wearing his perfectly pressed gray suit and gracious smile. That grin melts twenty years off his seventy-year-old face as his multitude of wrinkles smooth out. The shiny silver hair covering his head like a helmet accentuates his tan skin. He's painfully thin. I probably outweigh him by forty pounds. Ichabod Crane in Armani. I'm pretty sure I could take him without lifting a finger. Of course, that's exactly why I'm here in the first place.

"I was getting worried," he says.

"Sorry, I had to change my shirt." Which is code for I turned the car around half a dozen times.

He steps to the side, gesturing me to come in. His suitcase rests on a blue and white floral bedspread underneath a picture of a garden. Two double beds, a cheap dresser, cream-colored lamp shades. I've only been in hotels a handful of times and they always look the same.

"Were you surprised to hear from me?" I ask.

"Not in the least. I could tell you were intrigued. I knew that curiosity would eventually get the better of you. Just not so soon." He walks over to his suitcase and pulls out a water bottle. "Would you like something to drink? I'm afraid all I have is water."

"I'm fine." I take a seat in the chair next to the window. The view is pretty unimpressive, just cars passing on the freeway.

He walks over to the edge of the bed closest to me and sits. It barely moves under his thin frame. "So, care to tell me what happened tonight that prompted your call?"

My back goes ramrod straight. "Nothing," I say not too convincingly. "I was just curious. Don't get to meet a parapsychologist every day."

"There's no need to lie to me, Beatrice," he says. "There are no judgments here."

"Nothing happened," I say again.

"Beatrice," he chides, "I don't have to be psychic to know something is upsetting you. In the hospital earlier today you were very adamant for me to leave and then five hours later you call. Now please, tell me what happened. I might be able to help."

"I—I can't." I shake my head vigorously. "This was a bad idea. Uh. Maybe I should just go."

"Listen to me, Beatrice," he says in a sympathetic voice, "whatever it is, I can assure you I've heard much worse."

"I doubt it," I say on a quick exhale.

"You'd be surprised. Please. Nothing you say leaves this room. You came here for help. Let me *help you.*"

I look into his cauliflower eyes. Sympathy. Huh. Haven't seen that in a while. Lately it's just been *fear* everywhere, and that gets old after a while. Even in the hospital, where bleeding drunks come in ranting and raving about aliens implanting devices into their heads, *I* was the freak. A few machines dance in the air, an orderly has to be sedated, and suddenly you're Freddy freakin' Krueger.

He's right. If I want him to help, I need to tell him everything. And once I start talking, I can't stop. I confess about tonight and what I did to my brother Brian. About the first time something

3

flew across the room when I was six, knocking my mom's boyfriend unconscious. I tell him about my mother's suicide.

Finally, I tell him about Leonard.

He just sits there, occasionally nodding but saying nothing, that sympathetic expression never wavering. When I'm done, he walks into the bathroom and comes out with a box of tissues. I take two and dab my eyes.

"Thank you," I say through the sniffles.

He sets the box next to me and returns to his position on the bed, crossing his long legs. "Are you all right?"

I sniffle again. "No. I almost killed my brother tonight, just like..." I shake my head to push the image of *that man* out of my head.

"What precipitated this incident? What did your brother do?"

Just the thought of that scene starts the tears again. The whole thing comes in pieces. The fight. Brian's rage-filled words spewing out as Nana tried to calm him down. My body tightening like a coil with every syllable, while the pressure inside my head increased twofold. My palms throbbing where the nails dug into flesh. Our dining room table rattling as if a five-point earthquake had hit, plates clattering to the floor. More words. *Freak. Abomination. She hated you as much as I do. She should have killed you before you were born!*

Then, no more pressure. The table flipping mid-air off its legs, landing a few inches shy of Nana's feet. A huge crack cutting across the back wall as if an invisible knife slashed through it. Then the screaming. Agonizing. Horrible. High pitched, like a lobster thrown into a boiling pot. Brian grabbing the left side of his face, clawing at it. Two red streams of blood dripping out of each of his nostrils. The whites of his brown eyes quickly turning red from

4

burst capillaries. Then Nana. My Nana looking at me as Brian always had. Like a monster.

Two minutes later, I tried to kill myself with a bottle of aspirin.

"Do you often lose control like you did tonight?"

I blink away the images, returning to the tacky hotel. Before I can form words again, I take a few breaths to lessen the sobs. "No," I manage to get out. "I mean, not like that. It felt like something broke inside me." Dr. Black stands again, retrieving the bottle of water. This time I take it.

"That's common with psychokinetics."

"Huh? You called me that before in the hospital. I don't know…" I trail off and sip the water.

"It's more commonly known as telekinesis. You move matter with your mind. Didn't you know there was a name for it?"

"No."

"You never did any research on your gift?"

"I saw the movie *Carrie*. Well, part of it. My friend April made me watch it, but I don't like scary movies. And that was just a movie."

"True, but people like you have been chronicled through the ages. Saint Teresa of Avila levitated during deep prayer. In the first century, Simon Magnus floated to the top of a column during a duel. There are others, of course, in Russia, India, England, all over the world. However, none have lifted an entire car before. Have you ever tried to use your gift? Consciously, that is?"

"I don't know what you mean."

He stands from the bed again, picking up the box of tissues. He sets it down on the desk a few feet away from me. "I want you to pick up this box and have it glide onto your lap. Can you do that?"

5

"I—I can try." I look at the box, concentrating on it, letting its image fill my mind. Okay . . . *lift!* It doesn't move. *Lift!* Still nothing. I squint until I barely see the box. *Lift, for God's sake!* Nada. "I can't do it. Sorry."

Dr. Black nods. "It's okay. You've never really directed your gift before, only when your survival depended on it. Can I assume it works unconsciously?"

"Yeah." I sip the water. "Um, sometimes I turn around and see cabinets opening by themselves. My bed floats some nights too. It's really put a damper on my social life," I say with a quiet scoff. "How can I have people over when my plates dance in the air?"

"Who else knows about your gift?"

"Just Nana, Brian, and my best friend April. I couldn't let anyone else know in case they decided to chase me out of town with torches and pitchforks or something."

"How lonely you must feel," Dr. Black says.

"Yeah," I whisper, willing the tears away. I've cried enough over loneliness for twelve lifetimes. "But I suppose the whole of America knows now after what happened with the car."

The car. Geez. Was that only three days ago?

I was about to get into my car after a long day at school, looking forward to reading the latest Jennifer Crusie book while watching the Doris Day marathon on Turner Classic Movies when I saw him. Randy Dodson, one of my students, playing that gangster video game I had confiscated two weeks before, walking oblivious to the world. Without glancing either way, he stepped into the street, fingers still jumping on the buttons. At the same time, a shiny black Hummer—a monstrosity every man and soccer mom seems to be driving in San Diego—rounded the corner like a demon chased by the Devil himself. The moment the behemoth came into view, I knew without a doubt that the car wouldn't stop. I knew it. I was about to watch the boy I helped with fractions earlier get splattered on the street. Instinct took control of my body. I moved faster than I thought myself capable of. As the car zoomed closer, Randy glanced up from his game. He couldn't move. Neither of us had time to jump.

There but for the grace of God, I reached him before that tank did, pushing him to the ground and shielding his small, trembling body with mine. In that same instant, I stared at the car, filling my mind with it. Its shape. Its wheels. Its weight.

LIFT!

It soared off the ground, flying over our heads with the wheels spinning midair, inches from us. The engine roared, almost shattering my eardrums while the exhaust burned my already tender eyes, and hot blood ran out of my nose and ears. My head felt as if it was underneath the tire, the pressure and pain so great I couldn't even scream. The two-ton vehicle landed with a crash a few feet beyond us, sparks shooting everywhere as metal hit concrete. That was the last thing I saw before passing out: the Fourth of July in March.

I woke up three days later in the hospital to floating machines, a blinding headache, and a well-dressed parapsychologist sitting by my bed, business card in hand, offering to help me.

It's been a heck of a week.

"I wouldn't worry about that," Dr. Black says. "It will be chalked up to simple physics in the end. The world relies on Occam's Razor: the simplest explanation is often the right one. Which would you believe, that the car hit an incline or that a school teacher lifted it with her mind?"

"I guess."

"You would be surprised how deeply the public's deniability of things they don't understand runs. We rely quite heavily on it."

" 'We'?"

"The people I work for."

"And who do you work for? Let me guess, the government," I say mock seriously.

"Yes, of course."

The image of me tied up to a bed being poked and prodded with sharp metal instruments in the name of science dances into my head. I stand quickly. "I have to—"

He stands as well. "Oh, no. Don't be afraid," he chuckles. "I haven't come to cart you off to some lab never to be seen again. I'm afraid television and films have given us a bad reputation."

"Us? Who's 'us'?"

"Technically, we're an offshoot of the FBI. A highly classified one, naturally, but we have several trained official agents on our team. When we're in the field, we carry FBI badges as part of our cover, but their rules and regulations don't really apply to us." He begins to chuckle, "If they did, I'm afraid we couldn't get anything done. But we also work with the military if the need arises."

"The need for what?"

"Our help."

That sends a shiver down my spine. They handle what the military can't? Not a glowing endorsement for *my* involvement.

"Please sit down, Beatrice," Dr. Black says with a smile. "We have a lot more to discuss."

Despite my apprehension, I sit. I've always been too darn curious for my own good.

Dr. Black sits back on the bed across from me. "Now, you've trusted me tonight, and I know how hard that was for you, but I'm going to ask you to trust me once more. Because what I am about to tell you may be a bit shocking and hard to believe, but it's all true. I ask that you keep an open mind. Can you do that?"

I nod.

"Good," he says. "You are not as different and alone as you might believe. There are possibly hundreds of people with psychic gifts in this country alone. These gifts manifest themselves in different ways. Some can read minds; others can see spirits and communicate with them. It's different for everybody. Moreover, there are others who can do extraordinary things, like transform into animals or walk through solid matter. Basically, every manner of creature you thought only existed in fairy tales and films does, in fact, exist. Trolls, werewolves, witches, vampires, all of them. And sometimes—not often though—these creatures harm others. That's when we come in. The creature responsible has an edge over humans, often preternatural strength or even immortality. We simply ... even things out a bit. Are you with me so far?"

"Yeah," I say, "Dracula and the wolf man are alive and kicking. Do they share an apartment with Elvis?"

All humor fades from his face. "I'm being serious, Beatrice."

I scoff. "Well, forgive me, but I have a hard time believing that there are vampires and werewolves and whatnot walking around and nobody's found out."

"Says a woman who can move things with her mind."

I shrug. "Still."

"If a werewolf attacks a human, it usually gets written up as a wild animal attack, which is exactly what it is. Vampires work hard to hide their existence, just as you do. Most don't even need to kill to feed. But you'll learn all about this more intensively during your training. Now—"

"What? My what?"

"Training. There's a flight leaving for Virginia tonight."

My eyes bug out of my head and my jaw drops. "Wait. You told me in the hospital you'd help me get this thing under control, you didn't mention *anything* about becoming Buffy the Vampire Slayer." I jump out of the chair. "Uh-uh. No. I don't even like killing bugs! After I saw *Dracula*, I had to sleep with the lights on for a week! You've so got the wrong girl."

"You ran into traffic and single-handedly saved that boy. You are definitely the right woman."

"Anybody would have done that."

"No. They wouldn't." Dr. Black stands from the bed again, taking a step toward me. "I do want to help you. We have scientists and military personnel who will train you to use your gift. And you'll have a chance to be with others like you. As of right now, there are six members of the F.R.E.A.K.S. Squad, all with—"

"The what?"

"Federal Response to Extra-sensory And Kindred Supernaturals. F.R.E.A.K.S."

"I am *not* a freak," I say, voice deceptively quiet.

He smiles. "Well, not yet, no."

"Look," I say with a glare, "I appreciate you listening to me and not, like, tying me to a stake to burn, but ... " I shake my head. "I teach fourth grade. The worst thing that could happen to me is I get glue in my eye. I think I'd like to keep it that way." I bend down and pick up my purse. "And I sure as heck don't want to be called a freak anymore than I already have. It was nice meeting you." I step past the frowning man toward the door. "Good luck with the trolls or whatever."

"Beatrice," he says as I pass, "do you honestly believe it's that easy? To go back to the way things were?"

I stop at the door. "What do you mean?"

"You said it yourself—something has broken inside of you. To be frank, I'm fairly sure it has. I've seen it before. The part of yourself you've worked your entire life to contain is out of your control now. What happened with your brother tonight, I'm afraid, may become a daily occurrence unless you learn to harness your power. I fear that you will be unable to resume your position at the school. What if a child or parent brings about your anger? You could kill them."

He might as well have punched me in the stomach. His words knock what little breath I have out of me. Because he's right. Lord knows the kids do tend to infuriate me on an hourly basis. Some days it takes all my strength not to scream at them for talking back or disrupting class or just behaving like a bunch of unruly nine year olds. Not to mention the parents! One time during a particularly intense parent/teacher conference, I noticed the bookcase in the back of the room floating a foot in the air. I counted to ten and it dropped. Next time I could lose it and brain an irritating parent with a desk. Or worse.

No. I feel like slumping to the floor in a heap. I love teaching. I've always wanted to be a teacher. The smiles on the kids' faces when they're working on an art project, the pride when they master a new math or reading skill, the thrill of reaching them, of shaping them into productive, good, decent human beings. I don't want to give that up. It's all I have left. After this horrific day and the last grueling confession, I don't even have tears left.

"I'm sorry, Beatrice," he says. "Perhaps after you complete your training you can return without fear of harm coming to the children." I hear him taking a step toward me. "I'm sorry. I am. But I want to help you."

I spin around. "For a price."

"Everything has a price. We're talking about millions in taxpayers' money to train you. They should get something in return, no?"

"They should get my life?" I ask incredulously.

"You'll be instructed in weapons, combat, and—most importantly—your gift. You'll be working with some of the strongest creatures on the planet. They will protect you, and you them. We haven't lost a member in over two years."

"But you have lost some."

"Unfortunately, yes," he says in a low voice.

"Then forget it. I'm a fan of breathing, so I'll just keep my life, thanks." I turn around again but this time I make it to the door.

As I'm about to step into the hallway, Dr. Black speaks. "What life, Beatrice?" he asks in the same low tone. "You can't go back to work. Your family's terrified of you, with good cause. You almost killed your brother. Who could be next? Your friends? Your grandmother? What's left for you?" He walks and stops only a few inches from me. I can feel the warmth from his body on my back. "I know you're frightened. I know you've been frightened all your life by what you're able to do. And I know how lonely you've been. Feeling different, *being* different, having no one to talk to about what you can do. Having to hide it. It doesn't have to be that way anymore. I am giving you a chance to *belong,*" he whispers. "A chance to be yourself for the first time in your life. A chance to help people with your God-given talent. Will you let me do that?"

I stand at the door looking into the hallway. My exit. The eternal dilemma: should I stay or should I go? All that waits for me down that hallway is a lonely life locked in my apartment, afraid to go outside in case someone makes me mad and I accidentally drop a dumpster on them. Behind me, a chance at a semi-normal life, that is if I survive. Damned if I do, damned if I don't. Just…damned. Story of my life.

I slowly turn back to Dr. Black. "Can I leave anytime if I want to?"

"Yes," he says, "but trust me, you won't want to."

"And you'll help me control this thing?"

"Yes."

I open my mouth to give my answer but the words are stuck. I gulp them down and sigh. Here goes. "Okay, you've got yourself a deal." I hold out my hand and he gives it a firm shake.

"You've made the right choice."

What choice?

TWO

THE GOVERNMENT SECRET

Two Months Later

THE PLANE TO WICHITA, Kansas, landed an hour late, delayed in Washington, DC, due to a severe thunderstorm. The storm came out of nowhere, as they often do there. In the eight weeks I was in DC, the weather ran the gamut from snow one day to clear skies with warm winds the next. Luckily, I was indoors most of the time so I only had to experience it through my window in "The Building."

"The Building," with capitals, just the way they said it, had been my home for the past eight weeks, located in the industrial district of Manassas, Virginia. The only way I knew where the heck I was, was that we passed the town sign. Once I was in The Building, I was only let out on training exercises to run around the woods and work on my marksmanship. The two-story dull white building looked like any other warehouse from the outside, except for the keypad needed to open the door. Inside was something out of a spy movie. There was a lab where they drew enough blood on my first day to fill another person and a gun range where my limited skills improved by all of three percent. Next to that was a gym where I got my behind kicked daily by a Marine twice my size. Upstairs were my living quarters, which looked like a thrift store expo complete with cigarette burns and water damage. The last room across from my apartment was the place I hated most: the gift room.

I still have a hard time calling it that, my gift. As if the ability to hurt people with your mind is something akin to a Barnes & Noble gift card. We began with the easy items like pencils and cups. These proved harder than I thought they would be. Besides the car and the other incident, I'd never consciously tried to use my gift. It actually took a frustrating week to get the hang of directing my psychokinesis, but all it really took was a lot of concentration. I'd just think *pencil, pencil, pencil* and visualize the item. Within seconds, it was up in the air. When my mind wandered, it dropped. After two weeks of this, I could just look at the thing and up it would fly. The objects they gave me got heavier and heavier, but we had to stop at a thousand pounds because I kept passing out.

Then at the end of the day, instead of curling up with a silly book or watching TCM—I missed *The World of Henry Orient!*—came Monsters 101. I read volumes and volumes of case files and books, everything from the Bible to Anne Rice. There are over a million different varieties of demons, monsters, demigods, psychics, and everything in between walking this earth right now. For the most part, they live under the radar, keeping to themselves. Living lives, going bowling, the usual. When they surface for either good deeds or (more often) bad, they pop up in the chronicles. I had to read about every one of their exploits and see the accompanying pictures. There wasn't a night I didn't have bad dreams.

So … for the past eight weeks I've been poked by needles, beat up, and embarrassed to no end. I learned about the scariest things on earth and turned into the Terminator. Then without even a day to collect myself and prepare for the next leg of my adventure, I was pushed onto a plane to Wichita, of all places. And here I thought the life of a government secret agent would be glamorous. Kansas is about as glamorous as a pair of clogs. I miss San Diego already.

Nobody in my family knows where I am or what I've been doing. After my conversation with George (as Dr. Black instructed me to call him now that I'm "part of the family"), I drove to my apartment, packed up everything I could, and met him at the airport. I didn't even have time to go back to Nana's and clean up my aspirin-riddled vomit. Everything else—canceling my lease, resigning from my job, selling my car—the all-powerful "they" would take care of. I did leave a note so none of my family or friends would call the cops and start combing the ocean for my rotting corpse. The note was short but sweet: I was sorry for what I had done, that I had to go and get my head together, and not to worry. I knew they would anyway, if they still cared about me at all. I've never been the impulsive type. Heck, I plan trips to the grocery store days in advance.

Every few days I was allowed to call home but had to lie through my teeth about what I was doing. My made-up self sure did have a lot of fun these past eight weeks. I've been to the Grand Canyon, Las Vegas, New Orleans, Orlando, New York City, and everywhere in between. Nana loved the post cards I've been sending, and so did my friend April. We always talked about driving cross-country together, but she got pregnant at nineteen and hasn't been able to take a vacation that didn't involve Mickey Mouse since. She says she's living vicariously through me now. If she only knew.

George clears his throat and closes the final file. He's been reading files marked "CLASSIFIED" since we landed and got into the car, oblivious to the fact that I'm about to leap out of my skin. My foot hasn't stopped twitching since Virginia and my lip is sore from my nibbling it. George does look at me and pats my hand reassuringly. "It's normal to be nervous," he says, "but you really shouldn't worry. Everyone can't wait to meet you."

"Really?" I ask in a tiny voice.

"Of course. You're the first new recruit we've had in close to three years."

This bit of information does nothing to calm the butterflies in my stomach. Instead, my hands start quivering. I'm the new kid again. Swell. Alliances and camaraderie have already been established, and if my nomadic lifestyle as a child taught me anything, it's that people loathe letting in an outsider. It upsets the balance. It always took at least a month before anyone would even let me eat lunch with them. And here I come to shake things up with a group of people who fought together and relied on each other to stay alive for years. Honestly, this scares me more than any ogre that might jump out of the bushes.

The car turns off the empty highway and onto an even more desolate gray gravel road. I understand why Dorothy was so eager to leave. So far, I am not impressed with Kansas. I can sum up the state in three words: *flat*, *brown*, and *empty*. Wichita was a common enough city, complete with skyscrapers and traffic, but when we got about fifteen miles outside of the city center, all the suburbs and mini-malls disappeared, replaced with stretches and stretches of wheat fields and cow pastures. I'm surrounded by those amber waves of grain I'd heard about but never had any desire to see. We've been driving over an hour and I've counted a total of twelve cars besides us. There have been even fewer houses. Every ten minutes, we pass a farmhouse, followed by nine minutes of cows. The smell not only makes me gag but feels filmy and clings to my skin even after we pass. The city girl in me is petrified. I pout, thinking about how I won't see the dark blue ocean, the sand, the Coronado Bridge, the gas lamp district anymore, but I quickly regain my composure. Monster-hunting faux FBI agents do not pout.

"You really have no need to worry," George says, breaking my train of thought. "They are the best group of people I have ever worked with."

"I'm not worried," I lie. George raises a gray eyebrow. "Okay, I'm nervous," I admit. "I'm in the middle of nowhere, about to meet people who've been together for years. Either of those things is enough to make a girl apprehensive. I mean, where are all the people? If it were any more isolated we'd be on the friggin' moon!"

George chuckles. "Yes, it's isolated, but that's the exact reason we chose it. There isn't a neighbor for ten miles in any direction, which allows for a certain degree of privacy required by some of our members."

My heart rate jumps a notch. "Is there anything around? A movie theater? Grocery store? Hair salon?"

"Beatrice, calm down! I understand this is a bit daunting for you, but there is really no need to worry. There is a town ten miles away, equipped with all the luxuries. A movie theater, yes, and a grocery store. And if there is anything you need, we can get it for you."

"So I'm allowed to leave the house?"

"Of course, but if you're needed, you are required to report right away. You're not a prisoner, Beatrice."

"Just a government secret."

George nods and turns toward the window. I do the same. Almost immediately, I see something strange, something I haven't seen since we landed. Green. Trees and grass in and around the brown, like an oasis in the desert. It starts slowly, with just a few oak trees on the side of the road. Quickly all the brown disappears and all that remains is green grass and trees, lots of trees. Maybe we aren't in Kansas anymore, Toto.

"The designer of the compound was originally from New England," George explains. "He found the flatness of the area disconcerting. The trees give it a more … homey feeling, no?"

"I guess," I say.

Out of nowhere, an eardrum-bursting sound of a jet engine booms above us. My jangled nerves can't take it anymore. I screech and jump like an idiot. As I look out my window, a small jet cuts across the sky above the trees and disappears behind them.

"Oh good, they're here," George says. "I was worried they wouldn't make it back for your arrival."

"They're on the jet?"

"Of course. You didn't think we'd drive an hour to the airport every time we needed to go somewhere? That's the whole point of having our base in Kansas—a quick deployment. It takes approximately two and a half hours to fly anywhere in America from here, except Hawaii or Alaska. We own the airstrip and hangar two miles away."

"You have your own airplane?" I ask, my eyes bugging out of my head. I was eighteen before I got to fly anywhere (one of the joys of being poor) and these people have their own airplane?! Maybe it's like the one Britney Spears has. I wonder if we have our own private flight attendants. Heck, what I really wonder is if I can borrow it sometime.

"The government is very generous."

"I'll say."

We drive for another minute down the wooded gravel path before I can see what appears to be a wrought iron fence complete with pivoting security cameras, red signs warning off trespassers, and a slight buzzing coming from the fence. It must be electric. Not exactly subtle. The driver punches the code into the black box and the gate opens.

"The locals give you a lot of trouble?" I ask.

"No."

"This is a *secret* government facility, right?"

George smiles. "Of course."

"Well, this is *exactly* what I'd expect a secret government facility to look like. The people in town don't suspect anything?"

"They suspect, but nothing more. To them this is a private institute where troubled individuals come to receive treatment. If anyone asks—and they won't—you suffer from depression and have come to get better."

Not too far from the truth.

The car slowly creeps up the gravel driveway. Within seconds I see what upon first glance reminds me of one of those estates Jane Austen's heroines always live in. It's a flipping estate. An *estate*! The gray stone building in the Georgian fashion, a perfect rectangle three stories tall with a row of windows spread out in a straight line across each floor. As we move along the circular driveway—which includes a bubbling three-tiered gray fountain in the middle, by the way—I notice wide stone steps leading up to a set of brown double doors. I half expect Mr. Darcy to throw open the doors—dressed in that wet white shirt of his, natch—and offer us tea. As we curve along the drive, I see that behind the mansion lies a wide patch of grass that dead-ends at a forest. Nice.

"Welcome to your new home."

The driver parks the car right in front of the stone steps. I hop out of the car and just stare up at the enormous building with my mouth open. It's even bigger than I thought. Looking up at it, it's twice as tall as I had guessed.

"How big is this place?" I ask with more than a little awe in my voice.

"Five stories, with two floors underground. On the first floor, there is a library, sitting room with television, video games, and every electronic marvel designed to pass time. Behind the stairs to the left is the billiard room, and beyond that is the movie theater. Back to the right of the stairs is the kitchen. Three times a week, when not on an operation, a chef comes and prepares dinner. The top floors are the bedrooms. There are eleven in total, each with its own private bath. Subbasement One houses our laboratory, meeting room, and an additional bedroom. Subbasement Two is used for training, and you'll find it resembles your last residence a great deal. Firing range, workout space, and of course, ability training."

I pry my eyes from the house and over to George. He's grinning from ear to ear, just like an artist when he looks at a piece he's extremely proud of. I can't help but smile too. Maybe this won't be all that bad. Private jet, mansion to live in, and my own chef. Maybe I haven't made an epic mistake, as I've convinced myself I have over the last two months. Maybe everything will actually be all right.

Yeah. Right.

THREE

THE F.R.E.A.K.S. SHOW

I follow George up the stone steps, my heels clacking on the granite. I decided to be Professional Bea today with a black suit, dark purple dress shirt, and boring shoes. The deep brown double doors open as we reach them as if by magic. Could be, for all I know. Or maybe they heard us coming.

A man with a standard brown Federal crew cut, olive skin, hawk-like features, and blue pinstripe suit appears on the other side of the door, walking toward us. "Welcome back, Dr. Black," the man says. "Op went out without a hitch. The hostile was taken out."

"Good. Agent Paul Chandler, may I introduce you to Beatrice Alexander, our newest addition."

Agent Chandler and I shake hands, mine firmer than normal. "Nice to meet you, ma'am," he says in a voice as firm as my handshake.

"How are you feeling, Paul?" George asks. "You look better."

"Completely recovered now, sir. Thank you."

"Is the team in the living room?" George asks.

"They're not back from the airfield yet. Should be about five more minutes."

"Okay," George says, "then Paul, why don't you show Beatrice to her room? Third floor, end of the hallway, across from Will's."

"My pleasure." After picking up my mismatched suitcases, he starts toward the door, and George and I follow.

Holy smokes! The entranceway alone is as big as Nana's house, with a huge, sweeping staircase like the ones in old Southern mansions like Twelve Oaks and Tara in *Gone with the Wind*. The entire room, staircase and all, is off-white with redwood trim along the walls. I can't be sure, but I think the floor is made of polished marble. Massive oil paintings of cherubs and naked people frolicking hang on the walls in gold frames. I'd bet one of those could pay the rent on my old apartment for a year. It's quiet in here, like a museum with that same smell too: old but not unpleasant. I'm petrified to touch anything. It'd be just my luck to break a ten-thousand-dollar vase on my first day.

The stairs only sweep up one floor into a hallway with redwood walls and the same style of paintings on the walls. I follow halfway down the hall past only two doors—these rooms must be enormous!—before we come to an opening with a cramped, badly lit staircase. The steps are so shallow that twice I almost trip and fall. The not-so-gallant Agent Chandler ignores me and continues up to the third floor. The stairs lead to an identical opulent hallway, right down to the style of paintings. When we reach my room at the end of the hall, past Romantic-era paintings of fields and the ocean, Agent Chandler sets down the bags, pulling a key out of his vest. He unlocks the door and we step in.

"Oh. My. God."

I am standing in my dream room. The walls are a powder pink with white lace curtains in the large bay windows. The window seat looks out onto a large pond and willow trees. The space itself is massive. It has to be roughly the size of two normal living rooms. And it has everything! A huge plasma TV with TiVo hooked up. A pink silk couch right out of the nineteenth century. A mahogany desk with a brand-new Apple laptop. A small refrigerator. A walk-in closet with shoe rack. And the pièce de résistance: a king-sized bed with matching canopy. My jaw literally drops.

As I take stock of the room with my hanging jaw, walking around the boxes filled with my old life, Agent Chandler walks past my bed into a dark room. As I open the computer to check it out, he turns on the light. "This is your bathroom. Your room can be redecorated if you so choose."

"No ... no, this is perfect," I say, running my fingers over the keys. A brand-new computer. It is definitely a day of firsts.

Agent Chandler places the key on the dresser. "I'll let you start unpacking. If you need anything, just dial zero on your phone."

"Got it. Thank you." Agent Chandler nods and leaves the room, shutting the door quietly behind him.

The second the door clicks, I find the remote and start flipping channels. TCM. I truly am at home now. After gawking around a bit more, I dive headfirst onto the bed, squealing like a little girl who's just got a new Barbie. The bed is cotton-candy soft. I lay on my back looking up at the canopy with a huge grin on my face. This is way better than I expected. Finally, my dream of being a princess has come true, complete with castle! Now all I have to do is find Prince Charming, slay a couple dragons, and live happily ever after.

Just as I'm contemplating rolling myself up in the covers like a Swiss Cake Roll, there is a knock on the door. The roll will have to wait. I scoot off the bed and onto my feet.

"Coming!" I open the door. A man stands in the hallway. A cute man. A *very* cute man.

Enter Prince Charming.

His large biceps and legs are perfectly toned under his semi-tight black shirt and blue jeans. This man spends a lot of time at the gym. He's over six feet tall with a ruggedly handsome face, almost emerald green eyes, thin lips, and a thick head of soft, dark brown hair cut so it flops on his forehead a little. I'd place him at mid-thirties with a few wrinkles around his eyes and a slightly crooked Roman nose. Bet he has a nice butt too. The sexy boy-next-door. Can we say "crush at first sight"?

When he sees me, his lips open a little, almost as if he wants to say something. But he doesn't. We stand there looking at each other in surprise for an uncomfortable moment. Not that I mind staring at him, but we can't stay like this. What can I say? Marry me? I've never been this wildly attracted to a man this fast. Or ever. If my mouth isn't put to good use, I'm liable to smash my lips against his. Say something, Bea! I finally open my mouth. "Yes?"

His jaw snaps shut like he's just remembered that I'm here, his cheeks turning red. I can't help but grin. It isn't every day I make a handsome man forget how to speak. And blush too. Actually, this is the first time ever. I've had extremely limited experience with men. I mean, when you're trying to keep a huge part of yourself a secret, it's hard to let people in. Nobody wants to date a monster. The one guy I really gave it a try with, my ex Steven, I didn't even like that much. I kept him at arm's length like everyone else, and when he asked me to move in with him, I broke it off. I don't get close to people, especially men. One orgasm and I could blow up their head.

Not that avoiding relationships was that big a problem. I am in no way supermodel material. I'm cute, that old standby that means I'd never win a beauty contest, but small children don't flee from me. This is me: twenty-six, dull brown eyes, a small, slightly up-turned nose, wavy medium-brown hair a little past shoulder length, tan skin—no self-respecting San Diegan is pale—and now only twenty pounds overweight but still curvy. I would have lost more, but after a long day of getting my butt whupped during training, all I wanted was McDonald's and a hot fudge sundae. So the way this man is looking at me is an entirely new experience for me. I may not have much actual relationship experience, but I have a very active imagination, which has taken a turn to the racy right now. My cheeks flame up as brightly as his.

"Um," the man says, wiping his hand on his jeans. He extends it to me. "Will Price."

I meet those stunning eyes and shake his hand. "Beatrice Alexander, nice to meet you."

He releases my hand first, snapping his away as if I'm radioactive. He shakes his head. "Um, I'm—I'm supposed to fetch you. Everyone's in the living room."

"Oh, okay."

After locking the door behind me, we walk down the hallway almost side by side, arms just an inch from each other. I can feel his heat from here. His arm accidentally brushes mine and he jerks it away. "Sorry." When we reach the evil staircase, he stops to let me go first. Handsome *and* a gentleman. If he cooks, I've found the perfect man. Glad I wore my slimming black slacks in case he's tempted to look at my booty. My temperature rises at the thought.

"So, what do you do here?" I ask at the stairs.

"Same as you."

"Oh," I say, trying to hide my surprise. "So you're … "

"Yeah," he says uncomfortably. "One of the F.R.E.A.K.S."

I won't press it. I still hate to talk about my curs—I mean my *gift*—and I can feel the nervousness coming from him. "So, you're Will from across the hall?"

"Yes."

"Is it just us on the third floor?" Because that means we can make as much noise as we want at the height of passion. Oh yes, my imagination is *very* active right about now.

"No, Carl's one down from you. Some nights one or two of the agents spend the night, but they don't live here. You'll get a tour later."

"Oh, okay." We walk a few seconds in silence. I can't stand silence. "So, how long have you been with the team?" I ask for lack of something better.

He glances at me then drops his eyes to the carpet. "Six years."

"Wow. Do you like it?"

Will doesn't answer, instead quickening his pace down the giant staircase. I'll take that as a "no." We enter the living room, where everyone has assembled. So this is them. The F.R.E.A.K.S. My new family.

All eleven sets of eyes are on me, looking me up and down. Appraising me. I just give a weak smile and gaze down to the ground. A shy girl's best defense. George saunters over to me, putting his arm around my shoulder. "Everyone, let me introduce you to Beatrice Alexander. Beatrice, everyone."

"Bea is fine, if you want," I say quietly.

A very tall, thin woman about my age with dark brown skin and long, straight light brown hair stands from the pale blue couch and walks over to me. She is supermodel gorgeous with plump lips, high cheekbones, a straight nose, wide almond eyes the color of night, and even a beauty mark on her cheek. "Hi, Bea," the Beyoncé look-alike says, shaking my hand, "I'm Irie Dempsey. Pyrokinetic. You need a fire, I can start one—" she snaps her fingers and a burst of flame ignites from them—"just like that."

"Nice to meet you."

The teenager who sat beside Irie stands up. She's a few inches taller than I am with blue-black hair cut to her shoulders, Bettie Page bangs, porcelain skin with too much make-up, and thick black frames covering her eyes. Her lips are bright red, her light brown eyes have too much eyeliner, she has a spider nose ring, and her petite frame is encased in black capris and an *Edward Scissorhands* hoodie. A Goth kewpie doll. "Hi, I'm Nancy Lake," she says with a burst of energy. "Teleportation. Locked rooms are, like, my thing. I can get through anything up to, like, fifty feet from where I am," she boasts. "Did you really lift up a whole car?"

"Yeah."

"Ohmigod! That must have been, like, so cool! Can you, like, do it again? I'd totally love to see that!"

"I don't think I can. Sorry."

Her red lips move into a pout. "Oh, that sucks."

A short man in his late thirties rescues me from the awkward moment by stepping forward. He has ultra-short, spiky dark brown hair and square glasses and clears his throat as he walks over to me, extending his gloved hand. My savior is baby-faced and pudgy with dark blue eyes, nicely pressed preppy clothes, and black leather gloves. "Carl Petrovsky, psychometry." That's why he has the gloves. If psychometrics touch an object with their bare skin, they sometimes have visions about its history. If they touch a person, they see his past as if they were living in his head, experiencing everything firsthand. Our hands barely brush before he pulls away.

I have a little of the same thing, apparently. I never thought it was anything, but at The Building they tested me for other skills. I ranked semi-high on the clairempathy chart. It means I can sense people's emotions if I'm around them and their emotion is intense enough. I always thought it was something everyone could do. I could tell when to hit up Nana for money because I'd know when she was in a good mood. We worked on it a little during training. Now if someone's feeling something strongly, I can sense it. I'm just doubly lucky, I guess.

Finally, the African American man with salt-and-pepper hair sitting in the back corner stands from his chair. He's in his late fifties or early sixties wearing dark sunglasses. The white cane he has in his right hand sweeps the area in front of him before he takes a step. He makes his way to me just as quickly as a person with perfect vision. The man stops right in front of me, holding out his hand. "Andrew DuChamp," he says with a Southern accent. "It's a pleasure to meet you." I shake his hand.

"Andrew's our resident medium," Irie says. "Ghosts love him, don't they, Andrew?"

"A little too much, I'm afraid. Pierce followed me to South Carolina."

"You really need to tell him to leave you alone," Carl says. "I'm getting sick of being woken up in the middle of the night having to listen to a one-sided conversation."

"Pierce is one of the house ghosts," Irie explains. "He used to live here a hundred years ago. Don't worry though; he leaves everyone but Andrew alone."

"Good to know."

George gestures to the men and woman standing by the wall. All the men look the same, mid-thirties, tall, built, wearing stockbroker blue suits complete with guns. The woman is tall and thin, in her forties, with short brown hair and eyes. "And the gentlemen and lady in the back are Special Agents Wolfe," the man with the natural blond hair and blue eyes nods, "Agent Konrad," the man next to Wolfe with dark brown hair slicked back nods, "Agent Rushmore," the severe man with a scar across his eyebrow does nothing, "you know Agent Chandler, and our physician/medical examiner is Dr. Lynette Neill," George says. "So, that's the team."

"I thought there were more of you."

"You'll have to meet Oliver later," George says, "he's ... unavailable at the moment."

"He'll find *you*, I'm sure," Will says with a hint of disdain. Irie shoots him a look of disapproval before rolling her eyes.

"Well now," George says, "I know Beatrice has quite a lot of unpacking to do. Irie, Nancy, why don't you help?"

"Cool!" Nancy says right before she grabs my hand and jerks me out of the room. Irie follows behind us. "So, you're, like, from San Diego! That is so cool! I've never been to California, but I've always wanted to! Is it true it's always, like, sunny and warm? Do you go to the beach a lot? Have you ever seen any movie stars? OMG, have you ever seen Johnny Depp? I am, like, totally in love with him. Do you like him? He—"

"Nancy," Irie snaps, "take a breath!"

"What!"

Irie walks up to us, taking a place on my left. I'm wedged between the two women all the way up the stairs. "So, are you nervous?" Irie asks.

"A little," I admit. "This is all so surreal."

"Don't worry," Irie soothes. "We'll take care of you. We're really not that bad. For a bunch of freaks."

"Don't you totally hate that name?" Nancy asks me. "I so do."

"Nancy, even if you couldn't do what you do and weren't a member, you'd still be a freak."

"Shut up!"

Irie chuckles. "So, here's the dish," Irie says. "CliffsNotes version of your brand-new life. Andrew and Carl are sweeties. You ever need to talk, anytime night or day, they are always there. The only thing you need to avoid is touching Carl. No hugs, usually not even handshakes with or without the gloves. It goes back to when he was a kid. He'd touch someone and poof! All their feelings or worse would pour out. He saw molestation, murder, all that shit. They recruited him about ten years ago when he was doing his second stint in a loony bin. I don't think the guy has ever had a girlfriend."

"Do you have a boyfriend?" Nancy asks me.

"Not anymore."

"Me neither, but there is this boy in town that is totally—"

"Nancy! Shut it! I'm trying to talk here."

"What?" Nancy whines. "I was just asking a question. I am allowed to—"

"Not now. Christ, you are so rude!"

"Don't blow a freaking gasket. We don't want to, like, replace the wallpaper again."

"Then stop acting like a two-year-old on crack."

When we reach my room, I start fumbling in my pockets for the key. Nancy rolls her eyes and then disappears right before my eyes. Like a wuss, I gasp and jump back. It's as if she was never there. I look at Irie, who rolls her eyes. "She does that a lot," Irie says. "Doesn't know the meaning of privacy."

The lock clicks and the door swings open. Nancy stands on the other side with a smile on her face and a hand on her tiny hip. "Cool, huh?"

"Yeah," I say as I pass her. Okay, that was a little spooky.

The girls immediately go over to my boxes and suitcases. They each pick one up and throw it on the bed. "As I was saying before I was rudely interrupted..." Irie glares at Nancy, who sticks her tongue out. "Just don't touch Carl. That's the way he likes it. So that's Carl. As for our Nancy here, as you may have guessed: she is a pain in the ass."

"You're one to talk! At least the house doesn't almost, like, burn down whenever I have PMS!" Nancy pulls out my black cashmere sweater and holds it up. "Ohmigod! I, like, love this! Can I try it on?"

"Knock yourself out."

"If only," Irie mumbles. In a blink, Nancy disappears. Weird, definitely weird. Irie pulls out clothes from the box and takes them to the dresser. I walk over to the other box and start unpacking. I'm not sure if these will fit me anymore. I lost twenty pounds, thank you very much, and the Marines at The Building weren't big on the shopping field trips. Irie holds up my jean skirt. "We have to take you shopping."

"I'd like that," I say with a smile. "Have you been here long?"

"Close to eight years. George found me after I burnt down my high school." She shares this bit of information as nonchalantly as someone ordering take-out.

My eyes bug out of my head. "You burnt down your high school?"

"It was an accident. I stayed late for band practice and these pricks tried to rape me. I lost my temper. That's my tip about me— don't piss me off unless you want a trip to the burn unit."

"I will try to remember that."

We both go back for more clothes. "What happened to the boys?" I ask carefully, trying to avoid the burn unit.

She lifts an eyebrow. "Guess."

I glance at her sideways. "You mean you … "

She meets me square in the eyes. "Here's another tip: forget the past. Every person in this house at some point in their lives has done something that makes them wake up in the middle of the night with an attack of conscience. There are no angels here, only seriously screwed up people looking for a little acceptance. If you don't judge, neither will we. Besides, most of the time it wasn't our fault. We didn't know what we were doing or didn't have control. I'm sure you have a story too. Care to share?"

Thankfully, Nancy walks out of the bathroom in my sweater. It's about three sizes too big but still looks better on her than it ever did on me. "I so have to borrow this!"

"Okay."

"Cool!" Nancy skips back over to us and picks up more clothes.

"Take our Nancy here. Nancy, tell Bea what you did before you were recruited."

"I helped my parents rob banks," she says as cheerful as a chipmunk. "We robbed banks from Michigan all the way to

34

Kentucky. Then they got caught and I went into foster care. *Tres* nightmare, but the robbing was totally fun. I'd just port in, turn off the alarm, port into the vault, and port out with the money. It was, like, so cool!"

"Only you would think grand larceny is cool," Irie says, closing the top drawer.

"Shut up! I loved moving around. It was so exciting."

"I moved around a lot when I was a kid too," I say.

"Really? Why?" Nancy asks.

"My mom had a restless spirit, or that's what she called it. She thought there was too much world to see to stay in one place."

"But I thought you were from San Diego," Irie says.

"I moved there when I was eight."

"Why?" Nancy asks.

"My mom ... died."

"I'm sorry," Irie says, shooting icicles at Nancy.

"It's okay. I went to live with my Nana after that."

Nana. A homesickness pang hits so hard I have to draw breath. For some reason I see her as I did the first time we met. Brian and I were at the police station, sitting on a wood bench with itchy blankets wrapped around us when she walked in. Five hours earlier, Brian had found Mom with her head in our gas oven. He hadn't spoken a word since. An officer, a woman in her early twenties, told me what happened. I was so numb, I couldn't even cry. It was just too much for my eight-year-old mind to process. I'd just seen her that morning, lying in her dark bedroom under the covers staring off into space. I kissed her cheek and went to school. Didn't even say "I love you" like I normally did. I really regret that.

I knew who Nana was the moment she walked in. It was the eyes, the same ones that looked out of my face and Brian's. There was something in her brown eyes that night, something I couldn't understand at my young age. She looked haunted. It seems Death surrounds some people, waiting to take everything from them as He did her: husband, parents, two daughters. Bastard.

That look would appear in her eyes when she was deep in thought. It was there the night I almost killed Brian. It was what made me throw up the pills when I tried to kill myself afterward. Much as I yearned to escape myself, I didn't want to add my death to her pain.

Irie clears her throat, bringing me out of my own head, God bless her. "Anyway," she says. "Next stop in the getting to know us parade is your neighbor across the hall. Will is our de facto leader, much to Oliver's chagrin."

"They so don't get along," Nancy adds, holding my Ann Taylor silk shirt up to her body.

"Having two alpha males in close proximity is never a good thing," Irie says. "But George *insists* we follow Will when we're in the field. He was a detective for the Washington, DC, police before he got bit. So he has experience with—"

"He was bit? By what?"

Irie scoffs. "He didn't tell you. Why am I not surprised?"

"Will's, like, totally a werewolf," says Nancy.

My throat closes up with that last word. Werewolf. Oh my, I have a werewolf living across the hall. The crime scene photos from my studies flash back. People ripped apart by fangs and claws. There was nothing left of the victims but bones and raw meat. The worry must show on my face—I am incapable of a poker face—because Irie smiles to reassure me. "Don't worry, he's a puppy dog."

"A totally bossy puppy dog," Nancy says under her breath.

"When it's time for him to go furry, we lock him in the basement. But he's another one to be careful of. Intense anger can bring on the change."

"I know. I read up on werewolves at The Building."

"You actually read all that stuff?" Irie asks, eyebrow raised. "Wow, I couldn't get past page five. Anyways, Will and his wife were camping in some park and got attacked. Will managed to kill the fucker but got bit. His wife … "

"Don't ever ask him about her," Nancy warns me. "He'll get, like, *really* pissed."

"Well, it is a sore subject," Irie points out. "She died. He's still not over it."

"Oh God."

"I know. George heard about the attack and got to Will early before he, you know, offed himself or hurt anyone else. He's kind of in denial about the whole furry thing, I think. Not that I blame him. I had guard duty a couple of times. What that guy goes through once a month … " She fake-shudders. "He's a good guy and all—"

"Bossy!" Nancy says, picking up more clothes.

Irie glares. "Yes, a little bossy, and really hard to talk to. Basically, if it doesn't have to do with an op—sorry, an *operation*—he won't talk to you. But there isn't anyone here I trust more with my life."

Nancy nods in agreement.

"So … The real agents try to keep themselves separate from us except in the field. They're all real serious. I think we scare them a little, so just avoid them like they do us. There, you're now up to speed. If you have any questions, please put them in writing. We will try to get back to you within three working days."

"What about … " I draw a blank, "the other guy?"

"Oliver?" Irie asks. "Well, Oliver is—"

"You so can't tell her about Oliver!" Nancy interrupts again. "You totally promised him!"

I look at Irie. "You promised him what?"

Irie sighs. "Our Oliver has a flair for the dramatic. He wants to 'reveal himself'—his words, not mine—to you."

"That sounds ominous."

"Well, that's our Oliver. I will warn you though: don't buy into his bullshit. He's all bark and no bite," she chuckles at this, "literally."

My telephone rings on the nightstand, and Nancy answers it. *My* phone. Someone really should teach her some manners. "Bea's room, Nancy speaking." She listens for a few seconds. "Kay, no prob. Be there in a few." She hangs up. "Irie, they want us in the conference room for debrief."

Irie rolls her eyes. "Great." She closes my already full dresser drawer and turns to me. "We might be a while; you're going to have to finish yourself."

"Okay. Thanks for your help."

"Well, that's what we do around here. It's like the military; you're only good as the person next to you. Don't want to have that person pissed off at you. Come on, Nance, they're waiting for us."

"I totally hate debriefs," Nancy whines.

Irie rolls her eyes again, tugs on Nancy's—well, *my*—sweater sleeve, and leaves the room. Nancy stops at the door and turns to me. "Do you like *Portal*? If you want, you can come by my room later and we can play after your 'getting to know you' dinner."

"Um, I'd like that."

"Cool!" she says with a bright smile. "Okay, well, bye."

When the door closes, I take a deep breath and slowly let it out. Alone at last. That went better than I thought. All acceptance cost me was a sweater. I walk over to the bed and toss off the empty boxes. I'll do the rest later. All of a sudden, I'm exhausted, like I've been up for three days walking through a hot desert. I stare up at my canopy and yawn. There's a seriously cute werewolf living across the hall from me. There's a mysterious man who wants to shock me for some reason. I suddenly have two bickering sisters. It's a tad too much.

I'm not sure how long I lay on the bed staring up at the gossamer canopy, just letting the calm I've been missing for two months take over. My eyelids begin to droop. Closing them seems like a very good idea. A yawn wracks my whole body. Just a little nap. Then I'll …

When I open my eyes again, the room is pitch black. Panic grips my body. Where am I? What … oh, yeah. I wipe the drool from my mouth. Crud. The sun set several hours ago by the looks of it. The clock next to me reads 8:56. Great, I've missed my own "getting to know you" dinner. They must think I'm an antisocial snob. Great start, Bea.

I fumble in the dark for the lamp, clicking it on. I manage to sit up but suddenly my stomach growls like a Rottweiler. I haven't eaten since the plane. Okay, where is the kitchen? Oh yeah, I missed the tour too. Considering I get lost in my own school, should I venture around the scary mansion? The Rottweiler makes the decision for me.

The hallway is as quiet as a church during Mardi Gras, as is the rest of the house. I make my way through the dimly lit hallways, finding the big staircase with no problem. There isn't anyone on the ground level either. Okay, George said the kitchen was on the … left? I walk behind the staircase and am very happy to find the empty kitchen. Stainless steel everything fills the large space. The counters are covered with every appliance ever invented to make food: toasters, blenders, and a few I've never seen before. There are two ovens built into the walls, each the size of a dishwasher. You could make a lot of cupcakes in there. I go over to a subzero refrigerator the size of a small car with enough food to feed three football teams. I'm sure more drool slips out of my mouth at this wondrous sight. I pull out ingredients to make a roast beef sandwich and cut myself two pieces of the chocolate cake that reads "WELCOME BEATR." Gee, they celebrated without me. Well, it is tragic to waste a perfectly good cake, especially one made in my honor. I grab a third piece.

I leave the kitchen and make it a few steps up the stairs before I notice a light on in one of the rooms that wasn't on before. Juggling my plates, I go back down the stairs into one of the most fabulous sights I have seen. Even more fabulous than the fridge and my room, and that's saying something.

Books. At least a thousand books. Old, new, ancient. Browns, greens, burgundies, whites. Two floors of wall-to-wall books. I can't tell where one stops and the other begins. It's like a college library. There's a railing around the square room and a tall ladder that reaches the ceiling. In the middle of the library are three burgundy hard leather chairs with brass buttons. A couch of the same material sits near the two-story bay windows that look out onto the dimly lit pond. Off to the side are two dark wooden chairs set up on either side of a chessboard. This is the smart people's room.

Like most social outcasts who inherited the shy gene, books became my best friend. During recess, you could find me sitting against the wall in the corner with my nose in a new adventure. On date night, when the other kids were performing various tentative sex acts, I'd be locked in my room with the latest Sue Grafton. Most of my paycheck went to Barnes & Noble. I even knew everyone there by name.

Letting my inner girl come out, I squeal and run to the nearest book-filled wall, putting the plates on the nearest table. Food can wait. I run my fingers over the hundred-year-old bindings, my eyes wide. Jane Austen, John Galsworthy, Charles Dickens, Charlotte Brontë (my favorite!), history books on every period. I pull out one about the French Revolution that looks and smells as if it was written back then. I don't know how long I'm skimming the book but I'm brought out of France by the distinct feeling that I'm not alone. My back tingles. I glance over my left shoulder at the door.

A man leans casually yet elegantly on the door frame, arms folded in front of him and a small smile covering his face. Wow. *Hello.* This is the most gorgeous man I have ever seen outside a movie, maybe even in them as well. His thick, wavy brown hair with blonde highlights stops just above his shoulders, tendrils curling under his ears. His flawless high cheekbones go all the way to his cat-like gray eyes and I'd call him feminine if not for that strong, square jaw with a cleft chin. He's pale, almost lily-white, which really brings out the red in his lush lips. Lips made for kissing, April would call them. Cupid's bow and all. I can't tell his age except late twenties, early thirties. His frame is perfect on him too. Not too thin, but not as meaty as Will. Adonis is dressed in tight black slacks that leave little to the imagination, a billowy white shirt cut so the V of the neck reaches a few inches above his naval showing abundant chest hair, and finally a velvet blood red robe. Standing before me—devouring me with his eyes—is a man who belongs on the cover of a romance novel.

"I was just…" I hold up the book.

The intruder says nothing, he just keeps grinning like a beautiful mental patient. I turn back to the bookcase and replace the book. I'll come back for it later. When I turn around the man is gone.

"I am over here," he says with a light English accent.

I completely turn around and see the man on the exact opposite side of the room holding a book in his long fingers. Okay, how did…? I only turned for a second. There's no way he could have crossed the room that fast. "How did you—" I swivel my head between the door and where he now stands, all in about half a second, but he's disappeared again.

"Magic."

Out of thin air, he appears not two feet from me. I literally jump a foot, gasping along the way. The grin returns on the man's face just as mischievously as the time before. My heart almost escapes out of my mouth.

"I am sorry," he says, "I did not mean to frighten you."

"Well, you did," I say, my voice a few octaves higher than normal. "You shouldn't do that to people."

"You are of course right," he says graciously. "I promise never to do it again."

I don't know if it's his laughing eyes or just my intuition, but I know he's lying. He's too close. I take a step back. "Let me guess, you're Oliver?"

"What drew you to that conclusion?"

"They said you had a flair for the dramatic."

He smiles again. It's a knockout smile. "Did they now? And what else, pray tell, did *they* say about me?"

"Nothing."

"In that case, I suppose we should formally introduce ourselves like civilized creatures." He stretches out his arm. "Oliver Montrose."

I glance at those long fingers before shaking his freezing hand. "Beatrice Alexander."

He lifts my hand up, laying a small kiss on it. "Enchanted."

I pull my hand back. "Right back at ya." We're silent for a moment. His eyes meet mine, but I look away toward the shelves. Oliver's eyes move side to side across my face as if he's trying to figure something out. I decide to break the silence. "So, what do you do?"

He continues to study my face as if the root of his dilemma can somehow be found here. After five seconds, the smile comes back. "My, my, you are just full of surprises, are you not, Trixie?" I flinch at that last word. That's what Leonard called me: Miss Trixie. He'd whisper it into my ear as he stroked my hair.

"Don't call me Trixie."

"Why not? You look like a Trixie."

"Just don't."

He takes a step toward me. "It is only a name."

"Just don't call me that, okay? It's not that much to ask, is it?"

I step away from Oliver and toward the door. He simply stands there with that same grin on his face, his eyes roving up and down. I don't need to be a mind reader to know I'm being mentally undressed. The leer tells all. He's not even hiding the fact. My students sometimes did this; not the mental undressing—even in this day and age, ten year olds are a bit young for that—but staring just to make me uncomfortable. I look away, doing my best to ignore him. I don't want a fight.

"So, what can you do? Can you run really fast or teleport or something?"

"Close," he says, moving toward me. He stops a foot away. Apparently, he's not into personal space. "I can move faster than humans can see." He leans in, almost so his face touches my ear. "But there is more," he whispers. "Guess right and I will give you a prize."

I can just guess what this so-called prize is. He stays stone still as I take a few more steps away. "Why don't you just tell me?" I suggest in an exasperated tone.

Oliver shakes his head. "Do not tell me they have recruited another human without a sense of humor."

"I have a sense of humor."

"Then play with me, Trixie."

"Don't call me that!" I say through clenched teeth. Out of nowhere, my stomach growls loud enough to be heard through the room. Oh heck. My cheeks grow hot.

That stupid grin returns. "Hungry?"

"I missed dinner." I seriously wish I hadn't. Maybe he wouldn't be so annoying, or scary, with other people around. "Was everyone angry?"

"I would not know. I do not dine with the rest of the F.R.E.A.K.S. Apparently it makes them lose their appetites." He steps toward me. "That is clue number two. Need another?"

"I—"

Before I can finish, Oliver bridges the gap between us so fast my brain barely registers it. Within a millisecond he's within inches of me, and something that feels like an ice cube covers my lips. His long finger. I'm too shocked to even gasp.

"Here is clue number three: I do not eat, and I do not drink…wine."

Oh God.

Instantly I leap back, away from his touch. Oh God. Oh God. He smiles again. "I believe the lady has figured it out."

"You're a vampire," I say so softly I can barely hear it. He's a friggin' vampire. He drinks people's blood. Blood! Eww. I'm alone with a…thing that can break me in half without even flexing a muscle! A corpse has been flirting with me. Okay, officially freaking out. A werewolf is bad, but at least he's only evil one day a month. This guy's a monster 24/7.

I am more than sure the surprise and horror register all over my face, if not all over my whole body. What do I do? The blood-sucking fiend is actually grinning from ear to ear. Okay, get a grip Beatrice. He obviously doesn't want to hurt you; he's on the team for God's sake. You didn't spaz when you found out about Will, don't do it now. He wants you to flip out. *Don't let him.* I look at the smiling dead man square in the eyes. "So, you're a vampire," I declare. "That's…nice."

"You can meet my eyes as well. That has not happened in fifteen years," he says as if his mind is a thousand miles away. "How extraordinary."

"Um, why?"

"I cannot capture your mind," he says as if it's a bad thing. "What kind of fun can we have now?" That grin returns. "I will just have to be creative." He takes a step toward me, and instinctively I take a step back.

"What are you doing?" I ask, trying and failing to hide my fear.

He takes another step, and so do I. "I am trying to kiss you."

"Why?" Another step.

"Because I think you are beautiful."

"Um…"

What on earth can I possibly say to that?

We each step again, but I have to stop. My back hits the book-case. Unknowingly, he's backed me into a corner. Oliver uses this fact to bridge the gap between us again. His face moves mere inches from mine, his eyes studying my face again. Don't know what he's going to find besides fear and annoyance. I can smell his aftershave; it's strong with a small hint of flowers. Wow, there isn't a blemish or wrinkle anywhere. His long hand comes up to cradle my chin, gently pushing my face up to meet his eyes. I don't know if it's his hand or the fear, but I shiver.

"Do I frighten you?" he asks in a low whisper. I can see the two white, pointed fangs as he speaks.

"Yes," I admit.

He cocks his head to the right. "And yet you find me desirable."

"I guess."

His hand drops my chin, and all semblance of playfulness vanishes. "You guess?" he asks harshly.

"You're cute, but…"

He steps away from me, and I can breathe again. *"Cute?"* he spits. "For centuries women have wanted me, desired me. Royalty requested me by name, and you think I am *cute?*"

"I—I'm sorry! You're just not my type."

"Not your *type*?" he almost shouts.

Okay, I've made the scary vampire mad. So not good. I quickly glance at the door. It's about fifteen feet away.

I think I can make it.

Oliver must have seen the glance because just as I'm about to make my dash, he jumps in front of me. "Where do you think you are going?" He sounds amused again.

Not scared, not scared, not scared. "I'm going to my room."

"I do not think so."

Okay, that's it. I'm done. I really didn't want it to come to this, but we just passed ridiculous. I'm about to push his smirking face into a wall using my power but a voice stops me. "Oliver!" a man barks from the door. We both turn. Will stands in the doorway, the scowl he sports making his handsome face look dangerous. I can feel his anger from here. He steps into the room, never taking his stone-cold eyes off Oliver. "What's going on here?"

"I was just getting to know the newest member of our happy family," Oliver replies, not losing his smile.

"By harassing her?"

Oliver scoffs. "I was not harassing her," he insists. He turns back to me. "Was I harassing you?"

"I—"

Oliver turns back to Will. "See, I was not harassing her. We were simply having a civilized conversation before you so rudely interrupted us. Do they not teach manners at the Metro police?"

Will passes Oliver with a glare. "I am not in the mood." Will stops a few feet from me. "Did you get something to eat?"

"Not yet," I answer.

"Then you must be hungry," he says, eyeing the door.

"Yeah, I'm gonna ... " I start toward the door. Oliver doesn't stop me this time; he just smiles as I pass. I grab my plates.

"If you get scared in the night, Trixie, my bed is always open," Oliver calls to me.

"I'd feel safer with an alligator," I say under my breath.

"But you would not have nearly as much fun."

I mentally slap my forehead. I forgot vampires have heightened senses, especially hearing. Ignoring this last statement, I walk out of the library with my head held high. Will comes out a second later, jogging to catch up to me on the steps.

"I am so sorry about him," Will says.

"I can still hear you!" Oliver shouts.

Will sighs in exasperation.

"I heard that too, William!"

We reach the top of the stairs without a word and start down the hall. "It should be safe now. I can't hear him, so he can't hear us."

That's a relief. "Jeez, is he always like that?"

"Unfortunately."

"I'm sorry, but what the heck is he doing here? I mean, I can't see him hunting fellow vamps out of the kindness of his heart."

"He isn't. They gave him a choice: join or die."

"What'd they catch him doing?"

I don't get an answer.

My already pulsating heart rate goes up another ten notches. I was just cornered by a killer, someone who *willingly* took lives. And if that little display shows anything, it's that he probably enjoyed it. A cold-blooded murderer lives in the same house and apparently has the hots for me. Just great.

"Is he dangerous? I mean, should I hang crosses on my door or something?"

"He knows better than to try anything. He's just ... an asshole. Pardon my language."

"That's okay. I was thinking the same thing."

That gets a quick smile. And he's got a yummy smile. "My best advice is to avoid him as much as possible. Don't wander downstairs alone, he loves to skulk." A skulking vampire, almost makes me miss skulking cockroaches in my old apartment.

"I'm so glad you showed up when you did. I really didn't want to assault one of my new team members on the first day."

"Trust me, no one would have blamed you."

Will takes the lead up the narrow staircase, giving me the perfect vantage point of his butt. I shouldn't ogle my teammate's heinie on the first day either. But I was right, it's perfect. "So," I say, trying to keep my mind off the beautiful sight in front of me, "you were a cop? For how long?"

"Twenty-six years. I joined when I was nineteen."

"But wait, that makes you ... "

"Fifty-one."

"No way. You don't look it."

"It's one of the effects of ... my condition."

"Mine's headaches. Trade you."

He chuckles softly. Good, I got a laugh. Sex can't be too far behind. "My ex-boyfriend is a patrolman. Chula Vista PD. We broke up almost a year ago." Which means I'm single, just so you know. "So, any other tips you can give me? About being a good agent?"

"Trust your instincts." He glances at me again, still looking uncomfortable. "Always."

Irie was right, he doesn't say much. Ah, the strong, silent type. A tough nut to crack. I have the feeling I'm going to have oodles of fun trying though. Like most well-read people, I can't resist a good puzzle.

We reach our rooms, separating to our respective sides. As I'm about to step into my room, Will says, "Alexander." I spin around. I notice his thumb is rubbing up against his ring finger as if a ring was on it. "Um, if you need anything—you know, a chaperone around the house or … " he runs his hand through his hair, *anything*—I'm just across the hall."

"I may take you up on that. Thank you. For everything. You really made me feel …"—beautiful, important, giddy—"…welcome."

A flash of a smile crosses his face but disappears as quickly. "My pleasure. Good night."

"'Night." I step into my bedroom and quietly shut the door, resting my head against it with a sigh. I do feel safer having him across the hall. I'd feel even safer with him here, but it's too soon for that, unfortunately. Tomorrow is another day. I deadbolt my door, though as the latch catches, I chuckle. A tank couldn't stop the things I want to keep out; what's one little piece of metal in wood?

I put the plates down and fall on the bed. My white cloud seems to have gotten more comfortable in the last fifteen minutes. For someone who just slept five hours, I sure am tired. And hungry. I grab my neglected sandwich and start chomping on it. I finish in four bites, a new record. I devour the cake just as quickly.

Without really realizing it, I've finished my food. Unfortunately, my hunger hasn't been sated. It never is. Give a moose a muffin … it wants the whole basket and a Reuben sandwich on the side. But I don't dare go downstairs for seconds. Heck, I wouldn't go downstairs if my room were on fire.

A prisoner in my own room, scared of one of the people I'm supposed to trust with my life. So much for the brave monster killer I've been psyching myself up to be for the past two months.

Since I can't do my first favorite thing (eat), I'll do my second: a bubble bath. My bathroom is as lovely as the rest of the house. Pale blue tiles line the floor and walls, and two fluffy towels hang on a gold rack. I run my fingers through the soft material and they all but disappear in the thick pile. Pictures of cherubs and naked virgins hang on the walls in frames. Whoever decorated this house really had a thing for naked maidens. And to top it all off, there is a cream-colored porcelain tub big enough to fit three people and deep enough to bathe a horse. I turn on the gold faucet placed smartly in the middle of the tub. When the vanilla-scented bubbles reach the top, I drop my tired body into the heavenly water, instantly feeling better. There is nothing in the world that can't be cured with some chocolate or a bubble bath.

I breathe in the vanilla scent. It does nothing to assuage my ever-growing hunger but smells so freaking good I almost forget my growling stomach. I wring out the washcloth under me and put it over my eyes. Peace. At this moment, all is right in the world.

But of course, being me, I don't allow the peace to last long. Reality swims back. I've been so busy with training and studying, I realize I haven't had time to process everything. Really I've just been avoiding it, pushing and pushing it away. The deepest thinking I've done in the past two months involved what size Band-Aid to put on my cuts. Now…oh heck. Let the thoughts flow.

I'm stuck in Kansas. I'm living in a house with two men who can rip me apart with their bare hands before they eat me—which is scary no matter how cute they are—a woman who can make me spontaneously combust at will, another who spent the first half of her life robbing banks, a man who will know all my dirty secrets if he touches me, and another one who sees dead people. Nobody knows where I am. I'm expected to fight creatures that kill without hesitation. Three months ago, I was grading spelling tests and the most exciting thing in my life was going to the movies with April. All the fear, all the apprehension I've been denying the last months hits me like a brick wall. If I wasn't sitting, I'd fall. I snap my head under the water, clutching my knees to my chest and I scream. I scream and scream until my throat aches and my lungs all but explode.

What the heck have I gotten myself into?

FOUR

BELLS AND WHISTLES

I'VE BEEN IN THE tub long enough for my fingers to prune, return to normal, and then prune all over again. I'm positive I've used all the hot water in the state. Miraculously, there's still some left, because I top off the tub again with steaming hot water and sigh for the twentieth time this hour. I had my freakout. It's over and done with. All is well now. The washcloth goes back under the water and then onto my eyes so all I can see is white. I don't think I've ever been this relaxed without medical intervention. It—

Suddenly a noise as loud as a foghorn cuts through the calm room, like a fire truck's siren, only twice as loud. I scream and jump when it starts, sending soapy water splashing onto the tile floor. I sit in the tub for a second, unsure of what to do. Is it the house alarm? Has something gotten in? Is there a fire? Sirens are never a good thing.

Finally getting my wits about me, I climb out of the tub, grabbing a terrycloth robe off the toilet next to me. The screeching is even louder in my bedroom, so loud I have to cover my ears. God, shut up! I look above the bathroom door and notice a square piece of plastic vibrating lightly. Then the alarm stops just as suddenly as it started. The silence lasts for all of a microsecond before the pounding begins. I turn to the door.

Once again, Will stands in the hallway about to knock again. I quickly close the gap in my robe. "What was that?" I ask breathlessly. All the tension I managed to soak away has returned with its entire extended family.

"It's the alarm. We need to get to the conference room." With that, he runs down the hall.

"Why? Is something wrong?" I call.

"Five minutes!" he shouts before disappearing out of sight.

"Great," I mutter under my breath. I shut the door and prop up my still semi-full suitcases. Of course, I open the one filled solely with underwear and shoes. Seeing as I only have five minutes to do my hair, get dressed, and somehow find the conference room, I just grab the clothes I had on before. I'm still wet so the silk sticks to my arms and torso like snakeskin. Great, I look like a wet T-shirt contest. Shoes? Where are my shoes? I check under the bed, the bathroom. Crud. Oh, there they are. Under the suitcase. My hair goes into a ponytail and I'm ready.

The house is deserted as I walk through it. Everyone must already be in the conference room, which poses a problem. I cannot, for the life of me, remember where George said the conference room was. I run through the entire first floor from the kitchen to the library, shouting for someone to help me like an idiot. I'm late for my first meeting, and I can't find the fudging conference room. If I were them, I'd fire my butt. Can't even find a simple room. Monsters of the world, beware.

As I come out of the billiard room for the second time, I stop dead in my tracks, my heart catching in my chest. Oliver leans against the wall of the stairs, arms folded across his chest with an amused grin on his face. My body tenses the last bit it can. I am officially a plank of wood.

"We were worried about you," he says in that silk voice.

"I—" I can't get anything out. It's from either the fear or the embarrassment, but either way I'm tongue-tied. His grin widens enough for me to see the tips of his fangs; my guess is this not an accident.

For some reason, as his grin grows, all the fear—okay, *almost* all the fear—leaves my body. Anger floats in like a raging river. I look into his eyes, square my jaw, and fold my arms across my chest just like him. His grin fades. I always told my kids to stand up to a bully, and that's what this creep is. This is his version of pulling my hair or throwing a ball at me. I'd be a total hypocrite if I didn't take my own advice. We look into each other's eyes for a good thirty seconds. The vein in his temple bulges more and more as he goes deeper into thought. Vampires are the ultimate control freaks, and it must be killing him that he can't capture my mind. I don't know why he can't, and I don't care. He looks away first. Yeah! I won! In your face, fang boy!

"This is ridiculous," he mutters. "They are waiting for us."

Oliver turns and pushes one of the roses on the wallpaper. Immediately part of the wall slides, revealing a large metallic room with a door on the other side. An elevator. When we're in, the door slides shut. We ride in silence as far from each other as possible, though I see him peek over at me. His eyes move away when I glance back at him. That's right, grin boy, look away. Right now, I have no problems kicking your alabaster booty.

Mercifully, the doors open and we step into a dimly lit hallway furnished with a burgundy carpet and wood paneling along the walls. There are three doors pretty far apart along the long hallway, one to the right of us and two to the left. Oliver walks to the first door on the left, and with a bow opens the door for me. This gets an eye roll.

Everyone except the FBI agents and the doctor have assembled in black leather chairs on either side of a long table that takes up half the room. A theater-size screen fills the entire north wall and a felt board takes up the east wall. Opposite the screen, where George stands, is a computer hooked up to cables in the table. I seriously doubt we've been called down to watch vacation slides. "There you are," he says. With my eyes averted to the ground like a scolded child, I scuttle to an empty chair next to Irie and across from Andrew.

"I couldn't find the elevator," I mumble.

Oliver sits down across the table diagonal from me. "She was wandering up there like a lost kitten. It was rather cute."

I give him the stare of death that scared my students into silence, but Oliver raises an eyebrow and smirks. Ignoring him, I turn to George. "It won't happen again."

"So," Oliver says, leaning back in his chair and lacing his fingers behind his head, "what do we hunt this time? Trolls? Mummies? Defense attorneys?"

"No," George says, "it's an UNCRET right now."

Irie leans into my ear. "That's an unidentified creature," she whispers. "They usually start out that way."

"How many dead so far?" Will inquires, as if he's asking for the house specials.

"Two confirmed. One a week and a half ago, a woman, and a man tonight."

"How were they killed?" Carl asks.

George raises the remote in his hand. The lights dim as the projector starts up. I gasp when the first picture comes on the screen, not prepared for what I see. Filling the screen is a woman, or at least what's left of her. The only way I can tell she's a woman is the few patches of long red hair still on her scalp and a high heeled shoe still on her detached leg. She's been ripped to pieces, literally. Her left leg, head, and right arm are barely attached to her split torso. What's left of her gray and bloody intestines hang out like huge spaghetti noodles in a pool of black goo and yellow cottage cheese matter. Her jaw is gone too.

"Holy heck," I say to myself. I can feel the color draining from my face.

Once again, all eyes are on me. Most look sympathetic, all except Andrew, who can't see me turning green, and Oliver, whose smirk has returned. Irie passes me a glass of water, which I down.

"Are you all right, Beatrice? Do you need to step outside for a moment?" George asks.

I put the glass down and in my strongest voice say, "I'm fine. Sorry. Please continue."

"Her name was Valerie Wayland," George says, "local bank manager at Bridge Stone Bank in Bridge Stone, Colorado. Thirty-seven at the time of her death. Husband's name is Walter, manager of the grocery store there. They had a daughter, Emma, but she died five months ago."

"Any connection?" Irie asks.

"Daughter fell out of a tree and broke her neck, so no."

George presses the remote and the picture changes. The next one is of a live and whole Valerie Wayland, one of the professional type done in front of a forest backdrop. She stands between her husband and daughter, smiling that phony smile done for photographs. She looks older than thirty-seven, more like forty-seven, with streaks of gray in her curly red hair and plenty of wrinkles. She's a good thirty pounds overweight but wears it well. A typical suburban mom. The husband also looks older, with a crown of salt-and-pepper hair wrapped from ear to ear and a shiny bald head to top it all off. Middle age hit early. All the fat traveled down to his stomach, creating a medium-sized spare tire. The daughter, Emma, who seems not to have gotten any of her parents' imperfections, has long brown hair, pink lips, and a sweet smile. She reminds me of Elizabeth Taylor at that age. A typical middle-class family. I bet they even had a dog. George flips to another crime scene photo and I turn away.

"How do we know a human didn't do this?" I ask. "Or an animal?"

"That's why it wasn't flagged before," George says, "but the second body denotes a pattern."

"Oh."

"What about tonight's vic?" Will asks.

"Davis Wynn, owns the local butcher shop."

"Any connection between the two?" Andrew asks.

"The body was discovered a little over an hour ago, so the local police haven't begun the investigation yet."

"What have they found out so far about Valerie?" Irie asks.

"Absolutely nothing, though I've only seen the case file," George answers. "No enemies, no reports of domestic violence."

"So, wrong place, wrong time?" Oliver asks. "Was tonight's victim in the same location?"

"No. Wayland was found a half mile outside of the town and Wynn was discovered ten miles away. You'll know more when you reach the scene."

"Any local scaries around?" Nancy asks.

George opens his mouth, but I pipe up first. "It could be a Wendigo," I instruct in my teacher voice, "a local Native American monster. A large half man, half animal, though the animals vary from tribe to tribe. They eat people. Beyond a Wendigo, the only things that can do that to a human are vampires, werewolves, ghouls—"

"And psychokinetics," Oliver interrupts. "A psychokinetic could tear a person apart with her mind, correct?"

Will clears his throat. "We'll do a full assessment when we get there. The rest of the team are already on their way. I'll bring them up to speed on the plane. Dr. Neill will re-prep mobile command and fly in with it tomorrow. Twenty minutes, people."

Before everyone stands, Oliver raises a hand to stop them. "May I voice a concern before we disband?"

"What?" Will asks.

"I do not believe our newest member should accompany us on this trip."

My mouth drops open. "Why?"

"Well, to be perfectly honest, I think you will be a liability. You have only just arrived today, and I do not think you are ready for the field yet."

"I completed my training!"

"Be that as it may, Trixie dear, you almost threw up at a picture. What will happen when you are seeing and smelling the real

59

thing? Besides, you could not even fend off a docile vampire to-night without the aid of a werewolf."

I jump up from my chair. "You—!" I push against his torso with my mind. The chair falls back onto the floor and so does Oliver. His arms flail trying to grab onto something to stop his descent, but he clutches at nothing but air. His head hits the floor with a thunk. Someone, I think it's Nancy, lets out a giggle. Oliver is stunned for a second but then stands. I meet his furious eyes with my hard ones, my jaw clamped so tight my teeth hurt. I half expect him to jump across the table but he just stares, hands balled into fists. We glare for only a second, but it feels like an eternity.

"That's enough," Will snaps. Oliver turns to him. "Oliver, I re-spect your concerns but the decision is not up to you." Will turns to me. "It's up to you. We'd all understand if you sit this one out. Do you want to come with us this time?"

Do I want to? What kind of question is that? Do I want to look at a man torn limb from limb? Do I want to chase after something that can rip people's jaws off? Would I rather stay in this mansion playing pool and watching old movies? Heck yeah! But *nothing* would give me greater pleasure than showing up that bloodsuck-ing jerk. I turn to Oliver, imitating his smirk. "I'm coming."

His grin drops. Game, set, match.

FIVE

RIPPED APART

MY FOURTH TIME ON a plane is no better than the previous three. This time, instead of being stuck in a huge tube with lots of people, I am in a freakishly small plane, a Cessna sixteen-seater. Luckily, Nancy plopped down in the seat next to me before anyone else— i.e., a certain undead jerk—could. But the second her butt was in the seat, her mouth began to move. Before we had even taken off I knew where she was born, her first pet's name, how when she was five she wanted to be a ballerina and then later a sharpshooter for the army, and how when she was two she teleported into a closet and it took her parents three hours to find her. Finally, after the bumpy takeoff, Irie changes seats with Carl so she can kneel in the seat in front of me, interrupting a fascinating story about Nancy's first trip to the dentist.

"How you doing? Nervous?" Irie asks.

"A little."

"Well, don't be. We've done this a thousand times. Chances are it's a werewolf, so all we have to do is sic Will on it, sit back, and watch." She sighs, mock wistful. "You never forget your first time in the field. Mine was a vampire. She killed three people. Took us two days to track her and all of five minutes to ice her. It's really not as bad as you might think. We usually never get hurt."

"Good to know," I say with a half smile.

"And speaking of vampires ... " she says in a playful tone, "what is up with you and Oliver? I thought you two never met."

"Oh, we met."

"So what happened? You turned him down, didn't you?"

"Turned him down for what?" Nancy asks.

"A game of Parcheesi," Irie says sarcastically. "Sex, of course!"

Nancy turns to me, her mouth gaping open. "He asked you to have sex with him?" she asks in a high whisper.

I feel my face go hot. That was all the answer they needed. Nancy's eyes grow so wide they rival telescopes.

Irie just chuckles. "I knew it! God, he can't keep it in his pants!"

As if on cue, Oliver saunters over, resting one arm on Irie's seat and one on Nancy's, but his eyes are on me. "I believe my ears are burning."

If only. "We were just talking about what a jackass you've been acting like," Irie says.

"*Moi?* I was simply trying to make our newest member feel accepted."

"Please! You were trying to get some."

His gaze turns to Nancy. "Are you trying to turn my Nancy against me?"

Nancy turns as red as I was before. Yuck, she has a crush on him. No accounting for taste. "Jeez, Nancy, could you be more obvious?" Irie asks. Nancy turns an even deeper shade of red.

"Nancy knows she is my girl, do you not?" Oliver asks with a wink.

"She's too good for you," Irie says, "as is ninety-nine percent of the population."

"Are you including yourself in that, Irie?"

"I am now. Now go away, your blood breath is making me sick."

Oliver removes his elbows from the seats. "Whatever milady wishes." He gives Nancy another wink and walks back to the front of the plane.

"I can't believe I slept with him," Irie says with a groan.

It is my turn for my eyes to bug out. "You—"

"Not my finest hour."

"You're a total slut!" Nancy practically shouts.

"Oh, please." Irie smiles at me. "It's sort of a rite of passage for us girls on the team. Lori held out the longest with two whole years. I lasted four months, and from what I hear, most hold out three. It's best to just get it over with, otherwise he'll never leave you alone."

"I think I'll pass."

"That's what they all say."

Nancy gets up in a huff, collecting all her things and moving to an empty seat as far from me as possible, which is all of three feet. Irie just raises an eyebrow and falls back into her seat. The only good thing about people being mad at you is they tend to leave you alone. Distraction time. I pull out my book and manage to get a few chapters under my belt. A chick lit murder mystery to get me in the mood. Of course, right when I get to a good point, my undead stalker plops himself into the seat next to me. Great. He gets bored and I suffer.

"What are you reading?" he asks, grabbing the book right out of my hands. "A mystery. You know these things can rot your brain."

I snatch it back. "Then you must be an avid fan."

"Feisty. I had you all wrong."

I open the book. "Darn straight."

"Irie says I should apologize for my ill behavior."

"She's right, you should," I say, pretending to read.

"I will not apologize for what I said at the meeting. I really do believe you should not have come," he says almost sincerely.

Now I look up from the book. "I don't give a rat's patootie what you believe. I'm here, and I am going to do my job. If you don't like it, then you can stay away from me. I *really* won't mind."

He's silent for a moment, just looking at me with his lips pursed. "You really do not like me, do you?"

"In the ten whole minutes I've spent with you, you've hit on me, insulted me, made me look like an idiot in front of everyone, and now won't let me read my book. So no, I will not be joining your fan club. But hey, you can leave me alone now and my opinion might soften a bit."

That grin returns. "You are fiery, my dear. I like that in a woman. It translates to every area."

"I bet you'd sleep with a toaster if it showed interest. And I am not your dear."

"Unlike some, I have never had to resort to electronics for pleasure."

"Oh, I'm sure women have been falling at your feet for centuries."

"You will too," he says with absolute certainty.

"Not in a million years."

"Why? Are you attracted to women?"

"No."

"Then you must be afraid of sex. Are you a virgin?"

The book falls to my lap with a slap. "I most certainly am not! And even if I was, it is hardly your business! You know, this may be a hard concept to get through your narcissistic brain, but you are resistible." He raises an eyebrow. "You're good looking, but that amounts to very little in my regard. You won the genetic lottery, you did nothing to earn it." I lift up my book again. "And even if you weren't rude, inconsiderate, and charmless, you're a walking dead man. I'm not into necrophilia. So please stop wasting both our time and give it up."

He's about to respond with what is I'm sure another rude remark, but Will appears beside us. "Is everything all right here?" he asks in a low voice. Déjà vu all over again.

"We're fine," I say harshly.

"You really must stop interrupting, William," Oliver says, sounding mad. Like, scary-vampire mad.

Will isn't fazed. "It looked to me like your conversation was just about over. Right? Ms. Alexander?"

Great, put me in the middle. "Yeah."

"Then why don't you leave her to her book."

Oliver looks over at me and then at Will, mouth gaping open. "Oh, I understand now," he says as if he's just discovered radium. Surprisingly, he gets up from his seat. "You can have her, William." He leans in a little and the mirth drops. "For now." With a wink my way, he moves to the front of the plane. I am more than sure I turn as red as Will. This is worse than middle school; we might as well be passing notes.

"Um, he … " Will says uncomfortably.

"He's a jerk," I finish.

"Understatement." Will runs his hand through his hair. "Do you mind if I sit?" Not waiting for the answer, he does. Not that I would have said no. "I am so sorry for his behavior. He should get bored soon and then leave you alone. If he doesn't, just come get me. I'll straighten him out."

Part of me wants to kiss him for offering to look out for me. No man ever really did that for me, not even my policeman ex, Steven. But in this job I don't have that luxury, especially not on my first case. "Look, I really appreciate what you just did, but … you need to stop it. If I'm going to get his or anybody's respect, you need to stop rescuing me. I *can* handle him. I've handled a lot worse."

His face falls. "I didn't mean to imply that—"

"Oh, I know! But if I need help, I know how to ask for it."

Will nods. "Okay. But just so you know, nobody here thinks you aren't up to the job. George has never been wrong before."

I scoot a little closer to him. He's so warm, I want to curl up against his side, but I restrain myself. "Well, just between you and me," I whisper, "I honestly cannot promise that when the bullets, or whatever this thing throws at us, start flying, I won't run away. Bravery is not really my strong suit."

"Good to know!" Oliver shouts from his seat.

I have *got* to remember that super-hearing. "Does he always do that," I ask, knowing full well he can hear me, "because it's *really annoying.*"

A chuckle comes from the front of the plane. Will sighs and shakes his head. "Just ignore him."

"I'll try." I so want off this plane. Maybe if I ask nicely, the pilot will make a small detour to San Diego and drop me off. I close my eyes, willing it all away.

"Are you all right?" Will asks.

"Fine, except for the fact I'm homesick, scared to death, and seriously annoyed."

"This must all be very overwhelming for you."

"You could say that," I chuckle. "I just don't want to let you—I mean, *everyone*—down."

"You won't. I know it." He smiles and my stomach does a somersault. I have a feeling that will be a common occurrence around Will. "I was ... um ... very impressed that you came with us. And of your knowledge of the creatures. I think some of us here couldn't tell a Sasquatch from a banana."

My mood has officially just improved threefold. I have to suppress a gleeful giggle. A gorgeous/not-scary man is not only *talking* to me, but he's impressed. By me. Usually the only men who give me the time of day are guys who still live with their mothers or just got out of jail, and now I can add the undead. The drool-worthy undead, but still. So once again, I blush. "Thank you," I say. "That means a lot. Especially—"

"Would you two please be quiet?" Oliver shouts. "Any more lovey dovey talk and I may throw up my dinner."

"Then stop listening," Will shouts back. He shakes his head in frustration and sighs. "Will you please excuse me?"

"Sure."

Will makes his way up to Oliver and sits down. I can't see anything but the tops of their heads, so I start my book again, but not before I see one of the FBI agents, Agent Wolfe, raise a blond eyebrow at me. I sure am making a great impression with the team.

An hour later, the plane lands on a small airstrip, like the one we just left, except instead of being surrounded by flat nothingness, big bulks of black fill the void. There is a control tower and a small hanger but nothing more. The Rocky Mountains lay in front, beside, and behind us. If I could see them, I'd be impressed, but now all I can see is the black asphalt of the runway, and boy am I glad to see it.

I'm the first one off, desperate to get out of the tense atmosphere. Nancy follows behind me and practically shoves me down the stairs, as if it's my fault Oliver has at least some morals and won't seduce a teenage girl. It seems that the chilliness from the plane escapes as soon as we do. It's cold, especially for May. Welcome to high elevations, I guess. I've never been good with the cold. If it's below sixty, I need two sweaters, earmuffs, and thick socks. Just another reason for me to miss San Diego.

Two black Suburbans and a van wait for us on the airstrip, but no people are visible. The whole thing—arriving by cover of night, not a soul presumably for miles, the night as still as a tomb—has a World War II feel. I half expect a man with a thick German accent to step out of the shadows asking for "zee documents." Okay, I really have to cut down on Turner Classic Movies. Unless a Rita Hayworth movie is on, then not even Beelzebub himself can drag me away from the TV. Everyone else deplanes while I contemplate adding Katharine Hepburn to that list. Each person walks hastily to the Suburbans without a word. Like a good little sheep, I follow.

Irie, Nancy, Carl, and Agent Rushmore get into the first one. I follow Agent Chandler into the second. Oliver climbs in right next to me, squishing me against the side of the car. There's plenty of room, but he makes sure our thighs touch. I'm about to push him away when Andrew is led in by Agent Konrad, who gets into the driver's seat. Will climbs into the passenger seat and before his door is even closed, the SUV takes off after the other. Here we go. No turning back now.

As we pass the plane, Agent Wolfe watches a black coffin-sized pod on a conveyer belt lurch toward the van that stays behind. Even with only half a moon, it gleams. I'll bet it's lined with plush red satin. I just wonder how they're going to sneak that behemoth into a hotel room undetected. I can just see the night manager's face when it's lugged through the lobby. Priceless.

The car remains silent except for the GPS giving instructions until we pull onto the desolate interstate. Everything is so black it's almost blank. Very faintly, the outlines of trees wiz by, but it's so dark they could be skinny giants for all I know. I don't think I've ever been down a road without a speck of light before, certainly not an interstate. There are no houses, no cars driving by, no streetlights—it's creepy. Guess I'm just a city girl.

"Alexander?" Will says, turning around to face us.

I look away from the darkness. "Beatrice," I correct.

He reaches into his pocket and pulls out what looks like a black wallet. But it's not a wallet; it's my official FBI badge. Cool. It has a seal with *Fidelity* (got that), *Bravery* (not so much), and *Integrity* (sure, except on the LA freeway, anything goes there) written on it. Uck, it also has a really horrible picture of me inside. My hair's frizzy, my eyes squinted, and my cheeks look double their real size. Maybe now they realize why I put up such a big fuss when they wanted to take it. ID photos are not one of my strong suits.

Oliver glances at it. "I suppose the camera cannot love everyone."

The badge goes in my pocket. "Shut up."

Will also reaches back and gives me something bulky. Holy crud, it's a gun. And a black side holster! He hands it to me very carefully. "Keep this on you at all times, it's an FBI regulation." I pull the gorgeous piece of machinery out of its holster. Glock 9mm semi-automatic. Nice. "Inside are silver-plated bullets. They'll stop anything and anyone. We'll get you a spare clip later."

The gun returns to its holster and clips onto the left side of my pants. My confidence certainly got a boost there.

"You remember the cover story?" Will asks.

"We're part of the Violent Criminal Apprehension Team of the FBI, here to investigate a possible serial killer," I say. "What if they ask questions about our procedures or rules?"

"William knows them all," Oliver says.

"Unlike some, I took the time to learn them."

"Teacher's pet," Oliver says.

"And do we actually get to do some investigating, like collecting DNA and stuff?" I ask.

"These creatures do not often make it to trial, Trixie," Oliver says. "And even if that were the case, you are not on the investigative team. You are on the muscle side of our little operation. Your one and only job is to look pretty and watch daytime television until something is in need of killing."

I very nobly overlook Oliver's choice of epithets and turn to Will. "So I don't get to interview the perp or chase down leads?" I ask, not hiding my disappointment. That was the one part I was actually looking forward to doing: finding that crucial piece of evidence and sweating a confession out of someone. Nuts.

"You watch too much television, my dear," Oliver chides.

"Oh, bite me," I snap. I mentally slap my head the second it comes out. Must remember not to say that to vampires.

"I have already eaten this evening, but I suppose a midnight snack would not hurt."

"Knock it off, Oliver," Will says.

"It's all right, Will," I say more harshly than I intended. Will turns back around, brow furrowed.

"Have the locals been notified that we're coming?" Agent Chandler asks.

"Yes," Will says.

"Are they going to be a problem?" Agent Konrad asks behind the wheel.

"Are they not always?" Oliver responds wryly.

"So what do we do? Tell them to buzz off and they do?" I ask.

"If we're lucky," Will answers. "Though sometimes they take a little persuading."

"And how exactly do you do that?"

"A magician never reveals his secrets," Oliver replies.

"He captures their minds," Will says, "and they do whatever he wants them to, including forgetting what happened."

"I am very handy," Oliver smiles.

"Oh, I'll bet."

After half an hour of driving and bickering, we reach our destination: the crime scene. I am at a crime scene. Someone died here tonight, and I am willingly coming here. This is surreal. Three brown police cars with flashing white and blue lights and two compact cars sit in a small cul-de-sac at the end of a lone road. Trees surround us closely on either side of the road, keeping watch tonight like all nights. At the end of the cul-de-sac is a small, circular clearing where all the action is taking place. Tall floodlights sit at random spots on the grass. Four men in khaki brown uniforms stand around a blue tarp on the ground. I've seen enough police shows to know what's underneath there. How they can just stand there looking like they're having a casual conversation is beyond me. Their attention diverts when we pull up.

By the time we pile out of the cars, the cops are there to meet us. Will walks over to the oldest man, hand extended. "Sheriff Graham? I'm Special Agent William Price with the FBI."

The sheriff, a man in his mid-fifties with a few laugh lines and sandy brown hair and moustache shakes Will's hand. He's in pretty good shape with only a small beer belly over his belt. "Brought a lot of you, didn't you?" he asks, eyeing the teenaged Nancy.

"We're a specialized unit," Will says, "dispatched only on certain cases."

"Well, the government usually knows what it's doing," Graham says, not totally assuaged. "Though I was a little surprised the FBI was interested in a couple of animal attacks."

Will gives Graham a great good ol' boy smile, eyes crinkling when he does. I love crinkly eyes. "If that's what they are." He turns to Andrew. "Agent DuChamp, why don't you walk the perimeter, see if you can't pick up anything? Miss Lake, please go with him."

Nancy nods her head and takes Andrew's arm. They begin walking toward the tarp. Sheriff Graham watches as they pass, still puzzled. "And what exactly are their specialties?"

"He can see ghosts and she can teleport," Oliver answers.

Will's jaw visibly tightens. Graham looks at Oliver, then at Will, and begins to chuckle. Everyone else joins in. "Oh, that's a good one," the sheriff chuckles. "Didn't know you guys had a sense of humor."

"There is a lot about us you would not believe," Oliver says with his sly smile.

Will clears his throat. "If you wouldn't mind, Sheriff, we'd like to get a look at the body."

Sheriff Graham's smile fades and it's back to business. "Yes, of course." Graham nods at his three officers—none of whom are old enough to shave—who start toward the tarp, followed by their leader. Will walks in stride with them and we follow a few feet behind, Oliver practically at my hip.

"Have you begun with evidence collection?" Will asks.

"Yes. I've sent some to the station already."

"We'll come by and pick up what you have in the morning."

"Who found him?" Irie asks.

"Jesse Barnes and Clementine Charlemagne. This place is a real hot spot for teens. They came out here and spotted him right away, called nine-one-one. Poor Clem had to be sedated."

Not a good sign. My stomach does a flip. "Is she okay?"

Graham looks back at me. "She'll be fine, miss."

"That's *Agent* Alexander," Oliver says pointedly.

"Sorry," Graham says.

We reach the body, forming a semi-circle around it. Immediately, an acrid odor assaults my nose like a carjacker. It was faint before, but now it clings to my nostrils like tar. My already unsteady stomach lurches almost clear out of my body and they haven't even lifted the tarp yet.

"Sheriff, would you and your men mind stepping back while we examine the body?" Will asks. "Our techniques are very sensitive; having others around hinders the process."

"Um ... " The sheriff looks at his men, who seem very put off by this idea. They glance at each other, then at the sheriff. "With

73

all due respect, this *is* our case, if there even is one. You can't just order us—"

Oliver steps in front of the four men, scanning their faces and stopping at their eyes. His eyes don't move from theirs, and not one of them blinks or moves. Weird. After ten long seconds, the men turn and walk back to their patrol cars in a daze then drive off. Okay, I have to admit that was pretty cool. Not that I'd ever tell him that. I glance at Oliver, who is blinking again and looking very smug. "I commanded them to come back in half an hour. They will not even remember leaving."

"Good," Will says. "Then let's not waste any time."

Nancy and Andrew walk back over to the group. "These woods are, like, totally creepy," Nancy says. "They stink too."

"I know," Will says, "I've smelled rotting flesh since we got out of the car. It's highly concentrated here."

"Could the body be the cause?" Irie asks.

"It is too strong," Oliver answers, "to be from only one source."

"Could there be another victim out there?" I ask.

"If a human can smell it, then there would have to be at least ten bodies," Will says. "This body has just started to go into rigor; you wouldn't be able to smell the decomp yet. Oliver? Go into the woods; see if there are any more bodies."

"Why cull me from the herd?"

"Please," he says through gritted teeth, "just go."

"Since you used the magic word…" And *poof,* he's gone. Disappeared into thin air. I, of course, gasp like a frightened child.

"Jumpy much?" Nancy asks with a smug smile. "Can we just get this over with? I'm missing *Teen Mom.*"

"In a minute," Will says. "Andrew, did you see anything?"

Normally I'd laugh at someone who says this to a blind man, but all humor has left me. I can't take my eyes off the tarp.

"His spirit must have passed on already," Andrew says. "I do sense a presence here, but it's faint, like after a woman leaves and you can still smell her perfume."

"So there was a ghost but it's gone now?" I ask.

"Not a ghost. Something stronger," Andrew says.

"Can we see the dead guy already?" Nancy asks impatiently, pulling my sweater around her small body. "I'm, like, freezing my butt off."

My body tenses up in preparation as Will bends down and begins lifting up the tarp. I will not puke. I will not puke. Oh crud, the bile rises into my mouth. If I've ever needed a reminder that humans are nothing but walking, talking pieces of meat, I get it now.

He's in pieces, really bloody gross pieces. The man's head is still attached to his neck, and one arm (sans hand) remains. The other arm, broken off at the elbow, is nowhere to be seen, left with just red and yellow chunks. The legs lie on the ground a few inches from the torso. Scraggy pieces of white skin hang onto the legs by tiny filaments, but the rest is just red meat. The few intact patches of skin have circular wound patterns that look familiar. White jagged bones stick out of his partially open chest. They look like they've been torn apart with bare hands. His head is nothing but a few patches of intact skin and an eyeball plucked out and resting on his meaty cheek. White liquid lies in a pool in the other eye socket. His jaw is gone, as is all but a few tufts of blood-soaked hair. At second glance, the legs are still attached but only by thin threads of tendons. The smell comes from his exposed intestines, cut and gnawed on.

Oh good God.

I look at it longer than I thought I could—three whole seconds—but then I turn and walk away, forcing vomit down. When I get far enough away that the smell is bearable, I take several deep, cleansing yoga breaths. Nancy giggles behind me, finding what so funny I don't know. I should have puked on her—it'd serve her right.

I take another breath and look down at the ground. There is something whitish under my shoe. When I bend down I can tell it's flesh, a piece about the size of a silver dollar. Bile rises again. There are more pieces a few feet away, bigger like swatches of white leather. "There's more of him over here," I call to them.

"What is it?" Will asks when he joins me. I point down. Will bends down right next to the skin, and suddenly his body goes rigid. His nose begins to twitch like a dog's from side to side. He takes a few steps, nose still moving. I turn to the others, all of whom are watching too. They seem to find this behavior nothing out of the ordinary. To me, seeing the future father of my fantasy children acting like a bloodhound makes me uncomfortable. Hope it doesn't show on my face. He stops dead about twenty feet from us. "The blood trail starts right here," he shouts. "This is where the attack began."

There's a blood trail? I look down at the ground but see only grass. Will walks back to the body and stares down at it, deep in thought. Deciding my stomach is strong enough, I rejoin the team. Nobody even registers my presence.

"So what are we thinking? Werewolf?" Irie asks.

"I don't smell one."

"Um … " Not sure of the butting in protocol, I do the polite thing and raise my hand. Everyone looks at me as if I'm a loon.

"Um, look at his left leg." I point down to the red circular scar on it. "That's a human bite mark."

Everyone's eyes narrow a little. "How do you know?" Irie asks.

"I was an elementary school teacher; I've seen my fair share of bites."

"Then it's a ghoul," Irie says.

Note to anyone who never had to take Monsters 101: ghouls are undead creatures whose soul is still in their decomposing body, feeling themselves rot as sort of a divine punishment. Only a truly evil person rises as a ghoul, like serial killers and people who work for the IRS. Most can't get out of their coffins, but those that do are understandably angry, scared, and often get violent. So I'd avoid the cemetery where Jeffrey Dahmer's buried.

"Let's not jump to any conclusions without more evidence," Will says. "We should start exploring the woods." My heart begins to race again. Go into the dark woods, looking for the thing that ripped this guy apart. Good idea. "The smell is strongest in the north, so we'll start there. Irie, take Agent Konrad and flank right. Nancy, you go with Agent Wolfe, flank left. Agent Rushmore, you're with me. One team should eventually meet up with Oliver. Andrew, Carl, Alexander, stay here. Start marking and photographing the locations of the skin and blood." This makes my back become very straight. "Everyone use extreme caution; this thing could still be around. Stay in constant communication. Radios on channel three."

Everyone turns on their bulky black walkie-talkie and turns the dial until the green light becomes a "3." The groups start on their merry ways, but I grab Will's arm before he can take a step. "May I speak to you?"

"You go ahead, I'll catch up," Will says to Agent Rushmore.

"Yes, sir," Agent Rushmore says with a thick Long Island accent.

He nods and starts into the woods, flashlight and gun drawn. I pull Will away from Andrew and Carl so we have a little privacy. "Why am I staying behind?" I ask harshly. "I thought I was on defense or whatever you call it."

"You are, and I need you here in case this thing comes back," he says.

"It's not coming back, we both know that. If it was, it would have attacked the police. I came here to help, not be a glorified corpse-sitter. Why do you keep—"

"You have your assignment, Alexander," he snaps. "I suggest you do it without questioning, or go back to the airport." With that, he steps toward the woods. I manage to keep my tongue from sticking out at his back until after he disappears from sight. Childish, I know, but it does make me feel a little bit better.

"He's like a really tall Napoleon," Carl, who I forgot was there, says. "He means well, though."

"I just don't understand," I say, walking toward them. "I was brought here to do a job, and it seems like nobody wants me to do it. You know, I'm sorry I was freaked out by Oliver and had to step away from the smelly dead man, but ... " I groan in frustration. "How can I prove myself to you people if I'm sitting on the sidelines?"

"Well, maybe you'll get lucky and this thing will come back and eat us, then you can show us your stuff," Carl says, exasperated.

"No need to be a snide," I say under my breath.

"Perhaps we should begin with our tasks," Andrew suggests.

"Good idea," Carl says. "Excuse me, Warrior Princess."

Great, I've made another friend.

Carl takes off his gloves and bends down next to the body. He reaches out to touch one of the intact pieces. Gross. The second he makes contact, his body jolts like electricity just passed through him. The spasms grow more violent with each passing second. One of my students was an epileptic and looked like this when she had a fit.

"Oh no, he's having a seizure!" I cry out. I'm temporarily stunned into inaction. We're all alone, and I have no idea what to do.

"Leave him be," Andrew commands.

"What?" I shout. "We need to do something!"

Andrew grabs my shoulder. "No."

I can only stand it for about five seconds. He could be swallowing his tongue or something. I kneel beside him and see that his eyes have rolled back in his head so only the bloodshot whites show.

"Andrew, we—"

"Don't touch—"

The rest of the sentence never reaches my ears. I touch Carl's vibrating shoulder, my finger resting on his bare neck, and instantly a burning sensation travels through me, so hot I can't even think. I'm on fire. My mouth opens to scream, but it hurts so much my vocal cords are paralyzed. The world disappears with a blink.

Almost as quickly, the world returns, only a little out of focus and brighter. The orange sun still peaks out from behind the trees. I close the door to my Chevy Impala, and the keys I'm holding go into my khaki pants. There's something not right about this.

I start walking toward the clearing, looking up at the oranges and blues. Carrie was right; this place is less spooky now than it is at night, but not by much. Hopefully they'll come before the sun completely sets. I'm here at seven sharp. They must be running late. An owl hoots, nearly knocking me out of my sneakers. Jesus, I'm forty-three years old, I shouldn't be acting like a scared four-year-old. The trees groan and creak as a gust of wind travels through the field. What the hell is that smell? It's like a slaughter-house on a warm day. There must be a dead animal close. Okay, five minutes, then I'm leaving. Don't know why I'm here in the first place. I should—

Twigs snap in the woods, then more.

"Hello?" I call out in a husky voice. There can't be anyone here, as mine's the only car. Maybe an anima—more twigs snap, this time much closer. Was that a grunt? Lord, the smell's worse, if that's even possible. I plug my nose.

Twigs continue to crack, louder and louder with each moment. Something moves in the trees. Suddenly the flapping of wings fills the near silence. A couple dozen birds fly from their perches in the pines toward the orange part of the sky. I watch them escape in perfect formation. It has to be an animal. Oh shit, what if it's a bear? Another twig snaps, and I turn toward the farthest part of the clearing.

Guess I'm not alone after all. A middle-aged man dressed in a mud-caked blue suit with pale yellow skin and eyes almost sunken in stands there, staring at me. I knew I should have taken out my contacts before I left, my eyes must be getting wonky. I step toward the man, and he staggers toward me like a marionette. It takes me a second, but I recognize him. It's Dale Cobb, the old math teacher. But … he died three weeks ago. What the hell?

"Dale, is that—" I don't get to finish. Dale grabs my arm, biting down on it with the force of a pit bull until he reaches bone. Oh, fuck me! I howl in agony and jerk my arm back. The flesh rips from me, blood pouring down my arm to the ground. Pain ripples along my arm into my spine. I scream again. Dale snarls, showing his blood-stained teeth like a rabid animal. "Fuck!" I spin around and start running.

I only manage to make it a few feet. Someone else grabs my other arm and jerks it out of the socket with a sickening pop. White-hot pain shoots through my back and again when another mouth clamps down on my limp arm, tearing more of me away. Blood spurts from the wound. Out of the corner of my eye, I see a woman gripping me, with black holes where her eyes should be. The combination of the putrid smell coming from her or the unbearable pain makes me throw up. With my halfway intact arm, I push her away and continue staggering away, my legs wobbling. I gain a few more feet before one hand grabs me by the shoulders, head, and arms, spinning me around. There are so many of them, at least half a dozen, all reeking of death. Some of their skin sloughs off onto me. I can barely move, I'm surrounded, and their grips are so strong. I can hear and feel my bones breaking. Some bite down on my arms, my neck, shoulders, every inch of me. Right before I pass out, I piss my pants.

My eyes fly open. I'm greeted by Nancy looking down at me as if I've grown scales. It's dark now, and the fuzziness is gone. The nausea is not. Nancy tentatively reaches across to me but I roll away, throwing up my pre-plane snack and some major organs onto the wet grass.

"Holy shit," Nancy says.

I heave once more before panting for air. While I'm doing a great impression of a dog, I look down at my limbs. No blood, no bites. This is good. This is really good. I turn to the group. Carl is lying on his back panting too. A pool of vomit rests a foot away from him. Good to know I'm not the only one who tossed their cookies. Andrew kneels beside him, taking his pulse through the latex glove he wears. "It's a little high," Andrew says.

"Like, will he be okay?" Nancy asks, as breathless as I am.

"I'm fine," Carl croaks.

Andrew releases Carl's wrist. "Stay on the ground until the dizziness stops."

I couldn't get up if I wanted to. My heavy head thumps to the ground.

"Will someone please tell me what just happened?" I pant.

"Hell if we know," Nancy replies. "I was, like, in the woods when Andrew radioed. I popped back here and found you and Carl in some kind of funny trance. We were totally afraid to touch you. We, like, shouted and shouted your names, but neither of you answered. Then all of a sudden, you both screamed like you were crazy. Then poof! You snapped out of it and started puking your guts out."

"Are you okay?" Andrew asks me.

What a question. "I think so," I say, wiping the residual vomit off my chin. I manage to get to my feet, but my legs feel like wet noodles. "It was so strange. I was a man. I think I was *that* man," I say, pointing to the body.

"We were," Carl says sitting up. "I think we were actually reliving his last moments. What he went through. We were inside him when he was ripped up."

"You actually saw and felt him dying?" Andrew asks.

"Yes."

"Bummer," Nancy mutters.

"Wait, I thought that's what you do," I say to Carl.

"Normally all I get are emotions, sometimes images, or words. What just happened … " Carl shudders. "That's the most awful thing I've ever experienced in my life, and that's saying a lot. I felt every bite, every bone…" The memory makes him stop. "It was horrible. You all have no idea."

"I do!" I shout.

The three look at me. "How?" Carl asks.

"I don't know."

"When you touched Carl, it must have connected your clairempathy skill to his psychometry skill," Andrew explains, helping Carl stand.

"Huh?"

"Your power plus mine equals bigger signal," Carl says. "Your clairempathy tapped into mine, and with the combined power we were able to see and feel more."

"I'll take your word for it. Let's never do that again."

Twigs crack in the woods, lots of twigs. Oh crud. My body tenses, and from the bug eyes on Carl, so has his. I unbutton my gun, as does Carl.

"What?" Nancy asks.

Will, Irie, and the rest run out of the woods, guns in their hands. "Is everyone all right?" Will shouts. "We heard screaming."

"Everyone's totally fine," Nancy says. "Chill."

"Then why the hell was there screaming?" Irie asks, out of breath.

"Carl and Bea just had a bad trip, that's all," Nancy says.

"What?" Will asks.

"Beatrice and I concentrated our powers and saw the man die."

"Felt it too," I mutter.

Will looks at me either in shock or in awe. I'm hoping awe. "You actually saw the attack? You saw what killed him?"

"Yeah, it was…" I can't remember the darn word, "dead people."

"'Dead people?'" Agent Konrad asks.

"I think she means zombies," Carl says. "There were six of them."

"One was named Dale Cobb," I add. "The dead guy knew him. He was a teacher or something."

"What else did you see?" Will asks.

"He came here to meet someone," Carl says. "No idea who."

"Oh, and he mentioned the name Carrie, who said this place was spooky," I say. Irie raises an eyebrow. "What? It could be useful."

Another twig snaps in the distance. Carl and I once again become stone statues. Will looks at us, visibly confused. "What?"

"Twigs snapped and out came bitey zombies," I practically whisper.

Everyone grips his or her guns a little tighter. Another twig snaps. This time I actually pull the gun out. Another twig goes. All guns point toward the sound. Another twig. Shoot, I can barely breathe. The gun shakes a little but I grip it tighter. Will steps to my side, a comforting presence. "Stay close to me," he whispers. A figure moves out of the shadow of the woods, and we all take aim.

I'm actually relieved when Oliver appears holding something in his hand. He stops cold at the edge of the woods when he sees the barrage of guns. "Do not shoot!" he shouts.

There is a collective sigh from the group. All the guns return to their holsters as Oliver walks toward us. "Jumpy, are we?" he asks Will. As he gets closer, I can make out what he's carrying. It's a friggin' severed arm. A severed arm and he's holding it like a newspaper. What the heck is the matter with these people? Oliver lifts it up, practically shoving the thing in our faces. "Look what I found."

"Lord," I say. Oliver cringes when I say it. "Show a little respect."

"Where'd ya find it?" Agent Rushmore asks, examining it.

"Just outside the graveyard about a quarter mile from here. Some of the graves looked recently interred. You ask me, this looks like—"

"Zombies," Will says, "we know. Carl and Alexander combined their gifts and saw and felt this man die."

Oliver's eyebrow goes up. "Did they now?" He looks at me. "You really are full of surprises."

I smirk. I do so love to impress. "So we know that zombies killed him, the—"

"You are wrong there," Oliver says with a tisk. "It is not guns that kill people, it is other people. And in this case, it was a necromancer who, instead of using a gun, used zombies."

Shoot, he's right. Ghouls really aren't zombies because they still have their soul. They have control over themselves. Zombies, on the other hand, have no soul or higher brain function. Basically, they're just meat puppets with superhuman strength. A necromancer—a person who can control the dead—can raise the dead, but he has to tell them what to do. I should have remembered that. Guess being torn into tiny bits has affected my brain.

"Whoever did this must really have hated these people," Carl says. "I can't think of a worse way to kill a person."

"If you have a weapon, you will use it," Oliver says. He tosses the severed arm next to the rest of the body.

"So we find this necro and put a bullet between his eyes," Irie says. "Piece of cake. Should be out of here by tomorrow."

Boy, I hope she's right. But judging from the ache in my stomach, I have a feeling it won't be that easy.

———

Agent Chandler drives Andrew, Carl, Irie, Nancy, and me to our hotel after we're done documenting the scene. I don't even put up a fight this time. In fact, I'm the first in the Suburban. I lost my courage along with my last meal, and it is past time for me to go, in my opinion. Will, Oliver, and the agents stay behind to "work the scene," or more accurately, find the rest of Davis Wynn. We pass the local cops on the way. I'm sure it will be easier to pass as official without a blind man and a Goth teenager around.

I thought the life of a secret agent—that's what I'm going to start considering myself just for my ego's sake—would be a heck of a lot more glamorous but apparently not. The hotel we're in is grungy. I think I can hear the cockroaches scurrying in the walls. It reeks of Lysol with a dash of something I have no desire to identify. I wasn't expecting the Ritz, but my own room would have been nice. I'm stuck bunking with Nancy and Irie, and guess who gets the lumpy cot? If that wasn't bad enough, MTV is on, even though Nancy's asleep. I tried to turn off the TV, but she immediately woke up, turned it back on, and fell back asleep. Irie didn't even stir. She passes out the moment her head hits the pillow. Even if the TV wasn't on, I doubt sleep would be an option. Every time I close my eyes, I see those zombies attack, followed by buckets of blood.

After tossing, turning, and even watching MTV for three hours, I finally give up. I climb out of bed and quietly exchange my pajamas for regular clothes. We passed an all-night diner just down the interstate and since what little I had in my stomach is now fertilizer, I could use a little grub. My iPod and book go in my purse, and I'm out the door.

The road running by the restaurant and hotel is as deserted as the rest of this state. The only lights come from the hotel, and just as that light wanes, the lights from the diner take over. Good thing too. If it were totally black, I'd turn back, even if I hadn't been through the wringer already tonight. Sometimes I hate being a girl. Can't even walk when I want to.

The Treetop Diner is small, with only seven booths and five seats at the counter. It has a rustic motif with brown walls painted to look like wood and pictures of men chopping down trees. The thick aroma of coffee and grease is welcoming. Right now, there are only two people visible, and when I go in, there are three. The waitress, a young woman with black hair and even darker skin, leans on the end of the counter flipping through a magazine. She looks up and smiles. "Sit anywhere you like."

I already know where that is.

Will smiles as I slide into the seat opposite him, seeming genuinely happy to see me. His tie is askew. For whatever reason, this endears him to me even more. I give him a smile back. "Fancy meeting you here," I say.

The waitress comes over, putting his bill down. "What can I get you?" she asks me.

"Eggs, bacon, hash browns."

"No prob. Coffee while you wait?"

"You read my mind." The waitress walks off, writing everything down. "I am so hungry," I say.

"I'll bet." He sips his coffee. "I puked at my first murder scene, and it wasn't nearly as bad as the one tonight. You get as used to it as you can."

"Still embarrassing."

The waitress returns with the coffee before going back to her magazine. I dump three creams and sugars into the cup and take a sip. "Good coffee."

"Give me restaurant coffee over Starbucks any day," Will says.

"Amen." I gulp half the stuff down.

"Couldn't sleep?" he asks.

"Nope, and I doubt I ever will again."

He nods. "It must have been horrible."

"It was incredibly awful, yes. If you've never been torn up like that, I—" Looking up at Will, who has gone from Mr. Rogers to Hamlet in a second flat, I shut my mouth. What did I...? It hits me. "Oh, shoot, I'm sorry. I mean, you do know, and I—I forgot. Jeez, foot in mouth much?"

He looks up from his coffee to give me a reassuring smile. His eyes crinkle again. If he had an Irish accent, he'd be perfect. "It's okay."

I smile back. Time to change the subject. "So, did you find anything else at the scene?"

"Just the jaw and some skin chewed to the bone."

"Yuck, thanks for that image."

I get another quick smile. "Not what you expected, right?"

"You can say that, yeah. If I knew I would get *that* up close and personal with the nasties, I'd still be in San Diego. But it's not just that. Now everyone is afraid that I'll somehow suck out their power and torture them or something. Irie and Nancy went out of their ways to avoid me. In our own room! They looked at me like someone who has this terrible rumor about them circling the school, like I have lice or something. I got enough of those looks in actual high school, so no thanks." Now I'm on a roll. "And how is it my fault? I was just trying to help! I didn't think it was that big a deal to touch him. I mean, he was *seizing,* I don't think I did anything that out of line. I'm not a scary person, so don't treat me like one, all right? Is that too much to ask?" I've gotten myself into

88

such a tizzy, I'm almost panting. "Okay. I'm done now. Rant over. Thank you very much."

I expect him to run screaming from the crazy lady, but instead he looks into my eyes and says, "You don't frighten me."

"You're not afraid I'll suck out your werewolf powers and terrorize the moors?"

"No," he says with another smile. Such a nice smile. A gooey, melty smile. A smile that makes me momentarily forget all the crud of the day and smile myself. He reaches into his pockets and pulls out some money, putting it on the table. So I did scare him away? My smile fades. "Just give them some time. It is just your first day," he says as he stands.

"Yes, and I've managed to frighten or alienate the entire team."

"Well, tomorrow is another day. Try to get some sleep. I'll wake you up at nine so we can start finding this guy."

I raise an eyebrow. "I get to investigate?"

"Only if you want to."

"Heck yeah, I do."

"Good. I'll see you in a few hours then."

"Okay," I say, positively beaming.

Will starts toward the exit—I can practically hear April say, "I hate to see him go, but I love to watch him leave"—but he turns around at the door. "Just so you know," he says, once again playing with his non-existent ring, "you haven't alienated me. Quite the … opposite. I think you're doing a great job. I'm glad you're here."

A grin hits me, one that goes from cheek to cheek. I even blush a little. "Thank you. You have no idea what that means to me."

"You're welcome. Good night, Beatrice."

"Sleep tight, Will."

He steps into the night and out of sight. If this were an old movie, right now would be where I swoon or break into song with waitresses dancing behind me. But seeing as this is real life, I smile and blush some more. Maybe there is a light at the end of the tunnel after all. Or at least a gorgeous man with crinkly eyes. I sip my super sweet coffee and hope the tunnel isn't too terribly long.

SIX

BEATRICE ALEXANDER ON THE CASE

AT NINE THIRTY, WITHOUT A wink of sleep under my belt, Will, Agents Chandler and Rushmore, and I pile into our Suburban and head into Bridge Stone, Colorado, which is now shy two of its residents. The rest of the team gets to sleep in until the mobile command unit arrives at the nearest military base and is hauled to an undisclosed location. What it is, what it does, I have no idea. I'll find out later.

Bridge Stone has approximately three thousand residents, and whoever decided to put a town here clearly did not want outsiders to invade. The snowy mountains that surround the valley are unskiable, with jagged rocks everywhere, so no ski lodges have sprouted among the faded white, weather-damaged buildings that comprise the town. There is only one road in and out, an offshoot of the interstate, so the town is basically a dead end. On that road is the town proper with an honest-to-goodness "General Store," among other anachronisms. In chipped gold letters on its window,

91

the store boasts the best milkshakes in all of Colorado. As we drive through the town toward the sheriff's station, we pass Sarah's Beauty Parlor, the Apache Theater showing *Strangers on a Train,* a small grocery store, the bank where Valerie Wayland worked, a hardware store, a diner, a bakery, Wynn's butcher shop, and a dress shop with the ugliest hats ever created on display. That's it. That's the whole town. The few people coming in and out of the stores actually stop to say hello to each other and chat. The only thing my neighbor in San Diego ever said to me was "Move your car." I feel like I've entered a time warp back to the fifties.

The sheriff's station is off the main road down a narrow two-lane street between the bakery and the butcher shop. The short road dead ends at another road where the police station and fire department sit next to each other. Unlike the white wooden buildings on the main drag, both these buildings are made of stone and concrete, giving them an appropriately rugged look. We passed a few houses on the way with the same design. A fireman, a fat man with thinning hair, washing either a fluffy dog or a big rat, smiles and nods at me as I walk into the station. Friendly town.

I'm surprised to find that the inside of the station is a lot like the one my ex, Steven, worked out of, only smaller. We walk through a small beige hallway with a bulletin board filled with community information on one wall and pictures of smiling officers on the other. The hall ends at a plastic partition where an elderly woman in a pastel flowered suit sits. On either side of her are doors with key pads that lead into the offices. Will shows his badge to the woman, who presses a button. The door to our right opens. I follow behind Agent Rushmore past about five men and women, some in light-brown uniforms, and others in work casual clothes, who all sit in cubicles filling out paperwork. Another man in uniform gestures us toward a back room.

When we walk in, the men give their names and titles to the officers but my eyes immediately go to the bulletin board covered with pictures of Valerie Wayland, both alive and dead. On the table taking up most of the room sit baggies of evidence and a file with "Bridge Stone Sheriff's Department" printed on it. After the formalities, Will takes the file off the table and begins reading. A second later, Sheriff Graham and his five o'clock shadow and bloodshot eyes step in. I see I'm not the only one who pulled an all-nighter.

"Good morning," Sheriff Graham says.

"Is this everything from the Wayland case?" Will asks, not looking up from the file. He looks delectable today in a dark-blue suit, white shirt, and blue tie.

"Everything we have," Graham replies. "Pictures we took, Dr. Harper's autopsy report, statements, what have you. The doctor is examining Davis right now, so he'll have that report done later today."

"Is that the same doctor who claimed Valerie Wayland was killed by an undetermined animal?" Will asks.

"At the time it was—"

Will's eyes whip up to the sheriff. "With all due respect to Dr. Harper, who in here it says is a family practitioner and *not* a pathologist, we'll have our own medical examiner take a look at both bodies."

"That's going to be a little hard," Graham says, "considering Val's body was cremated. Walter is off in California spreading the ashes right now."

"Are you sure of that?" Agent Chandler asks.

"I didn't get on the plane with him, but he said that's where he was going and nobody's seen him since. And I don't appreciate your tone. I still haven't seen a lick of proof that these weren't animal attacks. Bears and mountain lions come down all the time."

"No doubt, but that's not what killed them. These people were murdered."

"By who? Jack the Ripper?"

Will just looks back down at the file. "You only interviewed four people, three from the bank and her husband. Why only four?"

"Because it was an animal attack! And I really do not appreciate your tone, Agent Price. I investigated this case to the fullest extent. If you're implying—" Okay, way too much testosterone in this room. Fist fight any second. I clear my throat theatrically as if I'm about to cough up a hairball. The men look at me. "You okay?" Graham asks. "Do you need some water?"

I smile. "I'm okay now. Thank you." The men glance at each other with confusion. Better to be a weirdo than collateral damage. "Uh, Sheriff Graham, do you know if Valerie Wayland and Davis Wynn knew each other?"

"I'm sure Valerie and Davis knew each other, we all know each other, but beyond a casual acquaintance ... I haven't heard anything. Val and Walter seemed solid from what I can gather. I never really had any dealings with them. They were quiet, mostly kept to themselves, especially him. If they fought, I never got wind of it."

"Did Walter have an alibi for that night?" Agent Rushmore asks.

"Left the store at seven, went home—a neighbor confirmed his car was in the driveway all night—and about eleven, he called us to report Val missing. He had no idea why she'd be out at the cemetery that night except to visit their daughter. The man went into shock when I told him what happened. Doctor Harper had to swing by."

"Did you search the house?" This from Agent Chandler.

"He let us in without a warrant, and we did a cursory eyeball search. Nothing out of the ordinary."

"You didn't go back?" Agent Rushmore asks.

"It was ruled an animal attack the next day, so no, we had no reason to return. He cooperated fully."

"What did her friends say?" I ask.

"The night she was killed, she stayed late to count out the drawers. Their names are in the file."

"What'd they say about the marriage?" I ask.

"Like I said, it was ruled an animal attack. I didn't ask them or him about the state of their marriage. There was no way I was going to grill a man who just lost his wife—and had lost his child not too long ago—if I didn't have to."

"Do you know when her husband is expected back?" Agent Chandler asks.

"No idea. He said he was going to spread her ashes in Sacramento, where they met. That was not quite a week ago."

"What about Davis Wynn? Do you know of anyone who would want to hurt him?" I ask.

His lips say no, but this question raises his anxiety level enough that I feel his emotion in my stomach. He also starts playing with his wedding ring.

"Is the name Carrie at all familiar to you?" Will asks.

The anxiety raises another notch. "Carrie Ellison works at the butcher shop. She has for about a year."

"Did she know both Valerie and Davis?" I ask.

"Yes. She worked at the bank with Val till she quit."

"So, she worked with both victims?" Will asks.

"Yeah, but Carrie doesn't have a violent bone in her body. And besides, she weighs all of ninety pounds; she couldn't do that to a person even if she wanted to."

Will closes the file. "Thank you for your time, Sheriff Graham. We'll keep you posted on our progress."

Before Graham can protest, Will steps out of the room, Agents Chandler and Rushmore at his heels. Graham's jaw clenches. I leave before he can tear into me. The men wait right outside the hall.

"Agent Rushmore, stay here and collect *all,* and I mean all, they have on the two vics. Then run it over to mobile command when Wolfe calls to tell you it's arrived. Have everyone get started sorting through it. Make sure Carl touches something of each of the victims. See what he can find out about them. When you're done with that, get on the phone dumps for both vics: home, work, cell, whatever they have. Have Irie check Walter Wayland's alibi. Credit run, airport security feed, she knows the drill."

Agent Rushmore nods and walks away.

"Agent Chandler, stop by Walter Wayland's work and interview his co-workers. And call Konrad. Have him start at Wynn's house. When you're done with Wayland, help Konrad go through everything. Find his appointment books, financials, whatever. And keep me posted."

"What about the Wayland house?" Agent Chandler asks.

"We'll have to go through proper channels since the husband's still alive," Will says. "We need a warrant, and we don't have probable cause yet. We'll start with Wynn first."

Agent Chandler goes the way of Agent Rushmore.

"Alexander," Will says, "you're coming with me."

I've been in small shops before, but this bank is little more than a closet. How did Valerie Wayland stand this place day after day? The two tellers inside Bridge Stone Bank stand behind a counter. One is in her twenties with a mismatched suit/shirt combo, and the other is a very tall middle-aged woman with black and gray hair cut to her shoulders. A man in an outdated brown suit stands from behind his desk.

"May I help you?" the man asks as we walk in.

Will displays his badge for the man. "Special Agent William Price, FBI."

The man glances at me. Shoot, where is my badge? I reach into my purse but don't feel it. I'm a bad agent. "I'm with him."

"What's this about?"

"We're investigating the deaths of Valerie Wayland and Davis Wynn. Would you mind if I asked the staff a few questions?" Will asks.

"Let me ask my boss," the man says. He walks through a door and reappears on the other side of the counter. He says something to the tall woman, who just nods. She hands money to her customer, who promptly walks away. The customer smiles and nods as she passes us. We nod back. On the walk over here, almost every person who passed us nodded. I followed Will's example and nodded back. At this rate, I'll have whiplash by the end of the day.

The manager waves us over. Will flashes his badge and I flash a smile before we reach the woman. I do retrieve my Hello Kitty notepad from my purse—a present from a student—to take notes. I don't have the best memory when it comes to details.

"I'm Theresa Petrie, the manager," the tall woman says, eyeing my pink notepad. I cover Kitty with my palm. "Is this about Val?"

"Yes. We'd like to interview you and your staff," Will says.

"Well, I'm sorry, but we told everything we knew to Sheriff Graham."

"Please, Ms. Petrie," Will says.

"I thought this was an animal attack."

"That's what we're looking into. There was another death last night, so we're just erring on the side of caution."

She sighs. "Of course, I'm sorry. Take as much time as you need."

"Thank you," Will says. "We'll be as quick as possible. Did Mrs. Wayland have anyone she was particularly close to here?"

"Not really. Val was never very forthcoming when it came to her personal life. She listened more than she talked, especially after … " She looks down at the counter.

"Did she change much after the accident?" I ask.

"You would think so, but not really. Like I said, she was never that talkative, and I guess even less after Emma died."

"Well, from what you can tell, how were things with her husband?" I ask.

"They seemed fine. They were never what you'd call affectionate, but she never complained. Walter would come in sometimes to take her to lunch, but he never even acknowledged us. I never saw them hug or kiss in the fifteen years I've known them. It was a bit surprising, though."

"What?" I ask.

"Well, when my sister and her husband lost their son, their marriage completely changed. Everything changed. For Val and Walter, it was as if nothing happened, especially on his part."

"What do you mean?" Will asks.

98

"When it first happened, she asked for extra hours. I even found her crying in the bathroom once. She refused to talk about it and never showed emotion again. Walter was the same, but in my opinion worse. A few weeks ago, Val mentioned he'd never been to visit Emma's grave. Not once since they buried her. I couldn't believe it when she told me that."

"There is no one way to deal with loss," Will points out.

"I suppose, but it just bothered me. Though I never liked Walter to begin with."

"Why not?" I ask.

"I don't know. Have you ever just met someone and instantly disliked them? There's just something you can't quite put your finger on?" Theresa shrugs. "The few times we spoke, he was perfectly pleasant, if a bit standoffish. He's quiet. Keeps to himself. He just rubbed me the wrong way."

"What about Davis Wynn? Did you know him?" I ask.

"Oh, yeah. He and my husband played poker together for years until Dave quit. He was a great guy. I hadn't really seen him in a while though."

"When did he quit the game?" I ask.

"Three, four months ago, out of the blue."

"Any idea why?"

She shrugs. "Said he was tired of getting wiped clean."

"You believe him?"

"He is a really bad player." She bites her lower lip and shakes her head. "Shit, sorry. He was. Was." She shakes her head again. "Sorry. First Val then Davis. It's just so sad. My husband found out this morning. He was near tears."

"Do you think he'd mind if we interviewed him?" Will asks.

"Not at all. He'll be at work until four. He's the principal at Bridge Stone Elementary."

I jot that down. "Did Davis come into the bank a lot?"

"About the same as everyone."

"Was he overly friendly with Valerie when he was here?"

"Not that I noticed."

"So there was no relationship between them beyond the professional one?"

"I doubt it. The only time I know they met outside the bank was at a dinner party I threw about five months ago. They did spend a lot of time talking that night. Oh, and Emma's funeral, but everyone in town was there that day."

"Who were the guests at this party?" Will asks.

"My husband, Val and Walter, Davis and Carrie, Donna over there and her husband, two other couples."

"Carrie Ellison was there?" Will asks.

"Yes. *That* was uncomfortable."

"She used to work here, correct?" Will asks.

"Until about a year ago."

"Was she fired?" I ask.

"No, she quit. When our old assistant manager retired, both Val and Carrie were up for the job. Now, Val had been here a lot longer, but Carrie thought she was the best candidate because she had some management experience. When I gave the job to Val, Carrie just up and quit. Few days later I went into the butcher shop and there she was."

"If Davis knew about the animosity between all of you, why did he bring Carrie to your party?" I ask.

"When Stan, my husband, asked Davis, he said Carrie overheard him talking about it and asked to come. Of course, she spent

100

half the night chewing my ear off about how much better her new job was and how *wonderful* Davis was to work for. The other half she spent sulking on the couch."

"So she minded that Davis spent the whole night talking to Valerie?" I ask.

"Oh, yeah. She'd slip over to them occasionally and try to get into the conversation, but Dave ignored her."

"Was it possible that Davis and Carrie were seeing each other?"

"It wouldn't surprise me. Half the men in this town have had something going on with Carrie at some time or another. Of course there were rumors, them being found in parked cars and such, but Davis never admitted it to Stan or me."

Will reaches into his pocket and pulls out a business card. "Mrs. Petrie, if you think of anything else, please call me. You've been very helpful," he says, giving her a grateful smile.

"I just wish I could tell you more."

"Do you mind if we speak to your employees now? I promise we'll be brief."

"Of course. I'll send Donna right over."

An hour later, we leave the bank having learned nothing new from the others. Valerie rarely spoke about her home life, at least to her colleagues. Valerie and Walter had a decent relationship, at least on the outside, and her co-workers knew nothing about an affair. I walk out of the bank feeling more than a little frustrated. No smoking gun, only more unanswered questions. We start down the street passing more nodding people.

"Did you find anything in there a bit odd?" I ask.

"What do you mean?"

"I don't know, the fact that she barely mentioned the death of her only child to anyone?"

"People do deal with grief in different ways."

"I know, but … if a person doesn't even *talk* about something like that to a friend, therapist, whatever, it festers and rots. It can even kill. They did a special on the Discovery Channel."

A small smile creeps across Will's face. "You think she committed suicide by zombie?"

"And then rose from the grave to kill a man she barely knew? That's a bit of a stretch," I say. At least I hope so.

"I agree. So, what's your point?"

"That she had to have confided in *someone.*"

"Her husband?"

"Maybe, but he sounds more closed off than she was."

We reach the crosswalk and wait.

"Perhaps … Davis Wynn?" Will asks.

The little man lights up and we cross.

"I've seen enough cop shows to know there has to be a connection between the two. They were killed for a reason." We reach the other side of the street but instead of turning right toward the butcher's shop, Will turns left.

"Wait. Aren't we going to interview Carrie Ellison?"

"Not yet. No doubt she's heard we're in town by now. Let her worry."

He's the boss. I follow Will up the side street that dead-ends at the sheriff's station, past the buildings, and up the deserted street. Heels were definitely a bad idea. They are an invention of the Devil. My feet feel double their size and with each throb, they swell even more. Looking good shouldn't be this painful.

"Um, where are we going?" I ask.

"I studied the maps last night. The school's just up this road. We're going to interview Stan Petrie."

"And driving wasn't an option?"

"A little exercise never hurt anyone."

"Said the man without two torture devices strapped to his feet," I mutter.

The school is not "just up the road." It ends up being up the first road for a quarter mile, then up another tiny road for the same distance. My shoes come off during the second stretch. They go back on when we get inside the school.

It's like any other school in America, including my old one: one story with a flag flapping in the front, rows of classrooms on either side of a polished linoleum hallway (though we had an outdoor campus thanks to the mild California weather), pictures of various sports teams and class murals made from magazines and crayons hang on the walls here. Another pang of homesickness hits. I always loved watching the kids cut out flowers and pictures of celebrities while gossiping with their friends. With a sigh, I look away.

The office is down the hall on the right. A middle-aged woman in a pink linen dress stands behind the counter next to a yellow sign that reads "Don't forget to sign your children out." She looks up from her files. Will flashes his badge and asks for Mr. Petrie. The woman hops to with the speed of a woman half her age. A second later, she comes out of the back office, waving us in. We pass by the other secretary, who averts her eyes quickly and goes back to her work as if looking at us is a crime and we might arrest her for it. The receptionist leaves us with Principal Stanley Petrie. He's about the same age and height as his wife but with a severely receding hairline and ginger beard. He wears the same work attire my old principal wore: a too-small suit with a ghastly red and blue striped tie.

We sit in the chairs across from him—the "naughty chairs" as my fellow teachers always called them. If you had to put your behind in one of these, the news would not be good. Never thought I'd be back in one of them this soon.

Stan Petrie smiles at us. "I wasn't expecting you so quickly."

"I apologize for that, we should have made an appointment," Will says.

"No, it's okay. I want to help. Dave … he was a good friend. If someone did that to him … " Petrie shakes his head. "I just can't believe anyone would want to hurt him. Are you sure this wasn't an animal?"

"Fairly sure," I answer. "How long have you known him?"

"Ten years. We met when he moved here and opened up shop."

"He wasn't born here, then?" Will asks.

"No, he was from Denver."

"And you were close friends?" Will asks.

"Yeah. We played poker. Sometimes he came over for dinner."

"Did he ever mention Valerie Wayland to you?" Will asks.

"Not really. Just that he enjoyed talking to her that night."

"The dinner party?" Will asks.

"Yeah. I never would have put those two together. Both too quiet. I was surprised how well they got on. Her husband actually left early, not that he was talking to anyone. You could tell Walter didn't want to be there even before his wife began ignoring him. He barely spoke to anyone and left for home the first chance he got. Val didn't even notice. But after that night, Davis never mentioned her again."

"So you don't think there was anything between them, romantic or otherwise?" I ask.

"Anything's possible, I guess, but he never said a word to me. And let me tell you, if they were together, they kept it a damn good secret."

"What about Carrie Ellison? Was he involved with her?" I ask.

"Carrie Ellison," Petrie chuckles. "Yeah, that one came as a shock. I mean, I'm not surprised she fell for him, but why he was with her was a total mystery."

"How come?" I ask.

"I taught Carrie algebra ten years ago when I was still working at the high school. She was your typical little lost girl. Her father ran off when she was young, so she kept looking for his replacement."

"She came on to you?" I ask.

"Oh, yeah," he chuckles. "Always had a thing for older guys even then. Though she grew tired of them pretty quickly. Davis was the last in a long line."

"So *she* broke up with *him?*" I ask.

"I just know what the rumor mill says. From what I heard, Carrie was in tears at the grocery store three months ago."

"Three months? Around the same time he stopped going to your poker game?" I ask.

"I guess."

"And, according to the rumor mill, how long did they date?" Will asks.

"I think about seven months. A record for Carrie."

"But Davis wasn't serious about her?" I ask.

Petrie sighs. "I don't think Dave could have been serious about anyone. He lived here for ten years and only dated two women: Rosie, a former teacher here, and Carrie."

"Why do you think that was?" I ask.

"His wife, of course."

I nearly drop my pen. *"He's married?"*

"No, widowed."

"How did she die?" I ask.

"Car accident eleven years ago."

Will graciously nods at Petrie and stands. Guess the interview's over. "Principal Petrie, thank you for your time." Will hands the man a card. "If you think of anything else that might be useful, please call."

"Sure."

We see ourselves to the door. Will ignores the staring office workers as we pass. What they must be thinking. Nothing like having the FBI come in and interview your boss to break the monotony. The few times the police came to my school, it kept the water cooler conversation going for weeks. When we reach the hallway, I open my mouth to speak, but Will holds up his hand to stop me. My mouth snaps shut. The second we're outside, Will opens his. "So, what are you thinking?"

"Why did you end the interview so quickly?"

"He told us everything he knew."

"No, he didn't. We know about as much as we did before."

"We have the connection. Carrie Ellison. She had reason to want them both dead."

"No, she had a reason to *dislike* both. Getting passed over for a promotion a year ago and being dumped are not good reasons to raise the dead and kill people."

"When I was on the job in DC, I had cases where guys killed each other over a pair of shoes."

I shake my head. "I'm sorry, I just don't buy it. If the breakup was her breaking point and she was consumed with rage, she'd kill

Wynn first, the source. Valerie would be just an added bonus. There has to be more—"

The passing police cruiser stops our speculation. As it pulls over to us, Will shoots me a grave look. I take this to mean my mouth shall not open for the next several minutes. Sheriff Graham rolls down the passenger side window. He pulls down his aviator sunglasses on his nose and grins. "Seems you lot had a busy morning. Can I give you a ride somewhere?"

"The diner in town would be great," Will answers matching Graham's grin. "Thank you."

Graham's smile doesn't fade, but his eyes flicker a look of either anger or disappointment. Perhaps both, according to the vibes I'm getting off him. The feeling doesn't last long. "Not a problem. Must have worked up quite an appetite. Get in." Will opens the passenger side door. Guess that means I'm in the back. I've never been in the back of a police cruiser. It's not as bad as Steven had made it sound. There are no door handles and there is the Plexiglas separating the front from the back, but there's no blood or vomit, which he always complained about having to clean up. It smells pleasantly like Pine-Sol back here. Maybe Steven was just trying to impress me. Then again, this small town is no Chula Vista, California.

We ride in silence for ten uncomfortable seconds before Graham works up the nerve to speak. "So, how's the case going? You have a suspect who can command bears to attack yet?" Will just stares out the window. Graham looks at me through the rearview, but I follow Will's example. What wonderful trees. "I hear you've been asking questions about Carrie Ellison," he tries again.

Once again, neither Will nor I answer. I feel another surge of emotion and the word *frustration* pops into my mind. I'm getting a handle of this clairempath thing. Next stop, human lie detector. My hunch proves true because Graham suddenly stops the car. Will still doesn't look at the man. "There is such a thing as professional courtesy, Agent Price," Graham says. "You people cannot just come into *my* town, boss *my* deputies around, take over *my* investigation, and cut *me* out of the loop. And you certainly cannot harass innocent citizens and tarnish the name of a good woman!"

"We will do whatever it takes to stop the deaths of more of your citizens. If you don't like where the investigation leads, that's not my problem. Perhaps if you had done your job, we wouldn't be here doing it for you."

"I will not be insulted in my own cruiser," Graham snarls. "Get out. Both of you."

What did I do? Will jumps out, slamming the door so hard the whole car shakes. I think Graham was too preoccupied with his own anger to notice. He's seething, breathing twice the normal rate. Before the man explodes all over me, Will opens my door and I leap out. The millisecond the door closes, the cruiser speeds down the road. So much for our ride. I think I can hear my feet sobbing.

"You couldn't have insulted him closer to the diner?"

Will doesn't answer. He starts down the road and I of course follow, after the heels come off. He obviously has no desire to say anything to me, so I follow a few paces behind. Lord, he's as moody as a teenager. I am so avoiding him during full moons.

The town is busy now with the lunch rush. SUVs line the street waiting for the light to turn. One or two compact cars sit between the SUVs looking like children's toys. Four-wheel drive must be a necessity here. The sidewalks are congested as well, as the number of people on the streets has easily doubled. People go in and out of the stores as if they have revolving doors. The strange thing is all of them seem to have a smile on their faces. They smile when they see a neighbor, they smile as they walk out of the stores, they smile as they turn a corner ... it's unnerving. Maybe the whole town is under a gypsy curse or something. An entire town cannot be this happy. The Stone Diner is the first building on the other side of the street, and by the looks of the line outside on the sidewalk, it's the most popular place in town. We're going to be here forever.

Will joins the line behind a man in overalls covered in what I hope is dirt. I feel totally out of place in my black suit and white dress shirt. People here probably think Ralph Lauren was a character on *The Honeymooners.* Overalls glances at us then turns fully around. "You're two of the FBI guys in town, right?"

News sure does travel fast. "Yeah, we are," I say.

"Heck, you shouldn't have to wait for your lunch. Hey, Sam!"

The man in the front of the line turns. "Hiya, Dean."

"Do you mind if the FBI cuts in front of you?"

He shrugs. "Not really."

I look at Will, but he's already jumping the line. We reach Sam, who opens the diner door. "Hey, Ruby!" A woman my age with olive skin and brown hair standing next to the Wait to Be Seated sign turns. "Can my FBI friends cut?"

She looks at Will and subtly sticks her chest out. "Sure, Sam."

When we get to the front, Will gives a killer smile to the woman, who blushes. I'm surprised she doesn't lick him. Within two minutes, we're shown to a booth in the back. The diner is so loud it reminds me of the cafeteria at school, a few hundred voices chattering away. The waitress disappears with our drink orders, two coffees. I take off my jacket, hanging it on the coat hook above our booth. A few people turn and glance at us.

"Why do I feel like we're under a microscope?" I ask in a low voice, which means I still have to shout to be heard.

"Because we are."

The waitress comes back with our much-needed elixir of life. My sleepless night is catching up with me. "What can I get you?"

"Can I have a hamburger, medium rare, salad with ranch dressing, and fries?" I ask.

"I'll have a hamburger, two steaks—all very rare—and pork chops." Will says.

The waitress stares at him, dumbfounded for a second. I feel the same way. Will just smiles at the woman. "Atkins," he says. The waitress walks away shaking her head.

"Like meat, huh?"

He places the napkin on his lap. "I haven't eaten since last night. My metabolism is much faster than yours."

"Do you eat that much all the time?"

Will shrugs. Geez, and here I felt bad about ordering that side of fries. "So … " I say, and then draw a blank. I really should have gone to more parties. My small talk stinks.

"So?" he asks.

Okay, think. "You think Carrie did it?" Will scowls and eyes the man obviously listening to us. It doesn't take ten seconds to take a sip of coffee. "On … *General Hospital?* She did hate Colette for that drunk driving accident."

"I don't know," Will grumbles into his cup. Neither of us says anything until the eavesdropper downs his coffee and jumps off his stool. Good.

When the man's far enough away, I ask, "Are we off to the butcher shop after this?"

"Yes."

"So, *do* you think she did it?"

"She's definitely a suspect, but I don't want to jump to conclusions yet. If you focus too much on one suspect, other possibilities aren't weighed equally. But she did have motive and opportunity, and as far as I can tell, nobody else did."

"That we know of," I point out. "We so do not have the full picture yet."

"What makes you say that?" Will asks.

I raise an eyebrow. "Well, what happened three months ago? It's too much of a coincidence that he broke up with Carrie and stopped a ten-year tradition at the same time. I could understand if he stopped while he was seeing her, but why after?"

"What's your theory?" he asks with a smile. I do believe I am impressing him.

"Oldest one in the book. He dumped Carrie for Valerie."

Now he raises an eyebrow. "There's been no hint of that. You think they could keep something like that a secret in this town? Where's your proof?"

"Just female intuition. But you can see it, right? After her daughter died, she was seriously depressed. I mean, how could she not be? She might not be emotional in public, but it was there. She knew about Wynn's wife and wanted to share with someone who knew her pain. Her husband, who was cold and withdrawn like a typical hurting male, refused to discuss their loss, so he was no help. She and Wynn shared their stories, made each other feel better, and next thing they know they were sleeping together. Carrie found out she was passed over for Valerie *again* and snapped.

Zombie rampage time. Don't tell me it hasn't crossed your mind. That's why you ended the Petrie interview early. You got some validation of your theory."

"Very good, Agent Alexander. But again, do we have proof?"

"No, but it's early yet."

The waitress returns with our orders. Will's comes on two plates, both with small pools of blood on them. Yuck. Will practically devours a whole steak in a minute. I half expect him to rip it apart with his hands and teeth, licking the blood off his fingers. I just pick at my salad.

"I agree it's the most logical theory," Will says with a mouth full of meat, "but with no proof, we can't move on her. What about the other suspect? We haven't even begun looking at the husband."

"He's been in California, as far as we know. It's a small town, someone would have seen him around if he was back."

"We're checking that out, but I'm not sold on the affair angle. It calls for a lot of conjecture. Valerie Wayland seemed like a private person; I can't see her opening up to anybody, let alone a relative stranger like Wynn."

"She knew his history. He'd been through the whole grief thing. He'd know how it feels to lose the most important person in your life. Her husband was too lost in his own grief to be any help; chances are she went somewhere to vent. Damaged people seek out damaged people. I can personally attest to that. I mean, when your wife died, didn't you—"

I shut my mouth immediately. Will's gone all dark and broody again. His jaw is so tight I can see all the veins in his neck bulging. He stares down at his plate like the pork chops just slapped his mother and he's deciding what form of torture to use. I need a crib sheet of things that are off limits to speak about to certain people. Dead wife, number one on Will's list.

I look down at my salad and start moving the food around. "Sorry."

Will looks at me. "It's okay," he says quietly.

"I won't mention it again." I look up. "But … "

He tenses again. "What?"

"You can see how people could come together that way, right? I mean, there they are, sitting on his couch, she's crying, he reaches over to smooth her hair and wipe her tears. Next thing they know they're … you know." I sip my coffee. "Happens all the time."

Will grimaces. "Sounds like you've had experience in this area."

I feel my cheeks go red. Am I that transparent? "My therapist."

Will sits up straight, which makes him seem double his real size. "How old were you?"

"Nineteen. It just happened one session … and lasted two more. See? Grief is such a negative emotion, you want to replace the feeling with something else, *anything* else. Davis Wynn is clearly still hurting over his wife if he's only dated twice in ten years, so I can see Valerie seeking him out, either consciously or unconsciously."

"We still need proof."

"Yeah, well, it's there. We'll find it."

"Not a doubt in my mind, Agent Alexander."

"Why thank you, Agent Price," I say with a smile.

He grins back. "You're welcome. Now eat, we have a lot to do."

Don't need to tell me twice.

SEVEN

PRIME SUSPECT

THINGS SETTLE DOWN A little on the streets during the forty minutes we eat. Will orders seconds and we just talk. Not like first-
date talk, much to my chagrin, but about the job, my training,
and San Diego. Safe topics. I'm getting the feeling this whole
chemistry thing is all in my head. It wouldn't be the first time my
fertile imagination got the best of me, and it won't be the last, I'm
sure. He's not into me. Better to know it at the beginning before I
have any more fantasy children with him. I still like looking at
him though.

Everyone must have ran their errands and gone back to work.
The sun has finally come out from behind puffy clouds, and I've
got to say the town looks much better without the gloom. The yellow trim around the window of Wynn's Meating Place (groan!) actually looks cheery and not the color of an institution like the
other shops.

From the window, we can see two women in line and a teenager behind the counter handing one of them a white package. Poor guy, I guess he's never heard of Clearasil—or shampoo by the looks of his greasy brown hair. I wouldn't want this guy to touch anything of mine, let alone my food. The woman he's helping pays and walks out of the store. Will opens the door for her and is rewarded with a polite smile and nod.

"I don't see Ellison," Will says.

"She's probably in the back preparing the meat." A flash of Davis Wynn's mangled, bloody corpse pops into my head. I suppress a shiver.

"We should go in."

He takes a step toward the door, but I touch his arm. "Wait. Do you think maybe I should be the one to go in there?"

"Why?"

"Well, you know … all that blood and meat. What if you get excited or something?"

His eyes narrow at me. "I think I can control myself." Guess he never read the case of the werewolf who entered a butcher shop and ended up eating not only a whole cow but also the butcher. Obviously elementary students aren't the only ones who neglect their homework.

Will patiently waits behind the second customer, and the only sign of something odd is his nose twitching every second. I just smell antiseptic like in a hospital. His super-smell must have kicked into high gear. The place itself is somewhat antiseptic too. White walls with no hangings except a business license. The only decorative thing here is a display case filled with various meats. Salami is on sale. Above the glass case is a counter with two digital scales and a cash register. Simple, but it looks like it gets the job done. In the wall behind the counter is a metal sliding door where Carrie must be hiding. The teenager takes the money from the customer and gives her the meat.

"Thank you, Tommy," the woman says.

"Have a nice day, Mrs. Painter."

Of course, the woman nods at us as she passes. This place is a chiropractor's dream, the cases of whiplash he must get. Will and I step toward Tommy, Will's badge already out. Tommy's nervousness hits me. Oooh, maybe he has something to do with … I look into his bloodshot eyes. Oh. Add Visine and Lysol to the list of hygiene products this kid should look into.

"I'm Special Agent William Price; this is Special Agent Beatrice Alexander with the FBI. We're investigating the deaths of Valerie Wayland and Davis Wynn. Is Carrie Ellison here?"

The boy's nerve level drops to the floor. "Oh, um, yeah, I guess. She's in the back cutting meat. Should I, like, go get her?"

"That would be great, thank you," I say.

Tommy shuffles over to the metal door. A burst of cold air hits us as he opens it. "Be right back."

"Not the brightest bulb," I mumble after he disappears into the back.

"We should interview him away from Carrie. He might—"

Just then, Tommy comes back followed by a woman I presume is Carrie Ellison. It is obvious why men fall over themselves. Even in a large winter coat, blood-splattered apron, and sweat-soaked brow, this woman is beautiful. Thick hay-colored hair pulled into a ponytail, huge brown eyes, straight nose, and petite figure—except for the boobs, I applaud her plastic surgeon—that gives her a gorgeous, elfin look. Her type have been the bane of my existence since middle school. I so hope she did it.

Carrie doesn't even look at me but turns to Will with one of those model smiles that shows off her white teeth. "I'm Carrie, Officer . . . ," she says, still smiling. Oh, please.

"*Agent* Price," Will corrects, "and this is Agent Alexander." She briefly glances at me. "We need to ask you some questions regarding Davis Wynn. Is there someplace private we can talk?"

"Office in the back?" she chirps. Yes, actually *chirps.*

Tommy lifts apart the counter to let us pass. Oh goody, we get to go into the meat locker, my day is complete. Carrie leads us through the locker past a huge steel table covered with reddish and purple meat I hope was once a cow, but I wouldn't put anything past a girl who raises zombies to eat people. Across from the table is another counter holding a meat grinder with hamburger hanging out of it. Either the chill in this room or the *Texas Chainsaw Massacre* vibe makes me shiver.

The office is in another room right next to the meat locker. It's plain white, like the rest of the store. Just a file cabinet, desk covered in papers, and a yellow plastic chair, all of which barely fit into the room. Carrie sits behind the desk, never taking her eyes off Will. He takes the seat across from her, which leaves me leaning against the file cabinet. I pull out my pad as Will asks the first question.

"How long have you known Davis Wynn?"

"Known? About ten years, I guess. We didn't really get close until I started working here."

"What was he like to work for?"

"He was okay. Paid me on time, gave me overtime when I needed it."

"What about as a man? Was he a good man?"

Her nervousness spikes for a second. To lie or not to lie? "I guess so. He was never mean to me or anything."

"Why'd you open the store today?" I ask this time. "Your boss just died. I would have taken the day off."

She finally looks at me with a smile. I know about as much about her teeth as her dentist does now. "Davis would have wanted me to open the store. He had the strongest work ethic I've ever seen. Never closed the shop, even when there was ten inches of snow on the ground."

"You admired him," I say, "but you don't look at all shook up about his death."

Her eyes turn cold. "You don't know what I'm feeling." Actually, I do, hon. Right now it's nervousness and anger, a combo that makes my stomach hurt. Too many positive emotions and I get a headache; bad ones and I get a stomachache. I just can't win.

"You're right, I'm sorry. This must be very hard for you."

"Yes, it is. He was … " She looks down at the floor. "Sorry. It's just hard to believe. And the way he was killed. I heard they found him in pieces, is that true?"

"We can't comment on an open investigation," Will says.

"Oh. But I heard it was a bear attack or something."

"That's what we're looking into."

"Was there anything out of the ordinary that happened yesterday? Was Davis acting odd in any way?" I ask.

"Not that I noticed."

"Did he close the shop last night?"

"Yeah, I opened and he closed. Usually the closer has to stay about two hours after to clean everything and get the meat ready for the next day."

"That means he would have left the store around eight?"

"Well, he must have left a little earlier because the sausage wasn't done and the hamburger wasn't ground. He was supposed to open today, so I figured he was planning on doing it in the morning."

So he left work undone? Someone had an appointment to keep.

"So besides that, there was nothing different about Davis last night?" Will asks.

"Not that I noticed."

"Did you know of any reason for him to be out in the woods last night?"

"No."

My turn. "You've only worked here a year, is that right?"

"Yeah."

"And you worked at the bank before that? With Valerie Wayland?"

Nervous anger hits again. "Yes."

"And you left because you were passed over for a promotion? One that Valerie Wayland got?"

"No," she says, "I left because I was bored."

"And working with raw meat is more thrilling?" I'm digging being the bad cop.

"What does that have to do with anything?"

"Nothing. I was just saying it was quite a change. I mean, are you happier here? It takes a person with a strong stomach to be around this stuff all day."

She leans back. "It doesn't bother me."

I'm about to open my mouth again, but Will beats me to it. "Miss Ellison, wh—"

"Carrie. Please," she says with a smile.

"Carrie, was there anyone who made trouble for Davis? A customer who threatened him?"

"Or an ex-girlfriend?" I cut in, raising an eyebrow.

"Nobody that I knew of," she says, not missing a beat.

"So you weren't upset when Davis dumped you?"

Her cherubic mouth drops open. "That is nothing but filthy gossip."

"But you two *were* in a relationship," Will asks.

Carrie glances at Will with her mouth open, but his face remains stony. I'm liking this guy more and more each moment. Carrie looks back at me. "For about five seconds! We went out a couple times, but it ended months ago, and it sure as hell wasn't serious."

"After you two split, was he seeing anyone else?"

"Not that I knew of. It's slim pickings around here, in case you haven't noticed. He likes—liked—to be alone."

"Did Valerie Wayland come in a lot?" Will asks.

"No more than anyone else."

"He give her any special attention?" I ask.

"*Valerie?*" Carrie asks with a scoff. "Have you seen her?"

"What was left of her," I say. "So you don't think Davis and Valerie were having an affair?"

"No way. No way in hell would he ever touch her."

"You didn't like her very much, did you?" I ask.

"I didn't hate her enough to kill her, if that's what you mean."

"We have to ask," Will says. "Where were you last night around eight thirty?"

"I was at home with someone."

"We'll need their name."

"Can he be kept out of it? It's kind of a delicate situation. He's married."

"We'll try to keep it as quiet as possible, I promise," Will says.

Carrie sighs. "John Graham."

"The sheriff?" I ask in shock.

"Yes."

"And what about the night Valerie Wayland was killed, around nine thirty?" Will soldiers on despite my gaping mouth.

"Same." Carrie sighs. "You know, this is ridiculous. I heard what happened to them. There is no way a person did that."

"Anything is possible, Miss Ellison," I say.

Will stands up. "Thank you very much for your time. We may have some follow-up questions later."

"Okay." There goes that smile again. "I assume you know where to find me."

Oh, gag me. "We do. Have a nice day"

Carrie doesn't follow us out of the office. The front of the store is empty when we walk out. Could be because the door is locked. Through the window, I see Tommy standing outside against the wall smoking. He drops the cigarette and stubs it out when we leave the store.

"Sorry," Tommy mumbles.

"Cigarettes aren't illegal," Will says genially. "Do you have time to answer some questions?"

"I guess." He starts walking slowly down the street and we follow. I feel like today's been one long game of follow the leader. My feet may go on strike if this keeps up. We stop in front of the last store on the road, the bakery. The smell of fresh bread and cakes stirs my hunger again, not that it takes much.

"Uh, what do you want to know?" Tommy asks.

"How long have you worked for Davis Wynn?" Will asks.

"Um, seven months, I guess. I'm just part-time."

"Were you working yesterday?" he asks.

"Yeah, I opened with Carrie."

"Did she or Davis seem odd yesterday?" I ask.

"Not really. They ignored each other like always."

"They don't get along?" I ask.

Tommy scoffs. "No. It's tense as hell, like, real bad vibes. When Davis comes in, Carrie, like, makes it a point to stay as far from him as possible. She gives me messages to give to him. Real stupid shit—sorry, ma'am, *stuff*—like 'we're out of veal' and shi—stuff like that. I feel like a friggin' message boy."

"When did this start?" Will asks.

"Like forever. Three, four months, I guess. The first few months were okay. I even saw them kissing once in the office. Then, all of a sudden, Carrie keeps calling in sick and when she does show up, she's crying in the back all the time and it's awkward central."

"Has it gotten worse?" I ask.

"About two weeks ago they got into a screaming match."

"What about?" Will asks.

"Hell if I know. I was stuck up front during the lunch rush. I heard shouting, mainly Carrie, I think. She left right after."

"Do you know the exact day?" Will asks.

He thinks for a second. "I think it was a Wednesday, a couple weeks ago."

That would be the day before Valerie was killed. "Did you know Valerie Wayland?" I ask.

"Yeah, she lives down the street from me and my folks. *Lived*, I guess. Nice lady."

"Have you seen her husband around since her death?" Will asks.

"No. I heard he's in California. He left last week."

"Did Val and Davis seem particularly close?" I ask.

Tommy shrugs. "No. He actually kind of avoided her. Whenever she'd come in, he'd go into the back, and one time he did serve her, but they wouldn't even look at each other, which was totally weird for Dave. He was always harping on me for not smiling at the customers."

"Was she the only customer he did that with?" I ask.

"Maybe, I don't know. Look, I gotta get back before Carrie freaks out."

"Okay, here's my card," Will says handing it to him, "if you think of anything else."

"Cool. Good luck and everything."

"Thanks," I say.

Tommy nods and starts back toward the shop. Poor kid, all alone with an emotionally unstable killer surrounded by sharp objects. He should get hazard pay.

Will sighs. "That was no help."

"I'm sorry, were you listening to the same boy as I was? We now have proof they were having an affair."

"What, the fight? It could have been about anything."

"Sure, and I'm Wonder Woman. Not just the fight, the fact that Valerie and Davis were keeping clear of each other. When a person is trying to hide or deny feelings, they usually avoid the person they have the hots for. You never did that?"

Will doesn't answer, big surprise. He just starts walking back toward the butcher shop. "I'm still not convinced," he says. "In a small town there would be at least whispers. The fact nobody suspected—"

I stop dead. "Oh my God, how could I be so stupid?"

"What?"

I point across the street. "Look." Sarah's Beauty Palace or, as I'll call it, Sarah's Truth Palace. "If there is anything to know, it's in there."

After looking both ways, I dash across the street. Will doesn't follow. He walks to the crosswalk. Jeez, uptight much? I don't wait for him to go in.

Sarah's Beauty Palace is covered in faded pink paint with matching pink chairs and mirrors. The smell of chemicals and shampoo is heavy in the air. Another homesickness pang hits. I'm getting real sick of those. At least once a week, I'd pick April up at the mall where she works as a stylist, gossip with her and the other stylists, and then we'd go out for drinks or to a movie. She's been my best friend ever since I was eight. I knew we'd be best friends forever when I spent the night and accidently made her stuffed animals float because I was so nervous about my first sleepover, and she thought it was the coolest thing ever. We won't be having another girls' night anytime soon.

Two women sit in the pink chairs, an elderly woman with curlers covering her head and a teenager getting a haircut. The stylist giving the perm is middle aged with curly hair and thick black glasses. She looks up at me and smiles. "Be with you in a minute." The other stylist, with very blond streaks in her dark brown hair, then smiles as well. The teenager ignores me.

I sit in a plastic chair in the waiting area and pull out a magazine just as the door opens. Will steps in, and all eyes zoom to him. Beauty pageant smiles form on every woman's face. The streaked stylist eyes him from head to toe. "Well, hello," she purrs. Will flashes a smile back and joins me. The women exchange glances before going back to doing hair. Silence fills the Truth Palace. Guess what they were discussing isn't fit for strangers' ears. Will's phone cuts the silence after a few seconds. He smiles apologetically at the women and steps back outside. The old woman's eyes follow Will, focusing south of the equator. When he's gone, she looks up at her stylist.

"Not bad, huh? If I was thirty years younger … "

Everyone giggles. "Damn, Maxine," her stylist says.

"Excuse me," I say, standing up. "I'm sorry to disturb your work, but we're here investigating the deaths of Valerie Wayland and Davis Wynn. We'd like to ask you a few questions."

"Us?" Streaks asks.

"Cool," the teen says.

"How can we help?" the older stylist asks.

"Did any of you personally know either of them? Or Carrie Ellison?"

The old woman, Maxine, scoffs. "Don't get me started on that Carrie. That child's screwier than those women who inject botulism into their faces."

"Why do you say that?"

"She was having an affair with my Louie, may he rest in peace, who just happened to be thirty years older than her. Schmuck even left me for her but came crawling back a week later. She got tired of having to wash his shorts and cook his meals."

"I still can't believe you took him back," the older stylist says.

"Sarah, after forty years of marriage, you tend to forgive a little thing like your husband sleeping with the town tramp."

"If you say so."

"So Carrie sleeps around?"

"If he's over forty, he's undoubtedly been under Carrie," Maxine quips.

"Maxine!" Turning back to me, the older stylist, Sarah, says, "It's sort of a rite of passage—if your marriage can survive Carrie, it can survive anything."

"How long do most affairs last?"

"Until she tires of them. A month or two?"

"She ends the relationships?"

"Hon, what fifty-year-old man would give up a twenty-something girl?" Maxine asks.

"What about Davis Wynn? Did you hear anything about them?"

Streaks chuckles. "Oh yeah. I remember a couple of months ago I was doing her highlights, and she wouldn't shut up about him. 'He's the best thing that ever happened to me, blah blah blah.'"

"Do you know who broke up with whom?"

"From what I hear, Davis did the breaking up," Sarah says. "Joan Pulaski said she saw Carrie have a total breakdown in the produce section, and when Moira at the hardware store asked about Davis, Carrie blew up at her."

"Good for Davis," Maxine says. "Finally got some sense."

"Is Carrie violent, as far as you know?"

"I heard once she got in a fight with Mitch Connelly's wife and came at her with a broken beer bottle," Sarah says. "Ellie had to get stitches."

Jeez, men fall all over themselves for this woman? No accounting for taste.

Sarah gasps. "Oh, I almost forgot! Lily Goodwin over at the police station told me Carrie keeps comin' round to talk to the sheriff. You think they—"

"Oh, totally," the teenager says. "My friend Josie was walking home one night with her boyfriend and saw them parked on the street totally going at it."

"Poor Claire," Maxine says. "Her time at bat finally came up. I should bring her a pie."

"Yeah, starve a cold, feed an affair," Sarah says.

Okay, this is getting off track. "Does anyone know why Davis broke up with her?"

Everyone exchanges glances and shrugs. "No idea. Could be a number of things."

"He just finally wised up," Maxine says.

"So he wasn't seeing anybody else?" The ladies shrug again, all except Sarah. Her lips purse and she looks at the floor. "Sarah?"

"I wanted to keep it a secret," Sarah says with a sigh. "She'd been through so much and that husband of hers is such a cold fish. I've never liked him." All the women nod in agreement. Walter Wayland is not a popular man. "I figured the affair would run its course and the fewer people who knew, the better."

"Who are you talking about?" Streaks asks.

"Valerie Wayland, duh!" the teenager says. "Those are the deaths she's here to investigate, right?"

I nod.

"Val and Dave?" Maxine asks.

"Where did you hear about it?" I ask.

"Brooke Sanderson, one of my regulars, was driving past the Ramada in Lakeland and saw them. I told her to keep it to herself."

"I can't believe you didn't tell me," Streaks says, dismayed enough to pause cutting the teenager's hair.

"I didn't tell anyone, that was the point. I didn't want her marriage to end, not after everything."

"When you heard about Davis's death, why didn't you come forward with this information?" I ask.

"I did! The second I heard about Davis, I called Sheriff Graham. He said he'd look into it."

"What time was that?"

"About eight this morning."

Oh, that lying jerk! Looks like we're in need of another chat. "Just one more question. Has anything … strange ever happened around here?"

"What do you mean, dear?" Maxine asks.

"I don't know, like graves being disturbed or people seeing animals they thought were dead getting up and walking around?" Okay, in hindsight not the best question to ask. All the women look at me like I'm a crackpot.

"Like in a Stephen King novel or something?" the teenager asks.

"Never mind. Thank you all for your time."

"You're welcome," the women say as I walk out the door. "Good luck."

Will sits hunched over with his hands folded on a bench outside, just watching the people pass by. He stands as I walk toward him. "So, guess what?" I ask. "Davis did dump Carrie, and she took it really badly." The verbal diarrhea starts. "Then, get this—Davis and Valerie were spotted outside a motel. Guess who found out this morning? Carrie Ellison's latest conquest: Sheriff Graham."

"He lied to us."

"Oh yeah, big time. I think we should pay him a visit at the station and then check out Carrie's police record. She seems to like attacking people with beer bottles."

A smile creeps across Will's face. "You found out all of that in there?"

"Yep. Never underestimate a woman's need to gossip."

"Very good, Agent Alexander."

"Why thank you, Agent Price. So where to next? We gonna sweat the sheriff?" I ask gleefully.

"Later. First, we need to go to Wynn's house. The men found some interesting things."

Ugh, my buzz just disappeared. More walking. But wait, is that our black Suburban pulling up? The SUV stops right in front of Will, who opens the back door. What a gentleman. We both get in and Agent Chandler puts the SUV in gear, presumably headed toward Davis Wynn's house.

The town proper soon disappears and immediately the residential section starts. The houses on either side of us vary in architecture, some are one story and made of stone, others are two stories of aluminum siding or whatever they make houses out of. It's a far cry from the houses in San Diego, all of which look like they're made of mud and imported from Mexico. The homes here do have one thing in common: a front lawn of beautiful green grass. I'll bet if we came round here on Saturday, there would be someone in every front yard pushing a lawnmower.

We make a few turns onto other residential streets before stopping in front of the last house on the block. Another SUV is in the driveway and a police cruiser sits on the street. We pull up behind the SUV and get out. The house is a ranch-style one story with wood siding, sort of log cabin meets trailer. As with the rest of the houses, a beautiful lush lawn complete with holly bushes brightens the otherwise dark house. There must be a lawn law or something. We take the brick path up to the open door.

Agent Konrad, meeting us at the door, leads Will and Agent Chandler off to the right, but I turn left into the living room so I can snoop on my own. The living room has only a couch, a well-loved green recliner, a coffee table, and a huge TV, none of it matching. I go into the kitchen next. It's as big a disgrace as the living room. The one card table with two chairs must serve as the dining room. There's nothing in the cupboards but cereal, condiments, and peanut butter. This is why men marry—if they don't, they'll starve. Just as I close the fridge door, a young police officer I remember from the station steps in. "Excuse me, ma'am. They want you."

"Will you please keep searching the kitchen and living room for me? Thanks." The officer doesn't balk at my busywork assignment. Now he can't report anything back to Graham except that Davis hasn't been to the grocery store in a while.

The master bedroom where everyone waits resembles a disaster area with clothes strewn everywhere, drawers pulled out and hanging, and the bed half on and off its frame. The closet's been gutted and only empty hangers remain. All the contents—shoeboxes, golf clubs, suits— rest in a pile on the floor. It looks like my room when I was growing up.

Will sits on the bed with a shoebox on his lap looking through some papers. He picks out another from the box and starts reading. Just as I step into the room, Agents Konrad and Chandler come from behind, each with a box, and push me out of the way with the corners. "Ow!"

"Sorry," Agent Chandler says halfheartedly. "Sir, here are all the files from the cabinet in the garage."

"Good. Take them into the living room and start leafing through them. Look for the most recent credit card statements and put the rest in the trunk."

"Yes, sir," says Agent Konrad. This time I'm able to move out of the way before getting pushed.

"Look at this," Will says holding up a piece of paper. "Agent Chandler found them in the desk. 'My beloved Valerie, if only we could have found each other sooner, if only we were the only two people left in the world. Seeing you and not being able to touch you is beyond torture. I think of you every second of every day. Last night when I saw you with him, playing the role of wife to a man who knows nothing about your beautiful soul, I wanted to scream. You have bewitched me, I think of nothing but you.' It goes on from there."

"Cheesy, but sweet. Is there a whole box of them?"

"Only a couple to Valerie, some from Valerie. The rest are to a woman named Charlotte."

"That must have been his wife." I pick up the box and flip through the letters. The top five are to Valerie, all dated within the last four months. The affair was going on longer than I thought. In the first one, Davis apologizes for the kiss and for "what happened after," which I'm guessing wasn't just a firm handshake. He goes on to say he understands if she never wants to see him again but hopes she does. Her strength and sadness touch him. Then it gets really mushy. "I wonder why he has them," I say. "Do you think he gave them to her?"

"See how worn they are? She must have given them back so her husband couldn't find them."

"Smart."

"They also found this," he says, reaching under the bed. Out comes a tan cardigan, which is tossed to me. It's a little bland for my taste, but it might be just what a middle-aged woman in small-town Colorado would wear.

"So either Mr. Wynn's a cross-dresser, or he's had female company. And I have the distinct feeling Carrie Ellison doesn't wear anything without tassels on it," I say.

"I agree."

"Well, we have proof of motive now. Is it enough to bring her in or whatever? What do we do? Do we arrest her? Do we need a warrant?"

"One thing at a time. We need more proof before we confront her."

"And then what happens?"

"That depends on her," Will says, standing up. "If she goes peacefully, we take her to our underground detention facility in Montana. But they never go peacefully."

"Of course."

Footsteps come from the hall. Agent Konrad pops his head in a second later. "Sir, the sheriff just arrived."

"Good. Saves us a trip."

Sheriff Graham waits in the living room, talking quietly to his deputy. Their conversation stops short when we come into view. The deputy gives a final nod to Graham and goes back to the kitchen, no doubt to eavesdrop. I would.

"How is the investigation going?" Graham asks.

"Very well," Will answers. "We have several promising leads."

"Yeah, my deputy tells me you've found love letters between the victims."

"Yes, Mr. Wynn and Mrs. Wayland appeared to be having an affair. But then you knew that."

His nervousness hits me. "I beg your pardon?"

"This morning, over an hour before we came to the station," I say in my best condescending teacher voice, "Sarah from the Beauty Palace called you and gave you the name of a woman who saw the victims together. Did you forget that little piece of information when we spoke?" Oh yeah, I'm bad.

I can see his body tense up. "Sarah Wilson didn't call until after you left, *Agent* Alexander."

"We can check your phone logs to see the exact time of the call," Will says.

"You would take her word over that of a fellow officer of the law?" His tone is angry, but I still get nervousness in waves.

"Sarah Wilson doesn't have a reason to lie," I point out. "You do. You and Carrie Ellison are having an affair." I swear I hear a gasp from the kitchen. "She told us. You're her alibi for last night. Was she with you from six to eight last night?"

Graham doesn't answer right away. He knows we've caught him, and the wheels in his mind must be spinning like crazy trying to figure a way to minimize the damage. Good luck, two-timer. "Yes," he finally says, "she was."

"And the night Valerie was killed? The tenth?"

"I don't remember."

"We will check. On both of you," Will says.

"Why? Am I a suspect?" he asks, shocked.

"Two people who hurt the woman you're involved with are dead, and you've hidden evidence," Will says. "Of course you are."

"This is fucking ridiculous!" Graham shouts. "There was no murder! A wild animal killed Val Wayland and Davis Wynn, and the last time I checked, I wasn't Doctor Dolittle. Don't you people have terrorists to catch? Is this what my tax dollars are paying for? Investigations where no crimes have occurred?"

"Are you done?" Will asks. "Because if you are, I would like you and your deputy to leave. This is our case, and I don't want you messing it up anymore than you already have."

Sheriff Graham does not move. His anger is so hot I think I can see it all around him. "I'm calling Washington," he says through gritted teeth.

"You do that. Now please leave."

"Carmichael!" The deputy immediately steps out of the kitchen. "We're leaving." Graham gets right in Will's face. "This isn't over. I am going to do everything in my power to get you the hell out of my town." He gives the rest of us a sweeping glance and storms out of the room, deputy in tow.

"Can he do that?" I ask.

"He can try," Agent Konrad answers. "Sir, I think it might be in our best interest to have Oliver talk to him, if you know what I mean."

"Only if he continues to make noise." He looks at the boxes. "We need to get out of here before he comes back. Has mobile command arrived?"

"Yes," Agent Chandler says. "About two hours ago. Dr. Neill is performing the autopsy as we speak, and Irie and Wolfe are sifting through the evidence the police gathered. The phone records from the butcher shop, bank, both vics' houses and cell phones should be faxed in soon."

"Good. Let's go see if they've found anything."

—

Wow! The American government rocks! I was expecting a trailer or something, but this … it's bigger than Nana's house. No wonder they put it in an empty field well away from town. It would be conspicuous anywhere else.

From the outside, mobile command looks like a silver refrigerator with wheels, turned on its side. It has one large window right next to the door. Agent Rushmore walks past it, scowl affixed to his face. As I get closer, I notice things not common to a typical trailer, like a satellite dish on the roof and steam rising from the rear where a huge refrigeration unit is attached and humming. I can't wait to get inside.

We enter into a hallway with one door directly across from the entrance. To the left and right are two more doors like the metal ones at the butcher shop, except these doors each have an electronic keypad next to their frames. Will goes to the door directly in front of us and punches in a code. "Put those boxes in the conference room and start sifting through them," Will says to agents Chandler and Konrad. Once again, I'm pushed to the side by pointy corners. The men enter a much smaller version of the conference room at the mansion. The door shuts automatically behind them.

"I'd better give you a tour," Will says. He turns to the door on the right, punching numbers in, and the door opens. It's a white lab barely big enough to fit four people. Irie and Agent Wolfe sit at microscopes, both looking up as we enter. Some spinning instrument is working furiously on a counter off to the side. Right above it is a glass cabinet full of bottles containing different colored liquids. Must be chemicals for tests. The only non-medical piece of equipment is a computer with a scanner. It's about the only thing I know how to use in here.

"This is our lab, where we perform preliminary tests. Blood, fingerprints, things like that. Everything else is sent to Kansas for intensive analysis. But the lab here has DNA-testing capabilities as well as electron microscopes. Very useful. When we get back to

Kansas, someone will train you on it all. It's easier for us to operate the equipment rather than involve more personnel on the team. How's it going, guys?"

"Nothing really to report," Agent Wolfe answers. "We found traces of powder, which seems to be very dead skin on some of his clothes. Besides that … " He shrugs.

"I did, however," Irie says, "confirm that Walter Wayland was on a flight to Sacramento last week and checked into a hotel there, which he has not checked out of. He doesn't have a cell phone with GPS-tracking capabilities, but I've left a message. His credit card was last used there yesterday at a neighboring gas station. Nothing since."

"Excellent. Finish up in here. Conference in five minutes." He's out the door before he even finishes the sentence. When I step out, he's across the hall, already on the keypad.

"Do I get the code for these?" I ask.

The door opens. "Of course. 93010 for medical, 93011 for conference, and 93012 for the lab."

"Got it, thanks." We step into medical.

Okay, he probably should have shown me this room before I ate lunch. The first thing I see is a person in full blue medical scrubs complete with face mask and goggles carrying a gray human brain across the room and placing it into a very bloody scale. Up comes lunch. My gagging makes everyone turn to me.

"Are you all right?" the brain carrier, Dr. Neill, asks.

"I'm fine," I say swallowing down my French fries. Again.

"Okay. Brain, five point eight pounds," she tells her assistant, Carl, who jots it down. The brain comes out of the scale and back over to its body, which is thankfully covered.

"You're almost done?" Will asks. His nose is twitching like mad. Samantha from *Bewitched* would be put to shame. I smell faint blood but heavy antiseptic more, thankfully.

"Almost," Dr. Neill answers. "I wasn't left very much to work with. Lungs, stomach, intestines all partially missing, as are a few limbs. You only found the left arm?"

"Yes, in a cemetery."

"Then I agree with your preliminary assessment of zombies. I found human bite marks from at least three different people, but no saliva."

"Good job. Finish up, conference in five minutes. I'm going to show Agent Alexander around, if you don't mind."

"Be my guest. I can finish after the meeting. Carl?" Carl and the doc take off their coveralls and bloody gloves, Carl replacing his with his black ones before walking out of the room.

The medical room is about three times bigger than the lab and a whole lot chillier. Probably to keep the bodies from decomposing. Davis Wynn's corpse lies on a folding metal table attached to the wall. Next to him is a tray full of scary looking instruments like bone saws and scalpels, all covered in blood. Along the walls are glass cabinets filled with gauze, ointments, and bottles of pills. One of those machines that shock people with paddles sits in the corner next to a refrigerator. The only wall not covered with anything features another metal door, from which the chill originates.

"It's like a traveling doctor's office," I say.

"Exactly. Since some of us can't go to the hospital without being exposed, we bring the hospital with us. We have blood, plasma, antibiotics, splints, everything."

"What's in there?" I ask, pointing to the metal door.

"That's the freezer where we keep the body until the autopsy. It also doubles as a holding cell. Two inches of reinforced steel all around."

"Cool."

"I suppose so. We better get to the conference room. They're waiting for us."

I am more than happy to get out of the deep freeze. Will makes me enter the code for the conference room, which I screw up twice before the door opens. They're waiting for us. Everyone is gathered around a circular table covered in papers. Besides the table, there is a small desk with a computer and fax machine. One entire wall is covered with old books, making the room more than a little cramped. At least there is a huge window looking out onto the field so it isn't totally claustrophobic.

All the seats are taken, so I lean against the bookcase with arms folded. Will moves to the window and starts talking. I don't open my mouth once in the whole fifteen minutes. My only contribution is a few stifled yawns. The Sandman has caught up with me. Nothing I didn't already know is brought up. Affair, zombies, the sheriff and Carrie—all are revealed and discussed ad nauseam.

"I want a detail on Ellison," Will says. "Two one-man teams alternating round the clock."

"Why?" I ask. "Think she'll raise the dead again with the FBI in town?"

"If she does, I want to know. Carl, what'd you get when you touched the items?"

"Terror from the shirt Valerie Wayland was wearing when she was killed," Carl says. "The image of her daughter and husband too. They were fuzzy, but it was them and I think they were in an enclosed space. Oh, and the smell of pine was strong. I have no idea what it means. I mainly felt the terror."

"And from Davis Wynn?" Will asks.

"I touched the coat he left in his car. On the drive he was confused. Apprehensive. He didn't want to be driving there. The only image I got was of him kissing Valerie in the car. He must have been thinking about her a lot."

"Agent Chandler, what'd you find on Walter Wayland?" Will asks.

"He left for Sacramento six days ago, and no one in town has seen or heard from him since. He's supposed to return late next week. I also interviewed the next-door neighbor, and she confirms that he hasn't been home for six days."

"Did she tell you anything interesting?" I ask.

"Good neighbors," Agent Chandler says. "Quiet. Kept to themselves. She said they doted on that little girl. People at the grocery store said the same. Wayland wasn't loved, wasn't hated. He was a fair boss who didn't let the death of his daughter or wife affect his work or attitude."

"Sounds like a real warm guy," Irie says.

"The neighbor also said Valerie hadn't been home as much lately. She figured Valerie was working, but Walter barely left. Besides that, everything was normal, even after the death of the kid."

"Have the phone records come in?" Will asks.

"Yes," Agent Rushmore says. "The day of their murders, the same number called both Wayland and Wynn at their place of business. It's a public pay phone on Main Street. Could have been made by anyone. And there are no cameras in the vicinity."

"Of course," Will says, dejected. "Agent Rushmore, I want you to canvas the area. Ask people in the store if they remember who used the phone then. Irie, I want you and Agent Chandler to sift through the papers we retrieved from Wynn's house. If you need more help, drag Nancy away from her television. Agent Konrad, check the sheriff's schedule and see if he was on shift the nights of the murders. Hopefully, we can break Miss Ellison's alibi. Agent Wolfe, you're on Ellison watch. She's probably still at work, go from there. Carl, when you're done with the autopsy, take over evidence analysis. Thank you. That's all."

Everyone grabs their papers and gets up, muttering to each other as they file out. I catch up with Will just as he walks outside into the field with Agent Konrad. I feel like I'm having a hot flash, the temperature outside mobile command is so different. Agent Konrad nods and begins toward one of the Suburbans, off to bug Sheriff Graham.

"So what about me?" I ask as another yawn hits me.

"Back to the hotel," Will says. "You're exhausted."

"I'm fine. We still have time to re-canvas the murder scenes."

"Later. They'll still be there in a couple of hours. Come on." He walks toward the cars but stops, probably realizing I'm not following. With a sigh, he turns around. "What now?"

"Is this one of those protecting me things again?"

"No," he says, rolling his eyes, "it is an 'I'm exhausted and I'm sure you are too' thing. I'm going back to the hotel to take a nap, and I suggest you come with me. Unless of course you want to go though the victim's financials in all those boxes."

Heck no. "You promise you'll wake me up if anything happens?"

"You will be the second to know."

"And you promise no snooping without me?"

"I wouldn't dream of it," he says with an amused smile. "You seem to be better at this than I am."

"Don't you forget it."

Man, is he gorgeous when he smiles. It's amazing how some-thing as simple as a smile can totally change a person. And make my stomach flutter. As my grin grows, so does his, until we're just grinning like idiots at each other. That chemistry I thought was all in my head returns. Fertile imagination, my Aunt Fanny. He looks away first, blushing almost as much as me. We walk to the car and he opens the door for me. I know what I'll be dreaming about today, and it won't be dead bodies. Lust is a wonderful thing.

EIGHT

ATTACK!

FOR THE SECOND TIME in two days, I wake up in a fog with no idea where I am. I look around the dim, stuffy room and within seconds it comes back to me. Colorado, dead bodies, zombies. I pull the covers back over my head with a groan. Would they think less of me if I just spent the rest of the case under here? Yeah, probably. The covers flip off and I get out of bed. On my way to the bathroom, I check the clock. Four hours of sleep. Not great, but it should keep me on my feet until tonight.

After using the bathroom, I throw on my black slacks and royal blue V-neck and run a brush through my frizzy hair. I didn't mean to sleep so long. Who knows what I've missed. Dinner at least. Nancy and Andrew are walking up to his door when I come out of mine. She was nice enough to go torment Andrew with her soap opera when I shuffled into the room and fell face first on the bed. She did it without a word, the angel. I smile, but neither smile back.

"Hey," I say.

"Hello," Nancy says, her back ramrod straight. Still scared I guess.

"You guys just getting in?"

"Yes, we just had dinner," Andrew says.

"Oh. Is everyone back yet?"

"No." This syllable is followed by several seconds of uncomfortable silence.

"Okay, well, I'm gonna … ," I point down the hall. "Have a nice night."

"Whatever," Nancy mumbles as I pass.

I roll my eyes when the door shuts. The cold shoulder thing is beginning to get on my nerves. Bigger fish to fry right now, Bea. I knock on Will's door. Hope he isn't still asleep. The last thing I need is a cranky werewolf on my hands. Now a naked werewolf…

Will doesn't answer. Instead, a half-naked vampire sipping blood out of a black coffee mug saunters out of the room next to his. As if things couldn't get any more uncomfortable. I was right about him being a satin man. The only thing adorning his perfectly toned body is pair of black satin PJ bottoms and a bloody smile. A *literally* bloody smile, showing once-white teeth now covered with blood. Mondo grossness.

"Well, hello," Oliver coos.

"Yeah, um, hi," I mutter, unable to take my eyes off the coffee mug.

He must notice because he lifts up the cup to me. "May I offer you a cocktail?"

"I had blood for lunch, thanks. Is Will awake?"

"Why yes, he is. I heard him and Agent Konrad leave half an hour ago."

"What? Where did they go?"

"I asked that very question. He mentioned something about cemeteries."

My jaw drops. "What? That weasel!" I practically shout, going into full temper tantrum mode. "I can't believe he didn't wait for me. He purposely did this, you know. Made me come back here just so he could ditch me. Of all the … he is *not* getting away with this."

I stomp back to my room, the anger rolling off me like smoke. How dare he? I'll bet this is one of those protection deals. It is getting *so* old. I don't need some flea-ridden beast who's stuck in the fifties to keep me safe. I've done just fine on my own so far. No way is he getting away with this. I grab my cell, gun, walkie-talkie, and purse and am out the door in thirty seconds.

Waiting in the hall for me is a now-dressed vampire. The pajamas are gone, replaced by blue jeans and what look like cowboy boots. He's putting on a tight black shirt just as I step out. How he got dressed so fast is anyone's guess. Maybe another vampire perk.

"Where the heck do you think *you're* going?" I ask.

He slips on a black leather jacket. "Do you even have to ask, my dear?"

Ugh. "I do not need a chaperone. Why don't you go look in a mirror for a couple of hours, 'kay?" I walk down the hall toward the stairs, which thankfully are in the other direction. I get a few feet, but out of thin air, Oliver appears in front of me, which of course makes me nearly jump out of my skin. "Jeez! God! Will you please stop doing that!"

"I apologize," he says, none too sincerely. In my experience, someone apologizing shouldn't have a huge grin on his face. "But I feel it is my duty to deliver you to William. If something should

144

happen to you en route, neither I nor William would ever forgive ourselves or each other."

"Oh baloney. You just can't stand to pass up an opportunity to bug me."

"Regardless," he says with that freaking smirk, "I *am* coming." He pulls something out of his pocket. Keys. "And I am driving." He disappears again.

Great, just what I don't need. I mutter to myself the whole way downstairs. What a jerk. It's an epidemic. Oliver waits in the driver's seat with the engine running. I slide into the passenger seat and he speeds off, tires screeching.

"They issue vampires driver's licenses?" I ask as he does an illegal U-turn at forty miles an hour. I grip the armrest for dear life.

"Not that I am aware of." I clutch even tighter. We drive down the interstate like a rocket.

"Okay, some of us actually have a pulse and would like to keep it," I scream as he narrowly misses a silver Camry when passing.

"You are so tense, Trixie. Something should be done about that." He gets into the other lane with maybe an inch to spare between two cars. My fingernails ache from the armrest.

"Okay, that's it! Pull over now!"

"I cannot, dear. We are being followed."

"What?" I spin around and sure enough, a tan police cruiser pulls a daredevil move into our lane. "Oh, fudge. I think it's the sheriff."

"I believe you are right," he says, glancing out the mirror. "He has been following us since we left the hotel. I noticed him waiting in the parking lot. Do you perchance know why?" While we dodge and weave with the sheriff hot on our tail—I always wanted to say that—I fill him in on everything.

"So, the sheriff wishes to save his mistress. How noble of him. But why follow us?"

"No idea."

"Then we shall ask him." Oliver swerves down a small side road with a dirt ditch on either side and sure enough, the cruiser follows us. We park to the side and cut the engine. Sheriff Graham does the same. Nobody moves from their respective cars, and it's too dark to see inside the cruiser.

"Should we … "

"He will come to us," Oliver says, not taking his eyes off the rearview mirror. Five seconds later, Graham steps out of the cruiser. As the man walks toward us, Oliver rolls down his window. "May we help you, Sheriff Graham?"

"Where are you two going?"

"That is official FBI business and none of yours."

"If you all are official, then I'm Elvis."

"Costello or Presley?"

Graham's anger hits me like an ice pick. He looks Oliver square in the eyes. "There is something not right about you people, and I *will* find out what it is, even if I have to follow you all around the state of Colorado."

"I cannot allow that to happen," Oliver says. Graham's mouth snaps shut like a bear trap, and his eyes glaze over just like last night. "You will return to your car and call off all of your men who are watching us. You will leave us alone and let us investigate, giving us your full cooperation when asked. You will not follow us but will go home to your wife and beg her forgiveness for your adultery. Now go." Still unblinking, Graham walks slowly back to his car. Oliver watches him in the mirror. "Good boy. He will not be bothering us any longer." I stare at him with a mix of awe and fear. Oliver smiles. "Only one of my *many* talents, my dear. Perhaps someday I can show you my greatest one."

The awe and fear are instantly replaced by annoyance. "Can we go now, Romeo?"

"As you wish," he says, starting the engine. After another U-turn, we're back on the interstate, leaving the sheriff behind. No more death-defying car moves, thank you very much. We cruise in silence for a whole minute before either of us talks. "May I please have your cellular phone?"

I dig it out of my purse. "Why?"

"To locate William. I personally have no desire to traipse around a cemetery at night if I do not have to, do you?" Good point. I hand him the phone. "Hello, William," Oliver says after a few seconds, "I am here with a livid Agent Alexander riding shotgun. What is your location? ... And you are alone? ... Good. We will arrive in five minutes. No, they will not be a problem anymore. ... Tut, tut, you know me better than that. Five minutes." He snaps the phone shut. "William and Konrad had a few problems with the police but are no longer being followed. We are to meet them at the scene of Mrs. Wayland's untimely demise."

"A dark cemetery. Lovely."

"We will gather more information at night, it is a better environment."

"How?"

"A) Nobody will be able to see us should we have to use our talents, and B) the cemetery will be buzzing with leftover energy brought by the moon. Werewolves and vampires are extremely sensitive to every type of energy, especially the preternatural kind. We might be able to match that energy with the necromancer when we meet him." He pauses. "But most important, C) It makes us look tough in front of the ladies."

Without thinking, a smile crosses my face.

Oliver's face lights up. "My, my, did I just make you smile?"

"Shut up." Stupid face, always betraying me.

He doesn't talk for the remaining five minutes, but his smile never wavers. Probably thinking of blood milkshakes. I just watch the night go by. It's not completely dark, as some dark blue remains in the west. I can still see the details of the trees as they pass. I hope we'll be out of the cemetery before all the blue is gone. I can see pretty well at night but I bet Will and Oliver can see perfectly. I reach into the glove box and pull out a flashlight.

We're the first to arrive at the small parking lot next to the cemetery. There couldn't be more than ten parking spaces in all. Desolate too, trees on all sides, and quite a few in the cemetery. The cemetery itself is big. Newer and ancient headstones and little statues of angels sit randomly in the grass, separated by the trees. Despite the dark and the fact that it's a cemetery, it's not ugly like I expected. It's … appropriate. I wouldn't mind here as my final resting place.

As I get out of the car, I shiver. It's the cool air. I'm not used to it. Yeah, that's my story and I'm sticking to it. Oliver leans against the car, arms folded, eyes closed, nose up. "Do you feel it?" he asks. "It prickles my skin, like a hundred centipede legs."

"What?"

"Power." He opens his eyes. "After two weeks, I can still smell them … and her blood. The necromancer's essence permeates this cemetery. I felt the same last night, just as strong."

"Can you tell if it's a man or woman?"

"No, but whoever it is will feel like death. Their aura will be black and as stifling as the grave."

Well, that covers half the people living in Los Angeles but not Carrie. "Would Will know this?"

"Perhaps, but I do not believe so. One has to be tapped into death to fully comprehend it. He could feel it when the power is let loose, though, as would you."

So Carrie's back in the running.

"Should we wait for them or—" This question proves pointless as headlights flash down the road. Within seconds a matching SUV pulls beside ours and out climb Will and Agent Konrad. Will ignores my icy glare as he moves toward us. We'll talk later, buddy.

"I thought you liked to work your mojo alone, Oliver," Will says, eyeing me.

"I was afraid Trixie here would bring down the hotel if I did not let her accompany me."

"I accompanied *you*?"

Once again, I'm ignored. "Are you sure the sheriff won't bother us again?" Will asks.

"No. He should be on his way home preparing to grovel to his wife."

"Then let's stop the chatting and get on with this while there's still a little bit of moonlight."

"What should we look for?" I ask.

"Evidence of a ritual," Will says. "Most necros need to perform a ritual to raise the dead. A salt circle, dead animals, blood, charms."

"There was no evidence of anything like that at the fresh crime scene," Oliver says. "Do you honestly believe there will be anything at a two-week-old one?"

"Just look," Will commands. "And make a list of the corpses you think were raised. There could be a pattern. Two teams. I'll—"

"I will take Agent Alexander," Oliver cuts in. Oh, goody.

He glances at me, but I just glare. "Fine," Will says, looking away. "Stay in radio contact. We'll meet back here in half an hour. You take west, we'll take east. Any trouble—"

"We will scream like little girls," Oliver finishes. "Come on, Trixie." He begins toward the cemetery.

Will grabs my arm before I can take a step. "If he gives you any trouble ... "

I yank my arm away. "I can handle him, thank you very much."

His lips purse. "Listen, I'm sorry I didn't wait for you. I just wanted to—"

"Can we have this conversation later?" I click on my flashlight, pointing it right into his eyes. "I have to follow the bloodsucking vampire into the dark, creepy cemetery."

So I do. My partner waits by a black tombstone with that smirk on his face. "Lover's quarrel?"

"Shut up, and let's get this over with."

"For you, Trixie dear, anything."

I trudge down the small hill, sweeping my flashlight over the graves as I pass. Grass, grass, grass, grass. I walk and sweep in silence for a few minutes, Oliver staying a short distance behind me. I swear I can feel his eyes on my butt. Grass, grass, fresh dirt. "Found one." Putting the flashlight under my arm, I find my pad and scribble down her name and date of death. Jane Etheridge, dead three months. "No signs of salt or dead animals. Do you smell blood?"

"No. And I would not bother looking for any type of ritual. I do not think our necromancer has need of one."

"All the books say a blood sacrifice has to be performed."

"My dear, when you have been alive as long as I have, you come to learn there is no such thing as 'always.' People are never predictable. I believe that our necromancer is one of the most powerful puppet masters living today." He walks to the next grave, then the next. "More times than not, a necromancer requires power and focus to animate the dead. The blood adds power and the ritual helps him focus on the task. The one we are pursuing has all the focus and power he needs, hence no salt circle to protect him and no dead chickens laying about. Here is another one."

I jot down the name and date. Another recent corpse. We start walking again. "Then why are we looking for signs of one?"

"William has no imagination. His mind is placed squarely in a box with no use for the outside. All black or white. Not an ideal characteristic for a lover. I, on the other hand, live in a world filled with gray, blues, and especially reds."

I stop walking but he strolls on. "Eww. Are you really hitting on me in a cemetery? Because that is wrong on *so* many levels."

"Some find cemeteries highly erotic."

"And some people sleep with sheep."

"Touché. I will try to contain myself until we reach the parking lot."

"You can try afterwards too."

He doesn't quip back. He's stopped in front of a large headstone, his head cocked slightly to the right like an inquisitive dog that has just spotted a cat for the first time. I shine the flashlight down and sure enough, where there was once grass now lays dirt. I go to write but both my arms drop at the name on the stone. Emma Minnie Wayland, Valerie's daughter.

"Oh man," I whisper. "The sicko raised Valerie's daughter to kill her. That is … " I shake my head. As if this could get anymore gruesome.

"There is something odd here," Oliver says. Understatement of the decade. With that confused look, he bends down next to the dirt and practically puts his nose in it. Why did I have to be stuck with the vampire?

"What is it?"

"I get no sense of death at this grave. No scent, nothing. The magic is here, but—"

His attention diverts to something behind me. I turn to see what is so fascinating and find spotlights in the direction of the parking lot. I can't make out the source because of the slope of the ground.

"Oliver, do you copy?" Will asks over the walkie.

I unclip mine and hand it to Oliver. "We are here. I assume you saw the lights."

"Affirmative. Think it's the police?"

"Possible. We will meet at the rendezvous. Over and out." He hands the walkie back. "Apparently the sheriff's mind was stronger than I thought. I do hate it when that happens. Come on, my dear. Let us just hope he is not as strong as our necromancer. Otherwise you might have to use your tricks."

"I have tricks?"

"Two very lush ones."

I cross my arms across my tricks. "Pig."

Chuckling, he starts toward the parking lot as I reluctantly follow. His pace quickens into almost a jog, obviously giving no thought to the woman almost a foot shorter than him panting behind. It's not as if the cop is going anywhere, if it is a cop. It could

152

just be some perverse and/or horny teenagers who are in for a frightening experience when four FBI agents come out of a cemetery with guns. That'll kill the mood.

Our dash stops dead. Almost mid-stride, Oliver halts as if he's walked into an invisible wall. Seconds tick by and he just stands there like one of the trees. "Oliver?" Nothing. Wonderful. I face him and find a blank stare. No blinking, only eyes black as coal. Not even a glimmer of white showing. It's as if he has hypnotized himself. This is the part where I should panic, but the centipedes I now feel crawling on and under my skin, prickling every millimeter of my body, get my undivided attention. But there's no time to itch. The instant the crawling begins, Oliver's eyes roll back in his head, and he collapses. The seizure begins even before he hits the ground. Can vampires have epilepsy? He only seizes for another second, then lies as still as the grave his body landed on. My mind comes out of the haze of shock, and I realize I should do something. Calling for help would be good.

"Will?" I say into the shaking walkie. "Are you there? Something happened to Oliver. He had some kind of fit."

"Alexander? Where are you?"

"Um … middle of the cemetery? I don't know exactly. He isn't moving."

"He'll be fine, just calm down. Turn up your flashlight so I can find you. And stay put."

Like I'm going anywhere. I do the flashlight thing.

Still a little hesitant from my Carl/zombie experience, I don't dare touch Oliver. I kneel down and watch him. He's not breathing, but that's normal—I think. No way am I doing CPR on him. He'd never let me forget it. At least he looks very peaceful like this, except for the tongue hanging out. I think I prefer him this way.

One can just admire his unnatural handsomeness without his mouth ruining it. If he could just—

"AHHHHHHHHHH!"

Jesus Christ! His screams almost burst my eardrums. I yelp almost as loud as he does and fall onto my butt. His eyes, now back to their normal color, fly open, jumping around like a trapped wild animal. He doesn't recognize anything. This freaks me out more than anything. I crab-walk away in case he lashes out. I don't move until the screams subside, becoming low moans. He begins to blink again, and within seconds, the moans stop. The whole thing takes about five seconds, not the five minutes it feels like.

"What the *fuck* was that?" he shouts at me.

"Are—are you okay?"

Before he can answer, Will sprints over the horizon like an Olympian. I manage to stand but Oliver tries and fails. I grab his arm and sling it over my shoulder. He must be weak because he doesn't make a lewd remark or try to cop a feel. Now I'm worried.

Will reaches us, gun in hand. "Are you all right?" Will asks me.

"I'm fine."

"Good," he says with a sigh.

I help Oliver lean against the nearby tree his head narrowly missed when he fell. "I am fine as well, thank you for asking."

"What happened?"

"Well—"

The prickling that I hadn't even noticed had ended suddenly hits again, but this time it brings a two by four. I'm knocked off my feet, collapsing against Oliver, who seems to be hit by the same thing. We fall to the ground with Will crashing next to us. The world somersaults a few times before I can get a clear thought through the fog and itchiness. I'd scratch but I have no control of my body. The prickling stops as soon as it started, and I can move again. My frightened eyes meet Will's. A scared werewolf. We are so in trouble.

"What the hell is going on?" I ask.

"Magic," Oliver answers. "William ... "

"We are getting the fuck out of here."

We all find our feet, though if my supernatural companions' legs are as shaky as mine, those feet are going to get lost again. Then something hits me. "Where's Agent Konrad?"

The men look at each other. "Oh, shit," Will says. He pulls out his walkie. "Konrad, come in." No answer. "Konrad, come in." No answer. "I sent him to rendezvous with the car. Agent Konrad, answer me!"

The ground begins to shake under my feet. Do they have earthquakes in Colorado? I jump off the grave I am standing on with the speed of a rabbit. The ground keeps moving, shimmying, and falling down upon itself like a sinkhole. Dirt on dirt on dirt. All the grass is sucked underneath. That's when I notice that all the surrounding graves are doing the same thing. Oh boy.

"Is what I think is happening, happening?" I ask, eyes glued to the ground. "Guys?" Instead of an answer, hands wrap around my waist, and I fly up into the air like Tinker Bell, landing on my stomach in a tree branch. Will's arms are still up when I land. "Wha—"

"Shut up," Will commands. "We have about ten seconds before they surface, so just shut up. You *stay up there* as long as you can. I mean it. Cover Oliver. Do whatever you can, but stay up there. Call for help. Get everyone out here. Tell them to bring the tranq gun and incinerators. Oliver ... "

"Go do what you must," Oliver says.

Will nods. He pulls out his gun and extra clip and tosses them to me. "Just stop them from getting too close. Take out the legs, arms, teeth. Total dismemberment, remember that." I nod. "And if anything, and I mean *anything,* comes at you, don't hesitate." With that, he takes off in the opposite direction of the parking lot.

"Where the hell is he going?" I ask, near hysterical.

"Werewolves like privacy when they change. It is a very gruesome sight."

"He's—"

A gray, dry hand rises from the earth from a not nearly far enough away grave. Several more emerge from the surrounding ones. The eerie silence is interrupted as three gunshots echo through the graveyard, followed by a bloodcurdling scream. A man cries out in utter agony for a few seconds. Then silence. I don't know which is worse.

"Trixie! Call now!" Oliver shouts.

"Uh, right." I fumble to get my phone off my belt. Not easy when you're balancing on a branch half your size. The first few heads surface above the ground. Some are just skulls with dry skin in patches. A few are newer but the smell nearly chokes me. The rash of hands popping out gets closer and closer to us by the moment. I get the phone and push redial. Someone picks up on the second ring.

"Special Agent Chandler speaking."

"Weneedhelprightnowzombiesarecomingthey'recomingout nowWill'sawerewolfI'minatreeyouneed—"

"Slow down, I can't understand you. Who is this?"

Slow-moving silhouettes appear over the hill. A lot of them. They join a half dozen or so of their friends who have just freed

156

themselves from their not-so-final resting place. Oliver kicks the half-surfaced zombie by his side in the face.

"Oh, fudge," I say under my breath. "Valerie Wayland's cemetery *now*. Entire cemetery raised. Zombie horde coming. Will's a werewolf, bring tranq gun and incinerators. Gotta go." I slap the phone shut and put it in my pocket.

In mere seconds, their numbers have more than quadrupled. The corpses ramble with no real direction. A dozen more stagger over the hill, some looking like normal people, most partially or totally decayed. Some are nothing but sinew holding bones together. The stench is unbearable. The zombies closest to my tree hideout have fully risen. Oliver kicks like a karate master and punches them like a man in a bar brawl. If I wasn't so scared, I'd be impressed. Even with no eyes, they seem to know where he is. More freaking magic. "We're going to die," I say under my breath.

"Shoot them!"

"Um ... " I fumble for my gun, but my mind goes blank as three more stumble over the hill. One of their arms falls to the ground. There are too many of them. They're a freaking army. I —

"Trixie!" a choked voice says.

My eyes jolt back to Oliver. An elderly woman has him by the neck, the only thing separating her teeth from his neck are his shaking arms. She lunges at his neck like a snapping turtle on speed. There's a deafening noise as her head spins 180 degrees, and now she's snapping at air. I think I did that.

Oliver takes advantage of the reprieve and pulls both her arms off at the shoulders. This time I know it's me sending her flying into four incoming zombies like a bowling ball knocking down pins. Another zombie grabs at Oliver, but he rips its arm off. Aiming my gun at one a foot behind Oliver I fire, severing the leg at the knee. I shoot a few more times, hitting something important each time. Eat your heart out, Annie Oakley.

I'm aiming for another when Oliver shouts, "Get down from there!" He kicks another zombie away.

"What? But Will said ... "

The zombie he just dispatched comes back and gets a round-house kick to the head. "I said get down! Now!"

My brain shouts "no way" but my body obeys. I grab onto the branch and swing into zombie central. Immediately, I'm grabbed from behind by bony fingers. On reflex, I elbow it in the stomach. It releases me. I spin around and send the half-decayed thing flying into thin air along with two of his friends. Guess all those hours staring at pencils in The Building paid off.

"Come on," Oliver says as he grabs my wrist and starts pulling me toward our unknown destination, dodging and weaving between both the zombies and the holes they've left in the ground. "Keep them away from us," he says after releasing my wrist. We run closer toward the massive horde coming over the hill. Invisible hands knock any zombie within three feet of us away. With a sense of poetic justice, some fall back into their graves. We make it up the hill only to be greeted by more rotting corpses. This is getting ridiculous.

The ground suddenly disappears under me. I trip. My arms break the fall but this momentary misstep gives my pursuers the chance they need. I pull my foot out of a hole just as hands grab my shoulders. A mouth clamps down on my right shoulder with the grip of a pit bull. A wail escapes me before I push the creep away with my mind. You'd think after working in an elementary school I'd be used to being bitten, but each time it happens I'm shocked by the pain. Blood trickles down my back. Despite the pain, I get to my feet.

Oliver is oblivious to my plight. He's busy with the veritable wall of walking dead surrounding us. The moment he knocks one into a tree or tombstone, another seems to take its place in the line, like a zombie Pez dispenser. Two of them—one a man and the other of unidentifiable gender—grab Oliver, but he pushes them away. Another seizes my arm and tries to bite, but I kick it away. My martial arts trainer would be so proud. His girlfriend behind me grabs the other arm and chomps down on it. I scream. The gun in the other hand reaches her forehead and a second later, her head is nothing but puzzle pieces. Enough of this.

Then something I've never felt takes control. My body turns warm then hot in an instant, like someone's switched on my boiler. My breath becomes ragged and then stops. The breeze stops moving and everything but the dozen undead figures surrounding us turn black. There are no screams, no moans, no Oliver. The air moves toward me, inside me, through every pore of my body. It feels like two hands squeezing either side of my brain, but it doesn't hurt for once. I don't know what's happening to me ... but I like it. I close my eyes and feel the blood trickle out of my nose. I release. Power explodes out of me like a fiery gust of wind in a hurricane. It knocks me on my back. Several daggers plunge into my brain. I cry out, clutching my head. Oh God, now it hurts! Stop! Hands grab my shoulders.

"Trixie!" I hear a familiar voice shouting. I know that voice ... who ... "Open your eyes!" I do. It's blurry at first, but I blink until I see Oliver kneeling beside me. God, he's good-looking when he's worried. "My dear, can you speak?"

"Huh?"

"Never mind. Can you walk?"

Without letting me answer, he hoists me up by the arms, my injured one throbbing. When I'm up, the sight before me draws a gasp. Oh … my … lord. There's nothing left but the kind of destruction I see on TV after a tornado. Trees lie on their sides, tangled roots above ground. Every headstone within forty feet rests on its side, a few older ones are now nothing but pebbles and dust. The zombie horde is literally nothing but pieces. Twitching legs, arms, and jaws still trying to make their way toward us litter the grass. Every piece bigger than a foot still tries to continue its mission, but I doubt any of them is a threat to us now. A few fresher corpses remain intact but shuffle far in the distance.

"Did I … "

"Remind me never to anger you," Oliver says, serious as death.

"I don't—"

"We must get to the car." He hands me my gun. "Are you able to walk?"

"I think so." My head throbs and I feel nauseated, but I sure as heck don't want to stay here. I take a few steps and sure enough, I'm walking though my head throbs with each step. A hand grabs my ankle, but I kick it away. I really much prefer zombies without teeth. This is much better. Nice stroll through the body parts. Seems I've either destroyed or scared away all our attackers. Goody for me.

I spoke too soon. Several feet away, three zombies kneel on the ground surrounding something. Their faces are streaked red with what looks like ketchup but isn't. A leg dressed in a blue pinstripe pant leg pokes out of their feeding circle. The zombie in a white dress now soaked red with blood raises a hunk of bleeding meat to her mouth and bites down. The vomit rises, but I force it back down.

"Trixie, we do not have time for this," Oliver says.

"That's Konrad, isn't it?"

He lightly puts his hand on my good arm. "We need to keep moving." He tugs on the arm, and I start walking. "Avert your eyes, my dear." One of the zombies looks up from his feast and bears his teeth like a rabid dog. I raise my gun and shoot its jaw off. It falls onto its back from the force. I shoot the other two the same way and send all three into the air. Konrad looks exactly like Davis and Valerie—just meat, bones, and gristle.

"He didn't deserve this."

"No, he did not. But if we do not keep moving, we will join him."

Suddenly, coming from what seems like every direction, a howl echoes. For the second time tonight, Oliver looks frightened. If it's bad enough to scare a vampire...

"Was that..."

"Now I *insist* we depart." Grabbing my hand, he pulls me away from Konrad and drags me to the car at a run. You ever try to keep up with something that moves faster than human perception? I don't recommend it. The roadrunner would be put to shame. We maneuver around a few stray zombies who turn to follow us. I look back at them staggering slowly toward our fast-moving bodies, some dropping body parts and skin on the grass but never stopping. They won't stop until they're destroyed. I can't look anymore. Within thirty seconds, we're at the car. I officially have no breath left, and my head is filled with the entire rhythm section of a conga band when we get here, but at least now we're safe. I pull on the passenger side door handle but the door doesn't open. There's another howl in the distance. I frantically pull a few more times.

"Stop it," Oliver says, getting into the driver's seat. I let go of the handle, and he clicks the lock. The door opens. That's me, cool in a crisis. I swear I—

Something grabs my leg, biting my calf right above the Achilles tendon. I scream in pain. Oliver grabs my arm and pulls all but a bite-sized chunk of me in the car. Before the door even shuts, he backs up, hitting what feels like a speed bump. My biter lies on the pavement, half its body squished by an SUV. Ha! Oliver backs up all the way to the interstate without bothering to turn the car around. All I see is darkness, but we make it safely to the main road before spinning the car around and stopping. I'm so relieved, I fight the urge to cry.

"I do not see any of them following." He glances at me. "You are bleeding. There should be a first-aid kit under your seat."

There is. I take the aspirin first then start on my arm. I only realize how much it freaking hurts when I look at it. Oliver turns down another two-lane road. The teeth marks on my arm go deep. I don't want to see the others. I look up after disinfecting and bandaging the swollen area and recognize the gas station we pass. We're going toward mobile command. "Are we going to command? Shouldn't we wait for the others at the cemetery?"

"You are in need of medical attention. The others are on their way. They can—"

"Will is still out there! All alone!"

Oliver looks at me. "Believe me, Will does not need our assistance at present. You, however—"

"Look out!"

162

Too late. The person who just stepped in front of our huge SUV smashes into the front, the top half of his body folding onto our hood, then falling under the carriage. We hit another human speed bump. Oliver slams on the breaks, and the car comes to a skidding stop. We sit in stunned silence for a moment. He looks out the rearview mirror.

"Oh my lord," I finally choke out, *"we just killed somebody!"*

"Be quiet, we did not," he says, calm as can be.

"But—"

"Turn around and look."

I do. The man, who should be road kill and looks it, stands on his one attached leg. "Oh thank God, he's already dead. How did it get all the way out here?"

"I have no idea, but this is not good. They are not confined to the graveyard."

"The town's only half a mile from the cemetery. We need to get there! Now!"

"No, I need to get you to mobile command per protocol. You are weak and in need of—"

"For Christ's sake! I am not some china doll and I'm tired of people treating me like one! I am fine! This is me, fine. And we do not have time to debate this! They will kill people! We have a job to do, so turn this ... *effing* car around and let's stop them!"

He stares at me with no expression, but that smirk soon resurfaces. "Whatever you say, my dear. All you had to do was ask." He puts the car in reverse and hits the standing zombie again. The car shimmies on impact. That can't be good for the alignment. We're on the interstate within seconds. "You better call this in," Oliver says. "We are going to need help."

I pull out my cell and press redial. "Chandler."

"It's Bea. Where are you?"

"Seconds away from the graveyard."

"Look, it's possible some of the zombies have gotten out of the cemetery. There's at least one we know of. Oliver and I are headed toward town in case they make it that far."

"How many are in the graveyard now?"

"A lot, a whole lot. And Will's changed."

"Understood."

"We'll head off the ones going to town, just concentrate on the cemetery."

"Call if you need assistance." He hangs up.

"I hope they have better luck than we did."

"They will be just fine."

This is not going to be good. I can feel it. I push out the clip release on my gun and check the ammo. Almost empty. I put in the extra clip and get another from Will's gun from my pocket. "So, what's the plan?"

"You turn them into airplanes if they come near a civilian, or shoot them. Your choice."

"I'm allowed to use my power in front of people?"

"If they are being attacked by decaying corpses, I would say the supernatural jig is up. Protect them anyway you can, and we will deal with the consequences later." He glances out the window at the forest and the car comes to a screeching halt. "Gun, please," he says rolling down the window. I hand it to him and cover my ears. He shoots at an old man with yellow sagging skin twice, taking out the man's legs, then hands me back the gun. "Are we keeping score? Make a note about that one." And we speed away.

NINE

A MACHETE IS A GIRL'S BEST FRIEND

WITH NO MORE ZOMBIE interruptions, we reach the town's limits within the minute. There are only a few people on the streets, since most of the shops closed at six. The only lights come from street-lights and the glowing marquee at the Apache Theater. The Stone Diner is still open, but few people are outside. The desolation is good. Fewer walking meals.

Oliver doesn't so much park the car as bring it to a skidding stop in the middle of the two-lane road, creating a makeshift road-block. I doubt there will be much traffic, but the few people who drive by will think twice when they see the car. The people out and about stop to look at us and seem confused. I jump out of the car. "Everyone get inside now," I shout. Nobody moves. A gunshot echoes through the silence. Immediately fear replaces confusion and they run in the opposite direction, practically trampling over each other to get inside. I turn to Oliver just as he replaces his gun in its holster. Wish I had thought of that.

Only one person remains on the street. She continues shuffling down the sidewalk, oblivious to her surroundings and dragging her left foot. Oliver starts toward her but holds up his hand to stop me from following. As quick as lightning, he's by the woman's side, grabbing her head and twisting it off like a doll's head. A gasp escapes me. I watch with a dropped jaw as he tosses the head on the ground, but the body continues walking as if nothing happened. Without eyes, the zombie doesn't see when Oliver leans down to yank her ankles out from under her. With another quick tug, the legs come off. She must be a few years dead because only particles of dust scatter around them. Gross. Oliver drops the legs, and when I blink, he's inches from me. "She will not be a problem." She's still a crawling torso with arms but can do limited harm.

"You could have checked to see if she was one before you ripped her head off!"

"She stank of death."

"She could have just been *old!*"

Sirens and flashing lights from down the street put a halt to our bickering, as police cruisers barrel toward us. Took them long enough. I collect my purse from the floor of the car and pull out my badge, holding it up for the officers to see. Their cars stop a few feet away from us. The deputies jump out, standing behind their doors with guns pointed at us. I recognize a few from this morning.

"Put your hands in the air," the deputy directly across from me says.

"Special Agent Beatrice Alexander, FBI!" I shout. "This here is Special Agent Oliver Montrose. Please holster your pistols immediately!"

Like good boys, they take one look at the badge and put the guns away. "We had several reports of gunfire. What's going on here?"

"Ah … " plausible lie, plausible lie, "we have reason to believe that some violent felons we've been pursuing are on their way to town."

"Why weren't we notified?"

"We are better trained to handle this situation than you," Oliver says. "In fact, your presence is a hindrance, so if you do not mind … " He nods up the street. "We can handle this."

"Oh man, what is *that?*" another deputy says, pointing at the crawling zombie. All the men look, grimace, and turn back to us. Oops, busted. The guns reappear.

"There is a totally logical explanation for that," I say with a chuckle.

"Put your damn hands in the air!" The head deputy points his gun at Oliver, who isn't fazed in the least. My arms, meanwhile, are up as high as they can go.

"You are annoying me," Oliver says. "Point that pistol away now or—" We don't hear the rest. I blink, and Oliver is beside the stunned deputy yanking the gun out of his hand and pointing it at me. "Duck!"

I squat down as the gun fires. Behind me, an incoming zombie's jaw splinters into dust. Nobody moves except the zombie—who keeps moving. In my squatting position, the only thing for me to do is sweep its feet out from under it, so that's what I do. Its head lands right next to me, but I jump away toward a stunned deputy as it snaps at me.

"Thanks," I say to Oliver.

He nods. "Gentlemen," Oliver says, giving the gun back, "now would be a good time to fire."

The zombie gets to its knees. "Is that a … "

It's on its feet. "Zombie, yes! So shoot it!" I shout.

A barrage of bullets hit the woman, cutting off her legs, neck, and arms. I cover my ears with little effect. They stop firing after three seconds and fifty bullets. Overkill much? Still holding their guns, the men stare at the twitching thing with mouths open big enough for a train to pass through. A few lower their guns when they realize it isn't getting up again.

"Is it dead?" one of the men asks.

"That was not its problem," Oliver says. "I do not think it will be getting up again, though."

"What the *fuck* is going on?" the lead deputy asks.

"Your town is about to be overrun with the walking dead," Oliver says. His eyes leave the frightened deputy and move back behind the car. "And I am afraid it will be sooner rather than later."

All eyes follow his and bug out when they take in the scene. I count twelve—no, make that thirteen as another comes around the corner. They're spread out along the street and sidewalks, but all shuffle toward us. Another near-skeleton pops out from around the corner. The deputies just gawk at the advancing horde. One of the nearest, a child dressed in a dirty white communion dress, approaches her fallen comrade and steps on what is left of his leg.

"Jenny Cabot?" one of the men asks.

"Shoot it," Oliver says.

"But it's Jenny. My sister babysat her!"

She takes another step, arms outstretched toward Oliver, baring her brown teeth. I lift her with my mind, sending her toward the two closest zombies like a missile, temporarily knocking all three down. Not that it does much good; three more step out in their place. The men all glance at each other like a flying zombie is the strangest thing they've ever seen. Oh, boys, the night is young.

Three more zombies reach the car. "Guys, why are you not shooting?" I shout as I pull out my gun and take aim. The gun jolts as I shoot the nearest one, exploding the yellowish skin around its jaw. Another barrage of gunshots ring out and the closest zombies jerk from the multiple bullets hitting them all over. They're stunned but none fall down. The men missed all the sweet spots by hitting only the chests. Three more zombies make it to the car with two others close behind. To make matters worse, the officers need to reload. Stupidly, I watch them, giving the jawless one the opportunity to grab my arm and squeeze until I cry out. Oliver cold-cocks him, and it lets go. "Pay attention, my dear." Another zombie lunging at a deputy becomes airborne as if spring-loaded and smashes through the hardware store window. I wink at my partner.

Of course, just as the corpse's feet leave the ground, people begin exiting the movie theater, stopping dead as the shards of the window fly. Go see a scary movie and end up in one of your own, that's gotta stink. Like all normal people greeted by the rotting dead, the moviegoers just stand there like deer in the headlights while the zombies continue to approach. More patrons filter out, looking just as confused as their friends.

"Limbs and jaws," I shout to the men over my own gunshot. I pull the trigger again but only get a click. The men aim and splinter arms and legs, but for one middle-aged deputy in glasses, it is too late. A man with no eyes bites his outstretched arm. The deputy lets out a high-pitched scream I thought only six-year-olds were capable of. The zombie rips out a huge chunk of flesh as blood pours out of the wound.

Some of our audience join the deputy in his screams but none run away. Shock is better than Super Glue. Another deputy shoots the bloody zombie attacking his friend. Yet another pushes the injured man into the nearest squad car and shuts him in. A woman's shriek draws my attention. One of the secretaries from the school frantically swats at an almost skeletal zombie that grabs at her flapping wrist. It flies ten feet away, smashing into a dozen pieces on impact. I'm getting better at this.

The zombies have made it through our line. About half a dozen were smart enough to go around us and get to the scared-stiff civilians. Second problem: more keep popping out of the trees and around the corner. The town just *had* to be built downhill from a cemetery. There are too many to shoot or move with my mind. The men, finally getting their wits about them, start shooting the arms, legs, and heads of any zombie a few feet from them. Oliver swings at anything that moves, punching holes in their bodies as if they were made of dough. Even a few moviegoers start kicking and punching their undead assailants while others run away. Unfortunately, the commotion has brought anybody within a quarter mile radius out of their closed shops. I can't tell how many people are screaming or shooting right now.

"Trixie! Behind you!"

Something grabs my shoulder, and I try to elbow its nose. It's one of the zombies' missing limbs. Like we don't have enough trouble with the fully intact ones. This one glides through the air into the already smashed-up hardware store. I can only hope they aren't smart enough to use weapons. Wait! Brainstorm! Seeing a clearing through the carnage, I run past two deputies through the window of the hardware store. There are only a few aisles in the small shop. I run up and down them, finding nothing but bolts, paint, and a crawling two-limbed zombie, which I step over. Where are the chain saws and sledgehammers?

I'm halfway down the third aisle when something rattles in the back of the store. I eject my empty clip and push in a fresh one. Leading with my gun, I walk toward the back wall, checking the other two aisles as I pass. As I make my final careful step toward the end, teeth clamp down on my hand right below the pinky. With a howl, I drop the gun and pull my hand away, leaving a small chunk of my skin in its mouth. The zombie lunges before I register it. We fall to the ground with me on the bottom. All the air escapes my lungs as my head thumps on the hard floor. Immediately, the zombie starts wrestling me, snapping at my neck with only my shaking arms holding it back. If I survive this, I really need to work on my upper body strength.

I have about ten seconds before my arms give out and it latches onto my neck like a leech. I can't use my mind because it's holding onto my wrists with a boa constrictor grip and it'd just take me with it. I glance behind him but don't see the gun. It makes another attempt at my neck, moans of longing coming from its throat. My arms lower several inches. The second zombie I stupidly forgot about hops toward us, looking for her share of the meal. At least I'll be dead by the time that one starts chomping down. My arms lower another inch as I whimper.

Then I see it.

The machete, nothing but a foot and a half of cutting power, rests on pegs on the back wall. The metal blade is almost glowing from the streetlights outside, shining like the Holy Grail. It's not a sword but it's the next best thing. The machete floats off the pegs, moving slowly at first, then flying like a rocket into my attacker's head. Its body jolts, loosening its grip momentarily. I fling the corpse against the back wall. It crashes into the tools, falling to the floor amid saws and shovels. I flip to my belly. The zombie fragment, which is now close enough to touch, is yanked by invisible strings into the cash register. She flips over the counter, taking the register behind it with her. I'm on my feet the second she's out of sight, running toward the first one, who's struggling to stand. I pull the machete from its head with a sick sucking noise. The machete swipes through the zombie's neck and arms, severing all three limbs. It won't cause anymore harm. The second one finishes standing when I reach her, but I go behind the counter and cure her of that. Is it wrong that I'm enjoying this so much?

I emerge from the hardware store with two armfuls of potential weapons: shovels, pickaxes, hoes, and the two machetes. I tuck my gun into my waistband. I've got something better now. Outside it's bedlam. In the two minutes I've been fighting for my life in the hardware store, all the zombies have made it past the deputies, a few of whom now sit in their squad cars while the zombies surround them, pounding on the glass. A few windows are now nothing but shards. On the plus side, only a handful of people litter the streets and those who remain fight with nothing but bloody arms and legs. In most cases, it's three against one. A car maneuvering around our SUV draws both the attention of the living and the dead as it speeds down the road. Trying to avoid zombies, it swerves but not in time. The driver clips the corpse. He jumps out of the SUV before the car even comes to a complete stop, running toward the injured zombie. Before the Good Samaritan can get his nose bitten off for his trouble, I pull the zombie toward me with my mind like its on wheels. I drop all but my machete and with a swift swipe, off comes its head. The Good Samaritan gawks first at the headless zombie then at me, the wild-haired machete-wielding lady. The man jumps back into his car, zooming away between the undead.

My attention turns to one of the few brave deputies covered in blood, who hits an old man with the butt of his gun. The corpse won't let go. I pick up one of the shovels.

"Hey!" I shout. The deputy strikes the zombie again before looking at me. I toss him the shovel and the second he catches it, he swings. The old man's body falls to the ground with his head at an odd angle. Off the deputy runs to help a civilian. A woman bleeding from the collarbone comes up to the pile, gets a pickax, and returns to help a man fighting off two corpses. Immediately, four more people, not one in pristine condition, take a weapon and return to the fight. Oliver materializes like Houdini just as a man picks up the machete. Snatching it out of the man's hand, he says "Mine" with a smile. The man stumbles back. Good to know other people have the same reaction to his little tricks. Instead of the machete, the man takes a shovel and jogs off. "I thought I lost you there for a moment," Oliver says.

"I'm not that easy to get rid of." I smirk and go to help a blond girl about to be cornered by three zombies. Swiping away, I cut off a head, then another, finally an arm at the elbow. The headless creatures turn from the teen before falling into line next to each other like books on a bookcase. I cut through their torsos at the waist and they topple. The teen, who I realize is the girl from the Beauty Palace this afternoon, stares at me with a slack jaw. I wink and run off to the next potential victim.

I hack, cut, slice, all but mince fifteen of them, only using the gun when I have to. It's as if I'm possessed. Heads, legs, waists, nothing is safe. I'm like a homicidal ballerina, graceful in my carnage, twirling with my machete on Main Street. After I eviscerate one, I spin to the next. I don't know how long I have been chopping

173

away at anything that smells of decay, but when I can't breathe, I stop to look around.

Body parts lay scattered everywhere, some twitching, others moving toward the few humans left. Around those are pieces of skin and congealed puddles of yellow embalming fluid. I'm covered in the stuff, even my face and hair. Only a few people and zombies remain locked in battle. Shovels hit heads, axes cut legs. A deputy checks the pulse of someone lying on the ground. Nearby, Oliver swings his machete through the neck of a near-skeleton. Even though he's covered in the same dead junk I am, he still looks like a freaking model. So unfair.

"Oliver!" I shout. "I'm going to head the oncoming ones off at the pass!" Before he can say anything, I run in the opposite direction, past a few bleeding people helping others in the same condition. Oliver shouts something like "Watch for—" but I don't hear the rest. The road is clear up to the woods. Looks like the villagers get a temporary respite. Just as I get to the edge of the woods, an elderly man with no eyes in a tattered suit lunges at me. I grab him with my mind and push him into a tree. He falls to the ground, and as I pass, off comes his head. I embark into the woods with only a moment's hesitation. I think I'm forgetting something.

TEN

I KNEW I FORGOT SOMETHING

THE CEMETERY IS ABOUT half a mile uphill through dense, dark woods. I really should have brought a flashlight. Even with my better-than-average night vision, all I see are big black vertical lines until I get close enough to feel bark. Weaving around the trees, I continue toward, I hope, the cemetery. Twigs crackle to my left. A stumbling dark figure moves closer, and I walk to meet it. The second I smell death I bridge the gap, machete held high. Head and legs slice off, and I move on.

A few minutes and another zombie later, I realize I'm lost. Not surprising, since I got lost in my own school even after three months. There is no more uphill, which means I must have stumbled onto a plateau. I change direction for a few feet, but it's still flat. Great. Wonderful. Leave it to me to—

The cell phone chirps, and my heart leaps into my throat. I unclip the cell with shaking hands. "Hello?"

"What is your status?" a man asks.

"Who is this?"

"Chandler. What is your status?"

"Um, I'm in the woods making my way to the cemetery taking out stragglers. Oliver is still in town with the remaining zombies. We got hit bad, a lot of injuries."

"We'll send a cleanup crew and get Doc over there. Are you injured?"

He had to ask. All of a sudden, my whole body aches, and my bites sting like the dickens. I had totally forgotten I was in pain. Gotta love adrenaline. Too bad it wears off. "A few bites, nothing—"

A long, animalistic howl echoes through the woods, making the birds fly from their perches. I nearly drop my phone. Oh fu—dge. I've remembered what I'd forgotten. My breathing comes out in short spurts as what I pray is a bear growls not terribly far away.

"Alexander?" Agent Chandler asks.

Oh, I'm still holding the phone. I press it back to my ear. "Have you by any chance got Will yet?"

"Negative. Operatives are still tracking him. I suggest you double time it back to the town and wait for backup. A team has been dispatched with incinerators."

"Way ahead of you," I say as I run back the way I came. I was off the second he said *negative*. Honestly, I have no idea where I'm going since the ground is still fricking flat. Branches hit my face even after I brush them aside. It doesn't help that I can barely breathe after only thirty seconds of intense running. After zombie-busting for what feels like hours, I'm pooped. Me and my bright ideas. "Let's go into the dark woods and chase zombies!" That setup alone should have stopped me. But noooo, I had to play the hero and now Will's—

Something on the ground stops my legs, and I tumble onto something soft. It's covered in sticky liquid, and smells like—

A hand grabs my arm, and I push it away with a shudder. I crab walk backwards a few feet. I'm still close enough to see that the zombie on the ground is ripped to pieces. Poetic justice, if you ask me. The hand that grabbed me is attached to the only limb left on the caved-in torso. I don't see its head anywhere, but a leg twitches a foot away. Carved in the leg is a claw mark. So not good. There's another howl, and it's definitely closer this time. I can't move. My body has shut down from stupid fear. In the distance, but not far enough distant, branches break, and there's a faint snort. Okay, *think, Bea*. Remember your training.

Werewolves. Big. Very fast. Huge teeth and claws. Often track by scent, so he's drawn to my blood. He's faster and can find me anywhere. Best option: get off your behind and RUN! So I do. Machete in one hand, gun with silver bullets in the other, I run in the opposite direction of the breaking branches. The cracking sound and odd snorting continue getting closer behind me. Tree branches smack me in the face, but I don't care. He's hunting me. Just keep running, and when we get to town they'll... oh no. I stop running. If he's hunting me, then he'll follow me into the town. No one will be safe. Crud, now what am I going to do?

My cell chirps. "Alexander," I say through the pants.

"Are you in town yet?" Chandler asks.

"I can't, I'll lead Will right to them." He's silent for a second. I've stumped him. I am so dead. "Chandler?"

"Hold him off as best you can until the team gets there. Do you have any idea where you are?"

"None."

177

"Then just stay where you are and make some noise so they can find you."

"Okay. But what should I do if—"

"Whatever you have to." He hangs up.

I clip the phone back and eject my clip. Four bullets, great. Alexander's last stand and little ammo. Hope he doesn't get close enough for me to use the machete. "Help!" I shout. "I'm here! Over here! Help me!" I repeat myself a few times. Please God, let them hear me.

I'm on my third rotation of "Help" when branches crack louder than ever behind me. I twirl around, gun and machete at the ready, but see nothing in the darkness. Please be a zombie. A girl can hope, right? I spin again when more branches break to my left. He's circling me. "I could really use some help here!" I scream at the top of my lungs. "Oh God, oh God, oh God, oh God." He growls behind me. Once again I see nothing but night. "Will…" I whimper. More branches break. "It's me, Beatrice." A low growl. "Oh God, oh God, oh God," I whisper. "Just go away! Please just go away."

I see him. He starts as nothing more than a blob of black slowly stalking toward me. My first reaction is to run, but rationality says he'd chase me. I'd be dead in ten seconds. Instead, I raise my shaking hands holding the gun and the machete up high. "Will, I don't want to hurt you." He keeps walking and growling. Boy is he big. Werewolves don't lose height or weight, but when they change, it redistributes. In front of me is a six foot three, two hundred twenty pound animal with teeth and claws sharper than hypodermic needles. He resembles a regular wolf with long snout, vertical ears, four legs, a wagging tail, and very visible ragged teeth. He's only a few feet away when he stops. You have to shoot him, you idiot! His head arches back and out comes a loud yowl. *Shoot him now!*

I aim as best as I can with a shaking hand as my finger curls around the trigger. He lowers his head a second later, studying at me. He bares his teeth again, saliva dripping, but doesn't move. If I didn't know any better, I'd swear he's looking at me, waiting for me to make the first move. Why isn't he attacking? Heck, why am I not shooting?

A gunshot not too far away draws our attention. It came from behind him so he turns. A golden opportunity. I lift him off the ground, my head throbbing with each pound of his weight, and fling him as far as I can in the opposite direction of the shot.

I run.

My legs pump so fast I'm not sure they belong to me. "Help! I'm here!" I fire the gun up in the air in case they can't hear me. He's been chasing me almost since the moment I took my first step. It might be my imagination, or the pounding in my ears, but I think I can hear his paws hitting the ground right beside me. Don't think about it, just run. "Help m—"

My left foot falls into a hole. This time I drop sideways, rolling down a tiny hill like a log. I lose the machete but keep a strong grip on the gun. That is until my head bangs into a tree. Ow.

The world spins even though I'm lying down. My head throbs even more than before. I manage to sit up, but then rest my head against the tree. This brings white spots. Okay, I think I have a concussion if I remember the symptoms correctly. The spots start to fade as soon as they start. Thank God I didn't pass out. A growl across from me quickly changes that opinion.

My hand moves for the gun beside me, but I'm not quick enough. I blink and his snout is inches from my face, teeth bared, his paws on either side of me, straddling me. He breathes in short bursts right beside my face, his hot breath smelling of rotten flesh. My eyes water and it takes all my willpower not to let them become full-fledged tears. He's going to eat me.

I try to pick him up, but the concussion must have impaired my psychokinesis. Go to Plan B. My hand begins inching toward the gun again. Werewolf Will's eyes move from my face, to the gun, then back to me. He responds with a low menacing growl, complete with more teeth. My hand shifts back to the ground, and the noise stops. I'm out of ideas. I can't think over my pounding heart. Seconds tick away like hours as neither of us budges. His green eyes study my face as if it was a piece of fine art. How can his eyes be so human when the rest ... There's no anger in those eyes. No malice. Just sadness. "Will?" I whisper. His lips move into a snarl as his snout moves closer. My eyes close and my breath literally stops. This is it. Please just let it be quick.

But instead of teeth on my face, a soft, wet something moves up my cheek. My eyes fly open. We're face to face until he moves to my other cheek, licking from jaw to eye. Oh. My. God. This is too frigging bizarre. He returns to my other cheek, caressing it with his tongue. I must taste good. Or this is a werewolf French kiss. As if that wasn't creepy enough, his snout tenderly muzzles where he just licked. This is not how I imagined our first kiss. "Um, Will?" I whisper.

He moves away so our eyes can meet. I can't read his face, but I'm not terrified. Weirded out but not scared. If he was in human form, I'd be flattered. I have the strongest urge to touch him. His fur's the color of his regular hair and probably just as soft. But there isn't time. As twigs and leaves crackle near us, the growling starts again. The scary teeth are back too. No more Mr. Nice Wolf. The mood is dead and so am I if I don't act.

I do it without even realizing it. Will glides away, hitting a tree ten feet away. His brown body jerks from the force of the impact as I grab the gun and aim. He's on his feet, fur standing on end and all those jagged chompers visible. Springing from his hind legs, he flies toward me. This time there is no hesitation. I close my eyes and put pressure on the trigger.

Someone beats me to the punch. A loud puff of air shoots beside me. My eyes instantly open and see something silver hit Will's body. The moment it hits, his body jerks sideways as he yelps. He lands in a heap, skidding inches from my feet, his tongue lolling out. He doesn't move again.

"Elephant tranquilizer," a girl says. I look up. Nancy holds a huge rifle, a satisfied smile on her red lips. She pulls the bolt back, aims, and shoots Will again. "Totally works on contact but doesn't last that long. We should be able to get him back to mobile command now. Were you bitten or scratched? Are you okay? That was, like, so intense." She holds out her free hand and helps me up.

"Um, I'm all right," I say, not taking my eyes off the sleeping werewolf.

"Good, cuz one werewolf is so more than enough, thank you. Sorry we didn't get here sooner, but he was going super fast, I couldn't keep up. Are you sure you're, like, okay? You look super pale."

Not in control of my body, which feels as if it's made of air, I walk over and kneel down beside the wolf. His eyes are still open, but they look like glass. The world turns even blacker for a moment, but I blink the feeling away. Before I can stop myself, I'm stroking the top of his head between the ears. God, he's so soft.

My head is weightless on my shoulders, it's floating away. "This is so surreal."

"Yeah, well," she says with a scoff, "welcome to the F.R.E.A.K.S."

The black of oblivion envelops me before I hit the ground.

ELEVEN

OKAY, SO I MADE A MISTAKE

SOMETHING COOL WIPES MY face. It feels nice as it crosses my forehead, down my right cheek, then the other. Just like—

"Will!"

My eyes fly open as I jerk up into the sitting position. What...

I'm in the back seat of a car wrapped in a blanket. Where are the woods? Where's Will? Carl stands by the open car door, white washcloth in his gloved hand, staring at me. He seems as confused as I am. Behind him, Bridge Stone is lit up like Las Vegas. Police cars, ambulances, and fire trucks line the streets with their flashing lights. People with varying wounds sit in cars and on sidewalks being attended to by the cavalry. And on the streets, something I never thought I'd see outside of a movie. Men in silver fire suits use flamethrowers on twitching body parts. When one body part is thoroughly doused, they move on to the next, a burst of orange flame shooting from the tip of the silver baton. Cool. I woke up in a *Rambo* movie.

"Are you okay?" Carl asks.

Arms, legs, eyes, check. "I think so. What happened?"

"You passed out. Do you feel sick, or are you seeing spots?"

"Not anymore," I say, feeling the bump on my head. I've grown an egg. "How long have I been out?"

"About half an hour. We would have sent you to command, but Doc said it was only a mild concussion. She said you passed out from shock and exhaustion."

"Wonderful." I notice my bites are re-bandaged but blood is already seeping to the surface. God, they throb.

"I had to clean and re-dress the bites. You were bleeding all over the place. I think you might need stitches, but you'll have to wait until morning. Their hands are full right now. You've had a tetanus booster, right?"

"Yeah, six months ago." Great, scars by my second day. "Was anyone killed?"

"Agent Konrad didn't make it."

"I know. I'm really sorry."

"He was only here for a few months, so I didn't really know him, but ... "

"He was still one of us," I finish. "The others?"

"The rest of the team's fine. Two civilians suffered severe blood loss. They didn't make it. Another had a heart attack, but he should be fine. A few more had broken bones or serious bites, and they just left for the hospital."

I look back at the wounded on the street. This must be what a war zone looks like. Fires, shattered windows, blood on the pavement. A living nightmare. An old woman holding a bloody rag to her cheek rests her head on her husband's bandaged shoulder. He strokes her head. "Who were the two?"

"I think I heard a middle-aged man and a teenage girl."

My body tenses. "A teenage girl? What did she look like?"

"I don't know. Blond, thin, had on a blue sweatshirt. Why?"

"Oh, no," I say under my breath. "I knew her, I *met* her. She told us about Graham and Carrie. She was so sweet."

"I'm sorry."

I thought I saved her. Why didn't she run after I stopped them?

"Are you okay?"

"It's just … so unfair," I say more to myself. "What did she do? She just wanted to see a movie!" I shout. "What kind of sick freak would put all these people's lives in danger? I just—"

"Calm down."

"She was seventeen! Seventeen! She'll never get to go to prom or college and why? It's not fair!"

"No, it's not, but you need to calm down. There is nothing more that you can do."

I turn away, my breathing jagged. I *really* don't like being talked down to. This is not okay. A young girl is dead, it is *not okay*. Something needs to be done. "Can you leave me alone for a little while? I'm just—I'm not—"

"No problem. I'll be over there if you need me." He half smiles and walks toward the medics.

Pretend distress melts to righteous anger. She's not getting away with this. No way. You don't kill teenagers and get off scot free. Not if I can do anything about it. Okay, Columbo, how do we find the witch? Call her? Worth a try. I unclip my cell, which miraculously survived my tumble, and dial 411 to get Carrie's number. Luckily she's listed, and I press the button to be connected. The tension in my body grows with each unanswered ring. After the fourth, the machine picks up. *"Hi, this is Carrie and I'm not here, as you know.*

185

Leave a message or call my cell at 555-3674." I hang up and dial the new number. She picks up after the second ring.

"Hello?" she guffaws into my ear. There is a lot of background noise: laughing, rock music, and loud talking. Club or bar.

"Hi, Carrie, it's—" I mumble. "Where are you?"

"Guys, it's Kate," she says. "Down at McGinley's. Hey, do you know what's up in town? We heard a trillion fire trucks go by."

"No idea. Gotta go." I hang up. She's at a bar, probably toasting her latest victory. Bitch. No amount of hair flipping or smiling is going to save her tonight.

God is smiling down at me on my quest. The keys dangle from the ignition, just waiting for me to turn them. I jump out of the back, make sure nobody is watching, climb into the front, and start the car. Starting slow so as not to draw attention, I roll down the street. I make it a few feet before, in the mirror, I see Carl running after me, mouth moving and arms flapping. He disappears quickly enough as I race down the road, maneuvering around the roadblock the police have set up. McGinley's bar is only a couple miles outside of town right off the interstate. We've passed it a few times.

I don't have a plan. I realize I'm not really thinking. This is pure rage and instinct. Twice in one night I've felt this and been in a justice-driven zone. I almost wish I had my machete.

I pull into the bar's full parking lot a few minutes later. The place practically pulsates with the music and laughter. Those patrons are having a good time while people lie bleeding on a sidewalk. So wrong. A man and woman walk out of the bar, laughing and holding hands. Another man notices me staring and makes a kissy face at me as he passes. I push him with my mind hard enough that he falls onto the pavement. As I get out of the car, I turn back to the confused couple and smirk. Guess I don't need that machete.

The place is jumping for a Thursday night. Not a stool is empty, not a surface is devoid of a glass or bottle. A thick gray smoke fills the air like a putrid cloud. "Tainted Love" plays on the jukebox, almost drowned out by laughter. Nearby two men are playing pool while two women watch, one of them with blond hair I intend to rip out in huge clumps. With my jaw set and hands clenched, I worm my way through the inebriated patrons. Each person I pass stares then steps away as if touching me would infect them. Carrie sips her beer but sets it on the pool table when she sees me. Her sweetest smile emerges. I stop at the end of the pool table, my face hard as diamonds.

"Hello, Agent ... "

"Alexander."

"Right, yeah."

"God, what happened to her?" one of the men asks the other.

"No offense, but you look like shit," Carrie giggles. Her perky friend in a tube top joins in.

I crinkle my nose, and the beer bottle in front of her explodes, shards flying into the foursome like fairy dust. "What the fuck?" the other man shouts, jumping back.

Moving nearly as fast as Oliver can, I'm in front of a wide-eyed Carrie, backing her into the wall. She falls into the pool cues, the wooden sticks clattering against each other. Her friends just stare. Smart people. With my thumb and pointer finger holding her chin, I move her eyes to mine. She refuses to meet them. "Look at me." Her scared eyes look into mine. I let her face go. "Three people are dead. They are dead and you are here getting drunk."

"I don't—"

187

I squeeze her throat without moving my hands and her words stop. "You don't get to speak, you get to listen." I release her throat. Her hands pat her neck checking for hands. "You," I say in a low voice, "are a monster. A teenage girl had her throat ripped out by one of your buddies tonight, and you don't seem to care. You are a selfish bitch with a black hole where your soul should be. Was it worth it? Do you feel better now for being rightfully dumped for an older woman? How many bodies will that take? Ten? Twenty?" Carrie looks at me, her whole body trembling. "You may speak now."

"I don't know what you're talking about," she almost whimpers.

"Liar!" The pool table behind me rumbles as if caught in an earthquake. The crowd grows quiet. "Valerie. Davis. He dumped you for a middle-aged bank teller, and you couldn't take it. You lost it then like you lost it *tonight!*"

"You're nuts! Leave me alone!"

She tries to move past me but instead slams against the cues then remains held by my invisible force. Her eyes double in size as she struggles against my kinetic blanket. The whole bar is quiet, but nobody moves toward us. I guess chivalry really is dead. I lean into her ear. "I know what you are. I know what you can do. And I am going to make sure your friends drag you into their graves right with them. You can count on it."

"Fuck you, you freak!"

The energy pours from me as I look into her eyes, flowing into the anatomy of her brain. She starts whimpering. I'm doing this, I'm killing her, but I don't care. I really don't. A drop of blood rolls out of her nostril, then another. Tears stream out of her increasingly bloodshot eyes. Not so pretty now. She clutches her temples, almost clawing them, but still I feel no remorse. She's a child killer and deserves no sympathy. High squeals escape her mouth.

"Someone do something!" someone shouts.

"What's happening to her?"

"Someone call an ambulance!

Carrie falls to her knees still clawing and screaming. "Help me!"

Arms wrap around my torso and arms, hands meeting at my stomach. I don't take my eyes off Carrie. "Alexander!" I'm spun toward the slack-jawed patrons. Carrie stops screaming as soon as she's out of my view. "We're leaving," Carl whispers in my ear. The barflies part as if Moses was before them. Still holding me, Carl pushes me through the bar past the staring people.

"But Carrie—"

"Shut up."

He releases my right side to open the door and literally pushes me outside. "Are you out of your goddamned mind?" he shouts when the door shuts. "What the hell were you thinking?"

"She doesn't even care! She's in there drinking and playing pool an hour after she killed three people!"

"Alexander, you could have killed her!"

"So what? Isn't that what I was hired to do? Kill monsters so they don't kill again? If anything deserves it, it's that *thing* inside!"

"No, she doesn't!"

"Then who the hell does?"

"Right now … *you.*"

I scoff. "Don't you dare compare me to her. She is just going to keep killing whoever she likes!"

"No, she won't, Alexander. That's the point. She isn't the necromancer."

My stomach drops to my feet. "What?"

"She isn't our perp."

"No, she—" I shake my head, "she has to be. It all fits."

He steps toward me. "Wolfe was following her. He was in the bar watching her when he got the call about the cemetery. It cannot be her."

Oh God. No. *No.* The world topples in on itself, folding like origami. Oh God. Oh God. I double over and what little is left in my stomach comes out onto the asphalt. Carl kneels beside me. "Christ, are you okay?"

I hold out my arm to stop him from getting closer. If he touches me, I'll totally lose it. I wipe the spit off my chin. "Are you sure about—"

"Yeah."

"Oh God," I whimper. "I was gonna kill her. If you hadn't come in ... Oh God." I shake my head. I can't deal with this. Not now. Push it away. Bad thoughts, go away.

"Alexander?"

"Are you going to arrest me now?"

"What?"

"I assaulted a civilian."

He doesn't say anything for a few seconds then sighs. "Look, you've had a really crazy couple of days, you know, with ... everything. You lost it, it happens to all of us. Just don't do it again. Ever."

"I won't. Never again. Never."

"Then it'll be our secret."

"Thank you."

"You're welcome. Now get up. I better take you back to the hotel before the police show up."

"What about Carrie? I may have really hurt her."

"If it's bad, they'll take her to the hospital. You didn't touch her, did you?"

"Only once, but not when … " I can't finish.

"Good. I'll check on her tomorrow."

"Thank you." I manage to stand. "What a night."

"Yeah."

"Is it always this bad?"

"No. Most of the time it's a hell of a lot worse."

———

Taking a shower was not one of my best ideas, and after what happened tonight, that is saying something. Note to people with multiple zombie bites: hot water plus open wounds equals intense pain. Each of my four bites feels like a dozen bees are stinging them at once. The one on my arm and shoulder still bleed, but the others simply throb. Still, the feeling of all that sticky embalming fluid and blood sloshing off my body is worth it. I've only been in here for five minutes, four of those getting said goo out of my hair. I can spend maybe thirty more seconds in here before screaming in pain. The last of the conditioner is out and so am I.

The hotel room was empty when Carl dropped me off. We didn't talk the whole way here. I was thankful for that. He didn't come in but waited until I was at the door before he took off to clean up my mess. What a guy.

I made it all the way to the bathroom before I literally peeled off my clothes. It will take about ten dry cleanings just to get the smell out. Not that I'll bother. They're ripped up to heck. Too bad, those pants were so slimming.

I hate hotel towels. Not only are they about as soft as broom bristles, but they barely fit around my whole body. I tie one around my chest and hope it holds. The first-aid kit Carl gave me sits on my roll-out bed. It comes back into the bathroom with me. I clean and bandage the bites. The one on my left forearm is the worst: a welt of red pulp the size of a quarter. My very first scar. I cover it with Neosporin and an oversized Band-Aid. Out of sight, out of mind. For the one on my shoulder, I need the mirror. Eww. Bad idea. Bruises dot my arms, back, upper chest, and shoulders. Don't think about it, just bandage.

Everything in me aches to the bone. There isn't an inch of me that doesn't feel like road kill. I've probably done enough physical activity to equal a marathon. My head is killing me too with an alteration of throbbing and stabbing pain. The two headaches I had tonight decided to join forces in an effort to kill me. Not like I don't deserve it.

After I'm done patching myself up with a fair amount of whimpering, I flop down on my lumpy fold-out bed—avoiding the bitten areas—and stare at the slightly water-damaged ceiling. I don't want to think, but I can't bear the noise from turning on the television. Maybe I'm bleeding internally and will be dead by morning. Wouldn't that be nice.

I close my eyes. Carrie's contorted face greets me. Then Agent Konrad's mangled body. Will stalking toward me, teeth everywhere. My eyes fly open. Okay, I will never close them again. Ever. I curl into a ball with my knees up to my chin. I can't do this. Who the heck was I kidding? I'm no monster hunter. I want to go home. I want my Nana. I want to crawl into my purple bed in my peach room with my Brad Pitt poster staring down at me. I want all of this to be nothing but a bad memory. If wishes were horses...

Well, maybe I can ride a wish horse right out of here. I'm a secret. The whole organization is a secret. It's not as if they'll drag me into court for breach of contract. They won't do anything. Heck, let them try, I don't care.

Not even bothering to get dressed, I go around the room and bathroom picking up my few belongings and tossing them into my suitcase. If I forgot something, I'll buy a new one. My clothes from the night go into the trash. I would throw it all out, every reminder of the last few months, but I have to wear something. I'm pulling out some clothes, not caring if they match, when someone knocks on the door. Crap, so much for my quick getaway. Should I get it? They might get suspicious if I don't. I toss the covers over my suitcase and peak out the hole.

Oh, crud. I open the door a crack.

Oliver leans in the door frame with his stupid smirk present. I have to stop myself from smacking it off his face. "What?"

"I heard someone knocking about in here. Thought it might be you. Do you greet everyone in a towel?"

"Go away." I shut the door but feel it open again and sure enough, Oliver steps in. "Get out of my room!"

"I thought you would be curious to know about Will. I just left him."

Will. His name makes my stomach tense up. Not good or painful, just weird. "Is he okay?"

"He is sleeping soundly at mobile command. I heard you faced him without losing a limb." He sits on my bed then lounges, supporting his head on his fist. "It would seem that beauty has once again tamed the beast. What am I lying on?" Oliver sits up and pulls back the covers. Crud. He glances down at the suitcase then back up at me. "Planning on stealing away into the night?"

"No."

"Liar. Turning red is a dead giveaway."

I have no energy to fight with him. "Will you just please leave me alone? *Please?*"

He stands. "Where do you plan on going? Back to elementary school?"

"None of your damn business, okay?" I scoff. "I don't even know why you care. Look, I am not going to sleep with you. Never. *Ever.* You repulse me! So just get the hell out of my room!"

He studies my face. "There is something wrong."

"Get out."

"I am not leaving you alone in this state."

"Get out!"

"My dear, you have been through more than your fair share tonight," he says in the calming voice my Nana uses. "You are highly emotional, and now is not the best time to make rash decisions."

"Stop patronizing me and get out, or I swear to God,"—I enjoy seeing Oliver wince at my choice of words—"I'll send you right through that door."

"I am not leaving."

"Get out!"

"No."

I push with my curse, and he stumbles back. "Don't think I won't do it. Get out."

"I will not."

My jaw tightens, and I get ready to push his butt through the closed door when he disappears. Just disappears. Arms wrap around me for the second time tonight, but these squeeze all the air out of me. His body envelops me. I panic. I kick his shins as hard as I can, but he squeezes harder. The towel loosens but doesn't fall. My arms, pinned by his, keep it up. "You must calm down," he whispers into my ear. I stop kicking and bucking. "You are upset, you are exhausted, and now is not the time for mindless action you will regret later. Now, I will let you go, but remember I can crush you with little effort and will, if I must." He releases me. I clutch at the towels as I jump away, securing them as best I can. For once, there isn't a hint of a smirk, just a total lack of emotion. "Now tell me why you wish to leave."

"I just do, and I can if I want to." Jeez, I sound like a fourth grader.

"Yes, you can. Quitting is always an option. But I have a feeling this is not something you would do in a right mind. You do not strike me as someone who gives up so easily."

"And you've known me how long? Like, forty-eight hours?"

"You were the one who insisted on returning to town despite my protests."

"Well, look how that turned out. Two people died."

"And a dozen more did not because of you. Remember them. Mourn the dead but, more important, celebrate the living." He steps toward me. "They live. As do you." Another step. "You were spectacular tonight. Cool, calm … ," he takes another step, "and going into that hardware store for weapons was inspired. Not to mention the way you dealt with Will … "

"Nancy was the one who shot him."

"You faced a werewolf and both of you remained intact. Very few can claim that. For your first time in the field, you showed immense level-headedness and bravery."

"Don't say that! You don't—" I stop myself. "Will you please just leave? Please? Nothing you can say will change my mind, so just *leave me alone!*" I scream. Stupid tears fall, but I swipe them away so he won't see them.

"Has something occurred?" he asks like a concerned older brother in the movies. "Did Will do something?"

"What? No! What would he ... never mind." I don't think I want to know.

"But something happened." He takes another step. "I am not leaving until you tell me what is troubling you."

"I—I can't," I say, voice trembling.

He takes another step. "There is nothing you can say that will lower my high regard for you."

"Oh yeah? And if I told you I almost killed an innocent woman tonight, you wouldn't lower your regard? That I squeezed blood vessels in her brain and made her blind with pain, *that* wouldn't make me less of a person? Huh?" I'm screaming now. "Then that makes you pretty messed up, because if I were you, I'd spit on the freak in front of me! I'd curse her and despise her and pray that the ground would swallow her whole! So just leave before I hurt you too! *Just leave!*"

A sharp pain rockets through my head like a white-hot poker, and my legs collapse out from under me. But I don't hit the floor. I fall into Oliver's chest, and his arms encircle me again. He lowers us both to the floor so I'm sitting in his lap. He smells terrible but I don't care, not even when he pulls me tight to his chest, holding me, rocking me. I couldn't push him away if I wanted to. Something broke. I'm broken. And he has me. My ears pound in time with the pain. "Shush now," he whispers, smoothing my wet hair. "Shush, shush, shush. Please do not cry. I cannot bear to see you cry. Shush."

"My head hurts," I weep into his shoulder. "It really hurts."

"That will pass," he whispers. "It will all pass. Do not cry, my darling."

"I can't do this, I just can't. I can't. Oh God—" His body jerks— "please help me. Please. I didn't mean to, I really didn't. Please forgive me."

"Shush my dear, your—deity—knows. He does not blame you."

"I was so scared," I bawl. "I didn't know what to do. She died. I couldn't save her. It wasn't enough. It's never enough. I hate this. I hate it."

"I know. I know, my darling. It will be all right." He kisses the top of my head. "You are safe now. I will not allow anyone or anything to harm you. I have you. You are safe." He kisses my temple. "You are safe."

I wrap my arms around his neck, embracing him as hard as he is me. My fingers run into his thick hair that is so soft it's like feathers. He hugs me tighter, stroking my hair and rocking me as my head rests on his shoulder. He's warmer than I imagined. Feels almost human. And wonderful. I haven't been touched in months, let alone held. I've missed it. We could stay like this forever and I wouldn't mind. I clutch him tighter, wanting to be absorbed by him. I should be tense, hours ago I would have clawed his eyes out for touching me like this, but with each of my sobs and dulcet whispered promise of his, it flows out of me. This is how I fall asleep some time later. In the arms of a vampire.

I can't remember ever feeling so safe.

TWELVE

OCCAM'S RAZOR

I WAKE NAKED IN my bed with what feels like a killer hangover, though I've only had that wonderful experience once before. This is so unfair, I didn't touch a drop. All the pain, none of the fun. Headache, body aches, slight nausea—all present and accounted for. I groan and pull the covers over my head.

Wait, I don't remember getting into bed. Last thing I remember is … I groan again. I must have fallen asleep. God, how embarrassing. He must have picked me up and put me in bed like a small child. Normally I'd be panicking having fallen asleep in the arms of an amorous man and waking up naked, but for some reason I don't. Heck, he didn't even try to cop a feel last night. Well, why not? In my state last night I probably would have let him … okay, why am I upset? Get a grip, Bea.

The towel lies underneath me, which means he didn't see anything. I wrap it around me before the covers come off. Nancy and Irie are asleep in their beds. Wonder what time everyone got in.

Tiptoeing to my suitcase, I grab my neatly folded clothes on top—I don't remember doing that—and go to the bathroom. Big shock, I look like heck. Frizzy hair, bruises all over, dark circles under my eyes. I hope no one mistakes me for a zombie. No wonder Oliver was a perfect gentleman! After re-bandaging my seeping wounds, I toss on the clothes, put my hair in a ponytail, and leave, grabbing my purse on the way out.

I hobble like an old woman complete with creaking joints to the diner, inwardly moaning with each movement. The sleep worsened the soreness so now even my eyelids ache. Okay, the second I get back to Kansas I'm starting a new exercise regimen. I will run three miles, use weights, and practice kung fu every day, no excuses. Of course, if there is a Gary Cooper or Clark Gable marathon on or ... yeah, it's never going to happen.

The diner parking lot is filled with semis and, no surprise, a dozen truck drivers sit inside guzzling coffee and downing bacon strips. After a few minutes, I'm in a booth ordering a huge breakfast and a chocolate milkshake. Nausea be darned, I deserve a treat. A newspaper rests on the other side of the booth, so I grab it. Sure enough last night's fiasco made the headline, but not the one I would have thought. "Satanic Cult Wanted in Three States Attacks Locals." Okay ...

> Last night, twenty members of "Lucifer's Hand," a satanic cult based out of Albuquerque, New Mexico, entered the town of Bridge Stone, killing two and injuring over a dozen more. Dressed in rags and wearing Halloween masks, the members bit their victims in a ritualized attack. "We believe they bite their victims to use the flesh in their rituals," Special Agent Paul Chandler of the FBI stated. The FBI were called in

earlier this week to investigate the deaths of Valerie Wayland, 37, and Davis Wynn, 43, both killed in a similar fashion to the night's attack. According to a source inside the FBI, Lucifer's Hand has been linked to similar attacks in Kansas and Oklahoma. Their leader, the Rev. Damien Nightshade, a.k.a. James Dike, was elevated to the FBI's Ten Most Wanted list last night. "He is a top priority," Special Agent Chandler said. "We do not think he is in the area, but his followers may still be."

The article goes on to give a number to call if they spot a smelly, ratty-clothed person. Then there are a few eyewitness accounts about how scared they were and how the authorities apprehended several members. No mention of machetes, flamethrowers, or people still moving when they have no limbs. I don't know how, but we may have gotten away with it.

My purse begins to vibrate before I finish the article. "Hello?"

"Is this Beatrice?" Andrew asks.

"Yes, Andrew."

"I thought I heard you leave. I'm sorry to trouble you, but the police keep calling Carl's cellular phone asking to speak to a member of the FBI. He's honestly in no shape to help. I've been going up and down Carl's call list. You're the first one who answered."

"Everyone else probably got in late."

"Yes, I know, but I'm afraid they may send someone to the hotel. Everyone really needs their sleep if Carl is any example."

"I so don't think I'm the right person to go and lie to the police. I only just found out what the cover story is."

"You'll do fine. Keys for the SUV are on the undercarriage." He hangs up. Perfect. The world's worst liar now has to sell a doozy to trained professionals. My food arrives and I inhale it while reading the article again. Twice. Okay, Lucifer's Hand, flesh for rituals, dress up to scare people, wanted in three states. If they don't ask specifics, I'll be fine. Huh. Nice to see I still have some optimism left.

———

The once-quiet sheriff's station is now *the* place to be in Bridge Stone. People sit and stand three deep in the reception area, most bandaged from last night's "satanic cult attack." None of the victims looks at me as I make my way through them. They don't recognize me. One would think machete girl would leave an impression. The phones ring faster than the already overwhelmed deputies can handle. "No comment," they all say. About half a dozen news vans and pushy reporters lie in wait outside, shouting at anyone coming in or out. I just keep my head down and don't say a word.

Just as I am buzzed back by the frazzled receptionist, Sheriff Graham leaves his office as if he was watching for me. "About fucking time. Get in here!" Assuming he means me, I follow him in. "Shut the door," he says when I enter. "Where's the other one? The tall one with you yesterday."

"He's busy. You're stuck with me."

"It's been nuts around here and you people haven't been answering your fucking phones and—"

"I'm sorry. I'm here now, okay? What do you need?"

"You can start by telling me what the hell is going on in my town and why the hell you fuckers didn't warn us!"

I worked out this one on the drive over. "We weren't sure the deaths were related, so we didn't want to cause a panic. In hindsight we should have shared our suspicions, and I do apologize, but right now we need to concentrate on finding the rest of the members that may still be around."

"You people." He shakes his head. "There is no way in hell I am taking the blame for this."

"We will issue a statement saying it's all our fault, okay?"

This must be what he wanted to hear because his complexion reduces from purple to red. "Fine. Don't you have any leads, anything you think us country folk are worthy of knowing this time?"

"Carrie Ellison is no longer a suspect, but we do believe that someone in town is responsible for, um, inviting these people here and having them kill Wayland and Wynn."

"Invited them?"

"Yes. We've obtained evidence that someone from town asked them to come here. That's how they operate."

"Who invited them?"

"We just ruled out Ellison last night, so we haven't had time to pursue any new leads. If we do apprehend anyone, we'll be sure to inform you."

"Are these freaks coming back?"

"Honestly, we have no idea."

"The ones you arrested, are they saying anything?"

They think we *kept* them? "Um, not really. *Omertà* and all that." Graham gives me a blank look. Okay, not a fan of *The Godfather*. "You know, code of silence. We'll keep trying."

"When do we get a try?"

"Ah, never. I'm sorry but this is our investigation and we've brought in trained interrogators. If they can't break them, then nobody will." Darn, that was good. Thank you, TV.

"Now look, missy—"

"That is Special Agent Beatrice Alexander, not 'missy.' I get that you're upset, and I am truly sorry this happened, but this is an FBI matter. You should be grateful we were here and did what we did; otherwise, this place would be another ghost town. You are in over your head, so back off and let us do our thing. Do you understand me?"

He lowers his eyes. "Fucking feebs." He walks out. What a child. He had the same look my students did when I wouldn't let them go out to recess. Men. They never grow up.

———

Back to square one. Our only suspect has an alibi. More bodies but no evidence. I go up to the whiteboard in the conference room in mobile command and write down the original victim's names, Davis and Valerie, then their significant others: Carrie and Walter. Both had motives, but both had alibis for last night and the nights of the murders. Maybe Valerie and Davis had another connection like drugs, or they witnessed something illegal and the perp needed to silence them. Okay, I'm reaching, and I know it. I write the theories down anyway. Perhaps with more investigation we'll find something.

Now for last night's attack. What does it tell me? This person is mega super-duper powerful. If I'm any indication, that means he or she had serious problems controlling their gift, unless they had formal training. And they must have had training because they raised specific corpses without a ritual, and if my own experience tells me anything, it is hard to focus that kind of power. I write "trained" on the board. Okay, back to last night. Well, we were the targets, that's obvious. But how did he or she know where we were going to be? Duh, the necromancer was following us, brainiac. They knew we were getting close to finding them, so they freaked and raised the whole cemetery. So maybe they're still following us. I write "following us" on the board.

That's it. That's all I got. So yeah, back to square one. But I can't shake the feeling I'm missing something I learned last night. It's in the back of my mind, I know it's there, but it just won't come forward. I hate when that happens. It'll probably pop up when I don't need it anymore.

Time to check on Dr. Neill. Poor thing's been cooped up with a smelly zombie all day. It seems we did capture a "cult member," and she's doing all sorts of invasive tests on it.

The relatively fresh but still rank zombie lies tied to the examination table by the torso, as it has no arms or legs courtesy of my machete. The top of its head lies on the table next to it. Once again, I walk in right as Dr. Neill carries a brain across the room. Oy.

"Hello," she says putting the brain in a bag with "Biohazard" written all over it.

"Having fun?" I ask with a grimace.

"This is absolutely fascinating," she says walking back over to stumpy. "Its brain is removed and yet it knows we're here and responds." She holds out her hand and the zombie lunges at it teeth first. "I would bet that the brain, though detached, still shows electrical activity. It is almost as if each cell in this entity's body has its own mind and energy from an outside force, yet they're dead. All the cells are dead."

"Do you think when this outside force no longer feeds it energy, the zombie will die?"

"With no energy, nothing runs. As best I can tell, this corpse is still drawing its energy from your necromancer, though only a tiny sum. And it will continue to carry out its main objective until it or the necromancer is destroyed."

"So it just kills. I mean, is that all they can do, kill?"

"They do what they're ordered to. If I had to guess, the energy given is infused with a message of some kind, and they have to do what they're told."

"So, basically they just act as puppets and this remote person can do anything it wants with the bodies?"

"Horrible, isn't it?"

The corpse turns his head and looks at me through cloudy pupils. "Yeah, um … I need to get some air. Call if you need me."

The smell follows me into the hallway even after I shut the door. Just as I reach the front door to get some air, it opens. My heart stops dead in my chest. Will stands in the doorway, the human Will. Looking at him you'd never guess that less than twelve hours ago he was a furry killing machine. A furry killing machine that licked me. His body tenses and his whole face turns deep red when he sees me. I'm hit by a wave of nervous energy that doesn't originate from me. Oh crap, he remembers everything.

"Um, hi," he mumbles as he looks to the side.

"Jesus Christ, Will, move it," Irie says, pushing him to the side. How is it her brown skin glows after last night and mine is the color of that dead half-man in medical? So not fair. "Hey Bea, great job last night," she says on her way to the lab.

"Thanks."

Will steps out of the doorway to let in Carl, Agent Chandler, and Nancy. Carl half smiles as he passes. Please let him have kept his trap shut better than I did. Agent Chandler completely ignores me as he heads toward the conference room.

"That was pretty intense last night, huh?" Nancy says in her usual enthusiastic manner. "First zombies then a freaking were-wolf! Will, she was, like, seconds away from blowing your brains out! It was so—"

"*Nancy,*" Will growls, "go."

"He's always grumpy right after a change. You'll get used to it." She grins at us both on her way to the lab. A few incredibly long seconds of uncomfortable silence begin when the door closes. He glances everywhere but at me, and I do the same.

"I—" we both say at the same time. "Sorr—" We both say again. I laugh first but he joins in, running his hand through his hair.

"God, this is awkward," he says, still laughing.

"I know."

"I just wanted to say I'm so sorry for … um, *everything.* I didn't mean to—I mean, when I'm in that condition, I have very little control of myself."

"I know. It's okay. It was stupid of me to go into the woods in the first place. I'm just glad we both made it out in one piece." And I didn't have to shoot you.

"Me too. And it will never happen again. *Ever.*"

"What? You turning into a wolf and chasing me?"

"No. Well, yes, that won't happen again either. Just, um, never mind." He holds out his hand. "Friends?"

I shake it. "Friends."

Then his thumb caresses the top of my hand, and I almost melt. A hot, yummy feeling cascades down my body like warm rain, and I meet his eyes. Oh boy, bad idea. Even after last night, it takes all my willpower not to kiss him until our lips bleed. I wonder what he tastes like. I wonder if he's as gorgeous out of that suit as he is in it. I—okay, stop there, Bea. What the heck is wrong with me? I quickly pull my hand out of his.

He looks down at the carpet at the same time I do. "Uh, maybe we should go into the conference room and figure out where the case will go from here."

"Yeah. Yes. Good idea. Be right in."

I move right to let him pass, but he steps the same way. The same thing happens when we step left. We chuckle but don't look up from the floor. I don't move as he passes me. He enters the conference room and the second the door closes, I let out a big sigh and run my hands over my face. Get a grip, Bea; you're acting like a teenager with a crush. Hormones do not rule your life anymore. And the totally strange thing is he seemed more upset by the licking part than the almost-killing-me part. A werewolf with intimacy issues. I sure can pick 'em.

The men are examining the whiteboard when I walk in. "What is this?" Agent Chandler asks.

"I was just brainstorming."

"Do you think there's a connection we missed?" Will asks.

"I doubt it, but it can't hurt to write it out. We really don't have anything else to go on that I can think of."

"What about the husband?" Will asks.

"As far as we know, he's still in California," Agent Chandler says. "Last night I expanded on Irie's work. We confirmed that he checked in at the airport on the way to California but his return ticket isn't for a few days. We also confirmed there are no other reservations under his name at any other airline."

"What about credit card activity?" Will asks.

"Nothing since yesterday at the gas station in Sacramento."

"Did you check bank statements?" I ask. "He could have paid cash so there wouldn't be a trail."

"Yes. He withdrew five hundred dollars three days ago," Agent Chandler says.

"Chandler," Will says, "get on the horn and have the Bureau send someone to wherever Wayland is staying and see if he's still there."

"Okay."

"Alexander, come with me."

I follow Will out and down toward the lab. Irie and Nancy look up from their stations as we enter. "What's up?" Irie asks.

"Finish what you're doing and meet us outside." He shuts the door.

"What are we doing?" I ask as we walk out the front door and down the stairs.

"Something we should have done yesterday." He stops at the SUV. "We wasted all day running down the wrong suspect."

"She was a *good* suspect."

"She had an alibi, and we ignored it."

"It happens, right? We did find out about the affair, that's something. But what if Wayland actually is in California? What do we do? Start looking at paranormal mob connections?"

"I was a policeman for close to twenty years. Nine times out of ten, someone close to the victim is responsible. Occam's Razor: the simplest explanation is usually the right one." Must be the team motto.

Nancy and Irie come out of the trailer, speaking softly to each other. Nancy giggles. "What, Will?" Irie says when she reaches us. "You need three babes to protect you now?"

"Maybe," he says completely serious. "Get in the car."

Irie and Nancy exchange glances. Nancy rolls her eyes, but they do get in the car. I climb into the back with Nancy. "So where are we going that you think we need so much firepower?" Irie asks.

"Wayland's house. Screw the search warrant. If Walter Wayland is there, I don't want to take any chances after last night."

"What? You think he keeps corpses around the house as some sort of security system?" Irie asks.

"Better safe than sorry," Will says.

She shrugs. "Whatever. I'm just glad I'm not analyzing blood. Kicking ass is a hell of a lot more fun."

Says you. Give me the microscope over punching today. "Totally," Nancy chimes in. She faces me. "So, were you, like, terrified last night?"

"Don't ask stupid questions," Irie says.

"What? It was her first fight. I want to know. You should just be happy it wasn't a family of ogres. They're the worst. Like, mega big and fast. About a year ago we found some, and they broke, like, every bone in Will's body, right, Will?"

Will's hands tighten around the wheel.

"It took him, like, three *days* to heal, and he couldn't move or change or anything."

"Nancy!" Irie barks.

"What? I'm just saying she should be glad her first fight wasn't with ogres! God, why are you being so sensitive? Anyways, ogres are the worst, but werewolves are almost as bad. You have no idea how lucky you are Will didn't eat you. He—"

"Nancy! Shut the hell up!" Irie shouts.

"She needs to know these things!"

"Well, tell her later because we don't want to hear it."

Nancy crosses her arms and thumps back in her seat. So this is what family road trips are like. I'm glad Nana was too lazy to ever take us on one. No one utters another word until we pull up to the Wayland's two-story red brick house. My eyes take in a few red-cheeked, smiling garden gnomes positioned around the front lawn. These things creep me out with their staring eyes and rosy cheeks. I used to imagine they'd come alive at night and attack me with their tiny tools. Heck, with everything I've seen lately, it wouldn't surprise me.

"Should we do this without a warrant?" I ask on the way to the door.

Will hands Nancy his gun, which she clutches to her chest. Giving a teenager a gun, good idea. "Warrant? We don't need no steenking warrant," Nancy quotes before disappearing. People come and go so quickly around here. A second later, the lock clicks and the front door opens. "Enter all who dare."

Will grabs his gun out of her hands. "Be serious, please. This could be dangerous."

Her smile vanishes. "Sorry. I will be." We all walk in, and I shut the door.

Nice house. Homey. Old photographs of Waylands past hang on the walls and sit on various end tables. The entire floor and stairs are covered with beige carpet that matches the walls. Huge blue winter coats with multi-colored scarves hang on wooden pegs. A grandfather clock ticks away.

"What are we looking for?" Irie asks.

"Anything you think is important," Will says. "Proof he knew his wife was cheating, books on necromancy, evidence he's been here in the last week and a half. You two take the upstairs and we'll take this level and the basement."

"Got it, boss," Nancy says. "Scream if you need anything." The women disappear up the stairs, whispering to each other.

"I'll take the kitchen," I say on my way there.

It's small and stale like the rest of the house, but the window overlooking the backyard makes the room feel bigger. Dead plants with dropping vines line the shelf of the window. Valerie's, no doubt. They died right along with her. I bet she liked this spot. I can imagine her standing here doing dishes and watching her daughter swing on the now rusted swing set. Such a shame. I shake my head out of the clouds and start searching. No food in the fridge, only a few frozen casseroles in the freezer. Nice neighbors. I check the rest of the kitchen. Besides a few canned goods, there's nothing else. No trash in the trash can, either. If Wayland was here, there was no eating going on.

I join Will in the living room where he's examining the books above the gray stone fireplace. The living room is furnished in leathers and plaids, offset by sienna-painted walls. "Judging from the kitchen, he hasn't been here in a while."

"He could be staying in a hotel or in his car. I haven't found out anything either except that someone loves horror books and movies." He holds up books by Anne Rice and Dean Koontz.

"Lots of people do," I say.

"Still, I don't think he's been here. I don't feel him."

"You don't what?"

"If he had been here in the past few days, I'd feel him. My skin would be crawling more. It's a defense mechanism in ... people with my condition. So we can prepare for a fight. With the combined psychic power of you, Irie, and the necromancer, it would be unbearable."

"I didn't know you could do that."

"It doesn't always work. The person has to be very powerful."

"Did you get a twinge yesterday, with Carrie?"

"No, but I didn't know our necro was as powerful as he is. If I did, I would have ruled her out a lot sooner. That was my fault."

"So, she didn't make your skin crawl, but I do?"

His mouth opens a little. "I didn't mean it like that. You're just powerful, and I can feel it."

"But I make your skin hurt?"

"It's not that bad."

"Being around me hurts you?" I stare, dumbfounded. He opens his mouth a few times, but nothing comes out. "Whatever. I'm gonna check the basement." Shaking my head, I step out toward the hallway.

I can't believe this. I don't even touch the guy and I hurt him. Just perfect. I literally make his skin crawl. This is my cosmic punishment for last night with Carrie. I flip on the light switch next to the door and open it. Found the basement on the first try. I walk down the creaky wood steps. I finally meet a gorgeous, relatively stable guy who might actually like me back and my mere presence gives him a rash. Jeez, what would happen if we actually touched? Would he break out in hives? Doomed before we even start. Probably for the best; office relationships are a bad idea. What the hell is that smell? It's like a pine tree crawled in and died in here.

The basement is typical: dark, musty, with tons of junk making it hard to move around. The water heater rumbles in the corner making the bike leaning against it rattle. There are mainly boxes, old furniture, a workbench with tools, and a multi-colored patch-work quilt hanging on the wall. It doesn't fit down here. April's mom was always making quilts when I went to her house. She'd be impressed by this one: tiny strips of fabric in a spiral pattern, though it's covered in dust and dirt. Yuck. Okay, stop commenting on the décor and look for clues, Bea. I go through the box closest to me but find only winter clothes.

"Find anything?" Will asks from the top of the stairs. "Do you smell that?"

"Like Pine-Sol?"

"Yeah. Look up."

Sherlock Holmes, I am not. About a dozen or more pine tree air-fresheners dangle from the ceiling like a miniature forest. "Now why would he … oh, I'm an idiot."

His nose twitches. "It's faint but I smell a corpse." He walks down the stairs nose first. "It gets stronger down here."

I eye all the boxes, making sure none are moving. "Wouldn't it have attacked me by now?"

"Not unless that was what it was ordered to do. Get Irie and Nancy down here."

"No problem," I say running for the stairs before he even finishes the sentence. Trapped in a basement with a zombie? Not this girl. "Nancy! Irie! Come down to the basement. Will smells dead people!" I stay at the top of the stairs watching as Will sniffs a few boxes then moves to the walls. There are footfalls on the stairs. Nancy and Irie come up behind me.

"He find something?" Irie asks.

"He's—" Will bends down with his nose right on the brick, sniffing up the wall. "—looking."

When he reaches the quilt, the nose twitches double time as if moving to some unknown beat. He rips the quilt off its pegs and sure enough, there's a padlocked metal door. I knew there was something off about that quilt. Will presses his ear against it. "I don't hear anything."

The three of us join him by the door. The other two seem calm but my stomach is doing somersaults. I know what's coming next. I do *not* want to go in there.

"We need to go in there," Will says.

"No prob," Nancy says.

"Nancy, don't—" Will stops speaking when Nancy disappears. "Shit! Irie, padlock now!"

Irie stares at the lock. It turns from silver to bright orange in an instant. Better than a blowtorch. Someone screams on the other side of the door and Nancy reappears the millisecond it ceases, panting like a dog. "Oh my God, something totally touched me!" The smoking lock falls to the ground. Will and Irie pull out their guns and aim at the door. I, of course, forgot mine.

"Alexander, open the door," Will says. I scoff. Sure, let me be the entrée. I step toward the door. "With your mind, Alexander." Oh, yeah, I guess that makes more sense. I step back to focus on the knob and pull the door open.

It's pitch black in there but the overwhelming smell of pine trees and decay paint a grotesque picture. The red ball rolling out of the darkness, stopping at my feet, tells the rest. As does the tinkling sound of a music box. Oh heck, I remember the important thing I learned last night. "Oh my God, that sick creep."

"What?" Will asks, not taking his eyes or gun off the room.

A tiny figure moves toward us, dragging her left leg. "Jesus Christ," Irie mutters, "is that—"

"Emma Wayland," I finish.

The seven-year-old—and five-month-dead—Emma shuffles toward us, her twisted leg behind her. Her long black hair is matted and chunks of her scalp show where the hair fell out. Her skin is the same yellowish color as other corpses, but her eyes seem almost normal except they're glossy and one is crossed. They have to be glass. Her Barbie nightgown is covered in dirt and yellow fluid where she leaks embalming fluid. "He's been preserving her," Will says.

She walks slowly, passing the still armed Will and Irie as if she doesn't know they're there. They just watch her, standing like stone. No, she walks toward me. I know what she wants. I pick up the ball at my feet. She passes a disgusted Nancy and stops right in front of me. The little girl grunts. And again as if trying to say something. "You want your ball?" She grunts. "Here you go," I say brushing it against her dry, sallow hand. She takes it with a grunt and smile, revealing black gums and missing teeth. Ball in her small hands, she turns back around and walks past my visibly horrified companions. When she fades back into the darkness, they finally put the guns away.

"This is totally screwed up," Nancy says.

"He must have raised her right after she was buried," Irie says.

"He's kept her locked up all that time? Gross," Nancy says.

"He wanted his daughter back," Will says.

"That's why Oliver didn't sense a body in her grave last night."

All eyes turn to me. "You knew about this?" Will asks.

"I just remembered it now."

"How could you forget something so important?"

I scoff. "He said it right before all heck broke loose. I had other things on my mind!" A loud groan comes from the black room. "Excuse me. I'm going to check on her. We probably scared her to death."

"Yeah, *she* was the scared one," Nancy mutters.

I turn on the lights before going in. Besides the brick walls and no windows, the place is perfect for a little girl. A small pink bed, bookcase, white dresser with a menagerie of stuffed animals and Barbies with more on the floor. She even has a television and plastic pink chair with various DVDs near it. The music box finally slows down. She must feel my presence because she jumps off the bed with a Barbie book in her hands. She grunts and thrusts the book at me. "You want me to read to you?" She grunts and I assume this means yes.

"She likes you," Will says.

We both look up. "I taught elementary school for three years, I just give off that vibe." As opposed to the skin-crawling vibe I give hot werewolves. Emma grunts and pulls at my arm. Dead or alive, children want your undivided attention. "Why don't we put on a video instead?" I pick up the nearest one and pop it in. Taking her flaking hand in mine, I lead her to the chair and like a good girl she sits without protest. Mickey Mouse pops on the screen and I'm nothing but a memory.

I meet the rest in the other room. "Lord, it smells in there."

"So, what do we do now?" Nancy asks.

"Want me to incinerate her?" Irie asks.

I gasp. "You will do no such thing!"

"Bea, that isn't a little girl in there, it's a walking corpse," Irie says. "She's not hurting anybody."

"What? You want to adopt the little zombie in there? She's dead!"

"In her mind, she's just a little girl. I doubt she even knows she's dead."

"We are not killing the child," Will says. Finally, someone with a conscience. "We may need to use her as bait." Maybe not. "If he is following us, then he knows we're here, and he'll know we have her. We take her with us and lock her up in mobile command. Agreed?"

"Whatever," Irie says, "but I'm not babysitting."

"Fine. Alexander, get some of her things to keep her calm and bring her upstairs to the car. Nancy, go with them back to mobile command. Irie and I will keep searching the house."

"We can't do this. It's wrong. She's a little girl, not a—a chess piece. What are we going to do? Threaten to harm her if he doesn't do what we say? How does that make us any better than him?"

"We didn't bring her into this, Walter Wayland did," Will says. "Now, he is out there, and you of all people know what he is capable of. It is our duty to do whatever we have to, to make sure he doesn't hurt anyone else. If that includes keeping the zombie as a hostage, then so be it."

"She's an innocent little girl!"

"This is what we're doing," Will almost roars. "If you have a problem with doing what is necessary then perhaps you better re-think your job here. Get her things!"

We glare at each other for a few tense seconds before I lose the battle and look away. Damn it. "Whatever you say, *boss,*" I say, passing without looking at him. Emma turns from the TV to me, pointing to the screen with a huge black smile for me. I know she can't see me but I smile back. "Yes, Mickey Mouse. I like him too, sweetie." She turns back to the TV, hugging her stuffed bunny tight. I walk over to her and bend down beside her, doing my best to ignore the smell. Hesitantly, I pet her dry hair, and she beams at me. God knows how long she's been down here all alone, waiting for her father to return, and now I'm going to kidnap her. It's enough to break my heart. I sigh.

She's the zombie, but I'm the monster now.

THIRTEEN

THE BEST LAID PLANS

IT SEEMS THAT ALL children, dead or alive, hate doctors. Poor Emma grunted, squirmed, and even threw a temper tantrum during Dr. Neill's exam. I had to physically hold her down and sing while Neill drew clumpy embalming fluid. As if this child hasn't gone through enough. I didn't know zombies could feel pain. To make matters worse Agent Chandler insisted she stay in the freezer with a guard. Guess who volunteered? At least they turned the thermostat up so I only have to wear one huge puffy coat. When the doc left for the evening, I opened the door. Being surrounded by claw marks and dents with a dead child is just a bit more than I can take right now.

At least Emma's calmed down. No more grunting and pulling out her hair. *If You Give a Moose a Muffin* seems to have a soothing effect, but I should have grabbed more books. I've read the four I brought with us twice. I'm tempted to pull *Advanced Forensic Techniques* out of the conference room. Dr. Neill seems to think Emma doesn't understand the words, only the inflection, like a baby. If we have to wait for Wayland much longer, I may end up giving forensic science a storybook voice.

We're drawing now. Well, I'm drawing, and she's making blobs. This sure beats running around with a machete though. Maybe this can be my job from now on, babysitting. We both look up when the door to medical opens. Carl with my McDonald's? Thank God, I'm starving—but instead Oliver steps in, and my stomach clenches. A weird, gut-wrenching thought pops into my head. *He's probably seen me naked.*

"I heard we had a visitor." Emma hisses like a cockroach when he walks toward us. "Lovely child. She has your eyes."

"Shut up, Oliver. Emma, it's okay," I say, smoothing her hair. More than a few strands come out in my hand. "He's a friend, he won't hurt you." I smooth and shush until, after a few seconds, she stops. "Good girl," I whisper. "Now keep drawing, I'll just be in the other room." I put the crayon back in her hand. Oliver follows me out. "You probably shouldn't go back in there. You upset her."

"Whatever you say, my dear. I have no desire to impede on your bonding session. I just came to make sure you had recovered from last night. You do seem to have improved since I last saw you."

The way he says it, along with his eyes roving my body, makes me goosepimply all over. He totally saw me naked. "I'm doing better, thanks." I pause. "You went above and beyond for me last night. Not many guys would stay with me like you did, especially after the way I've been treating you. You were really sweet."

"'Sweet?'" he asks with that smirk. "I do not believe in all my days a soul has called me that."

"Well, it's true. You were a perfect gentleman. Like a human being, even."

"We all have our humane moments, I suppose." He leans toward me. "Though if you are, by any chance, looking for a way to repay me, there is an empty conference room with a sturdy table in the next room."

I click my tongue. "Just had to ruin it, didn't you?"

"You bring it out in me, my dear."

"Will this sate you?" Cupping his chin in my hands, I plant a chaste kiss on his cold cheek. Of course the door opens just as I do it, and Nancy peeks in. I pull away instantly.

"Oops. Didn't mean to *interrupt*. Here's your dinner." She tosses the bag and shuts the door, glaring at me the whole time.

I roll my eyes. "Wonderful. Now I'm the office slut."

That grin is back. "If only that were true."

"Zip it. There are children present."

Emma, hearing the door, steps out of the freezer with her drawing. I push her back in before the hissing starts again. "Go on, sweetie," I whisper before returning to Oliver. "I think she's waiting for her dad to come and get her."

He folds his arms. "We all are, are we not? I do hope he takes the bait. It will bring me intense pleasure to snap that madman's neck."

I gaze at Emma coloring purple swirls on her paper. "Want to know something weird? I totally understand why he did it. All of it."

"You lost a child?"

I turn back to him. "No, but I'd die to protect one. It's how I got into this mess."

"And the deluge last night, you understand that?" he asks, incredulously.

"I understand. I don't condone."

"Well, I spent the remainder of last night manipulating the minds of an entire town, most in wretched shape. I do not understand nor condone. This man is little better than a rabid dog and should be treated as such. Remember what his wife and her lover became in the end? He will not hesitate, and did not, to do the same to us all."

"I know that. I just—I feel bad for Emma. All she wants is her father, and I can't give him to her. She doesn't deserve this."

"My dear, I think you should take a break from the child. You are growing far too attached. We *will* have to put her back. You must keep in mind she is nothing more than a re-animated corpse."

"So are you. Are you saying I shouldn't get attached to you either?"

"I believe it is a bit too late for that, is it not?"

Before I can quip back, and I have a good one too, the door opens. Carl pokes his head in. "Guys, the necro's on the phone."

"Really?" We file out and into the open conference room. Nancy and Agents Chandler and Wolfe are already waiting around the table with the black phone in the middle. Agent Chandler presses the speakerphone button. "This is the agent in charge."

"I'll ask again, do you have my daughter?"

"Who is this?"

"Who the fuck do you think it is? Do you have my daughter?"

"Yes. She's safe."

"Good, then I won't have to kill your friend here."

"What friend?"

"The blind one."

"Oh God," Nancy says, "he has Andrew. You son of a bitch! I'll rip your dic—"

"Calm down," says Agent Chandler. "How do we know you're not lying or haven't killed him already?"

A second later, "I'm all right," says Andrew. "Please don't—"

"That's enough," Wayland says. "So we'll keep this simple: yours for mine. I want the one with the glasses to bring Emma to Highland Cemetery outside Sunbeam, about half an hour outside of town. You have an hour."

"No. We meet on neutral ground."

"Excuse me? Who do you think is making the rules here? Don't think I won't kill him. Highland Cemetery, my girl. If I see anybody else, I kill him." The line goes dead.

"Shit," Agent Chandler says under his breath. "How the hell did this happen?"

"He was following us. He knows where we're staying," I say.

"I am so *not* going to a cemetery alone," Nancy says.

"You won't," Carl says. "I'm calling Will." He whips out his cell.

"Another cemetery. Who's up for an ambush?" Agent Wolfe asks.

"You are no doubt correct," Oliver says.

"Maybe we should just do what he says," Agent Chandler chimes in. "If only Nancy and the zombie go, then ... no, that won't work. She can't teleport both her and Andrew out if something goes wrong."

"Will and Irie will be here any second," Carl says. "He says to sit tight."

"I am not going! I don't care!" Nancy shouts. Everyone shuts up.

Oliver moves to her and puts his hands on her shoulders. "Of course you are not. Not alone."

"He's right," I say, "she can't go alone. Nobody can. He *killed* one of us already. If we give him what he wants, he'll raise the cemetery just to keep us busy while he gets away. Or if we try to trick him, he'll raise the cemetery anyway. He's going to do it either way."

"So what do we do? Not show up and let him kill Andrew?" Carl asks.

"What do you think, my dear?" Oliver asks me. "You seem to know the most about our villain."

All right, why are all eyes on me? Everyone in the cramped room stares, waiting for my next word. What do I look like, General Patton? I suck at *Risk*, I'm always the first one out. Plan. We need a plan. Okay, I can do this. "Um, of course we show up. But … um … we … go prepared. Flamethrowers, machetes, anything we can use. People wait in strategic locations to cover both the meet and entire cemetery."

"He's probably drained from last night, so he might not be able to raise as many as he did before," Carl adds.

"But there's no, like, guarantee," Nancy says.

"What we really need to do is get him to neutral ground," I say. "So we shouldn't bring Emma; we need him to come back here."

"If he will not?"

"Then … ah … " I look to the room for help. "Oh! Nancy! You can teleport in and tranq him before he does anything."

Eyes move to her. "I can do that."

"Good! Okay! So the second we see Andrew isn't in danger, you pop in and shoot him."

"If he's hiding Andrew or realizes his kid isn't there?" Agent Wolfe asks.

"Then he does his thing but we're ready with flamethrowers and stuff. But Nancy still shoots him. We don't want him getting away, and someone can always get Andrew's location out of him."

"With pleasure," Oliver says, emotionless.

I meet his eyes, getting a chill. "Um, okay, so the first thing we—"

The opening door stops me mid-sentence. A serious Will, Irie, and Agent Rushmore step in. They've been ripping apart the Wayland house looking for clues. "Okay, people, we need a plan," Will says the moment he steps in. "Nancy is—"

"We already have a plan," Agent Wolfe says.

"What?"

"Dear sweet Trixie here apparently has an untapped diabolical mind," Oliver says. "We send someone to confront the fiend and allow Nancy to tranquilize him."

"Yes, but what if he—"

"We're around the cemetery, out of sight, weapons ready," Agent Chandler says. "It should work, sir."

Will glances at me and squares his shoulders. "Fine. Someone fill us in, and the rest get ready. There isn't much time."

"But who's the one to meet him?" Carl asks. "He could see we don't have the girl and shoot whoever's in front of him."

"Agent Alexander," Will says.

Now all eyes are on me. My mouth gapes open. "Well, I suppose—"

"Good," Will says. "Chandler, come fill us in. The rest of you get as many weapons as you can. Make sure you replace the tranqs from last night with something less potent. We don't want to kill the man if we can help it." He walks out with Irie and Agent Chandler behind.

"What's his problem?" Nancy asks when the door closes.

"Trixie stole his thunder, damaged his frail ego." He moves behind me, putting his hands on my shoulders, and whispers, "Do not worry, my dear, he will get over it."

I shrug his hands away. "We have work to do."

I walk out, head high, but biting my lip. Mind in the game, Bea. Don't let some furry, cute jerk get to you, not tonight. Forget about it. I'll think about it tomorrow. That is, if I survive the night.

———

"Radio check, one, two. Team three, check."

"Team one in place," says Irie over the radio.

"Team two, check," Carl says.

"Team four ready and waiting," I say, putting the walkie back onto the seat next to me. "How many checks is he going to do?"

"He's nervous and totally impatient," Nancy says from the back seat of the car. The huge tranquilizer gun rests in her lap. She should be lying on the floor out of sight but after twenty minutes there, her complaints finally wore down my last nerve. "How much time now?"

"Two minutes since you last asked. He still has ten more minutes."

We're parked right on the edge of the cemetery in the lot facing the road. I'm about to jump out of my skin I'm so nervous and (yes) impatient. If something is going to happen, I want it to happen already. If I'm going to be shot or eaten, let's just get it out of the way. My fingers haven't stopped drumming the wheel since we left mobile command. That feeling of dread grows with each drum. The ambiance isn't helping either. I swear the guy picked the biggest, creepiest cemetery in the country. Headstones and even old crypts and mausoleums as far as the eye can see (which isn't far) are packed in together with huge trees crackling and swaying with the wind. All that's missing is the mist from the moors and a howling wolf. Even if he only raises a quarter of it, we'll still have double the amount we had last night. If everything doesn't go according to plan, we're dead meat. Literally.

"Come on! Get here already!" Nancy says. "This sucks! I'm so bored!"

"He'll show."

"Good for him. Just wish he'd do it soon." She sighs a deep, theatrical sigh. "So … you and Oliver already, huh?"

"What? No!"

"But you totally kissed him."

"On the cheek! Just the cheek. He was nice to me last night, and I was thanking him, that's all."

"Well, good. Keep it that way. 'Cause Will and Oliver already totally hate each other's guts. Don't need to make it worse."

"And how exactly could I make it worse?"

She scoffs like I'm the valedictorian of Idiot University. "Duh! Will totally has a crush on you! I mean he, like, actually *talks* to you. And *smiles*. I didn't know he could *do* that!"

"Nancy, he volunteered me for the most dangerous job, I think the romance is off. Not to mention I literally make his skin crawl."

"Well, no relationship's perfect. You would totally make a good couple."

"I barely know him. Besides, he doesn't think of me that way."

"Yeah right, and you so don't have a crush on him. Hey, maybe if you sleep with him, he'll actually loosen up and I can, like, have friends over. I know he was the one who talked George out of the idea. He could use a good lay. So could you, for that matter."

"Nancy!" A faint streak of light shines in the distance. Headlights? Thank you, lord. My executioner's here. "Get down and cover yourself," I say. "I think he's coming. Keep the radio on."

"Got it." She lays on the back seat, rifle clutched to her chest.

Showtime.

I climb out of the car and take a deep breath. This will work. It will all work out. Just stay calm. You can handle anything he throws at you. Yeah, right. The light grows in intensity with each moment, as does my oncoming heart attack. A small sedan comes down the road and stops near my car. The mass murderer drives a Volvo. Why does this not surprise me? The engine cuts. The driver doesn't get out for several tense seconds. Is he going to turn around? What do we do then? But the door does open and Walter Wayland steps out.

This is our notorious killer? In front of the headlights where he stands, I can tell he's maybe a few inches taller than I am with a round stomach pouching out over denim. His round glasses cover most of his ruddy face and his bald head shines. No wonder Valerie had an affair.

"You aren't the one I said to come," he says. "If I wanted you, I would have asked for the chubby one."

Oh yeah, this man is pure evil. "We aren't about to send a seventeen-year-old into danger, okay? If you want your daughter, then deal with me."

His eyes jut around the lot, then the cemetery. It's too dark to see far, but the team still better be hidden well. "And they sent you alone?"

"I'm expendable. They don't like me very much. Now, where is our man?"

Wayland reaches down and pulls out a gun, pointing it right at my face. Oh, monkeys. "First take off your guns and throw them to me." Moving slowly, I do as he says, unclipping the holster from my belt, then putting my arms in the air. "Any others? Take off your jacket and show me your ankles." I do.

"Satisfied? Now where is Andrew?"

"My daughter first."

"No, Andrew first. No offense, but I don't really trust you."

He flicks the safety off. My breath quickens double time. "I make the rules, lady. Now where the fuck is my daughter?"

Don't lose it now, Bea. "She's not here, but she's safe. Now I will tell you where she is when you show me Andrew."

His grip tightens around the gun. "You didn't bring her?" he shouts.

Oh God! Be Joan Crawford. Joan Crawford knows no fear. "It was a guarantee so you wouldn't snatch her and kill me. So if you want your daughter back, tell me where Andrew is!"

"He's about ten minutes away from hell, lady. And if you do anything to me, if I don't call off my dogs in ten minutes, you'll have one dead blind man on your hands. I know what you all did to Kennedy with that sniper rifle; I'm not going down like him. So you have ten minutes to get my kid!"

"I need proof he's—"

We both get distracted the moment Nancy materializes clutching the tranq gun to her chest. Oh, crud, she's early. Nancy moves her huge rifle into position, the thing looking as big as she is. Wayland doesn't hesitate. His gun swings toward her. He squeezes the trigger. No time to think. I pick him up and toss him sideways a millisecond before the bullet leaves the chamber. It misses Nancy's head by just inches. She pants and the rifle shakes. Will runs toward us, shouting something I can't understand because my ears ring from the shot.

The sudden rush of power just about knocks me down. A million somethings creep under my skin just like last night. The others must feel the same because Will stops mid-stride and Nancy screeches, releasing the rifle. The wall hits a second time, dropping all of us to the ground. My head hits pavement. Stupid white spots cover most of my field of vision. I barely notice a fat figure dashing toward the cemetery. I lift my head and shake the fuzziness away. Wayland runs into the darkness of the cemetery. I stand and rub my new bump, watching as Nancy does the same.

"What happened?" she asks.

"We're in deep trouble." I grab her sleeve and drag her to the trunk of our SUV. We don't have much time. I put my machete in my belt—I found it with the other weapons that were collected after the mayhem last night and have decided to call her Bette after the equally intimidating Bette Davis—and the extra gun clips right next to it. Better than Batman's utility belt in my opinion. Nancy grabs the flamethrower and I help her put on the straps of the gas can. "You know how to work this thing, right?"

"Yep." I blink and she vanishes. I shut the trunk and retrieve my gun and Wayland's, tucking them in my belt too.

Then I make the mistake of looking ahead.

The first have risen, mostly skeletons held together by next to nothing. Will punches one and it falls apart. More rise, then more, just like last night. They come up with their teeth mash-ing, clawing at the world with dirty hands. I don't want to go in there. My legs don't move. I don't even try to move them. I shut my eyes. I could get into the car and drive away. Drive all the way to San Diego if I wanted to. Home to Nana, home to April, maybe I can even get my old job back. It was a good idea last night, still a good idea today. I can't do this again, I just can't. I'll die. I don't want to die.

Someone shouts my name. My eyes jerk open.

Three zombies hold Will, his body jerking, twisting, trying to get away. Two hold him by the shoulders. The one holding his foot bites his calf and he falls. A fourth joins the pile. I yank it off without moving. Then the other two disappear in opposite directions like they were shot out of cannons. My legs pump toward him. By the time I reach him, another zombie is almost on top of him. Out comes the machete and off comes its head and arms.

"Thank you," Will says, looking up at me in a sort of shock. I told him I could take care of myself.

"Don't mention it." He takes my hand, and I pull him up. Another zombie grabs his shoulder but he elbows it away, knocking its head off. I smile. "Neat."

"Which way did Wayland go?"

"No idea," I lie. That creep is mine. "What should we do now?"

"Kill as many as you can," he says before running away into the fray. A burst of orange light appears and disappears a little ways off. Why didn't I grab a flamethrower? At least I—crud. A mummified corpse in pioneer-era clothes grabs my arm but I chop in time. Don't think, just do, Bea. Flashlight and machete in hand, I run the way Wayland went. A few corpses snag me but are either shot or cut. There are too many to give my undivided attention so I just do a little damage to the grabby ones and continue into the cemetery. Stop the source and there will be no more zombies.

He could be hiding anywhere. I run through rows of stony graves as high as my waist, occasionally dispatching an attacker, but there are so many wandering people with no hair it's hard to distinguish a dead bald head from a living one. Guess he wasn't as drained as we had anticipated. If I were him, I'd be holed up in a crypt, but like the zombies, there are too many crypts to check and most have things pounding on their walls from inside. I'm not stupid enough to open them. I keep running around with no real idea what I'm doing. Slash, shoot, run away, look ... it's all I can do. Just stay alive and find the killer.

A flash of orange against the star-filled sky out of the corner of my eye gets my attention. A few zombies see it too because they change course toward it. Going *toward* fire; yep, no brains left. Easy prey. Heads literally roll when I reach them. When Bette the Machete finishes with a woman in genuine bell-bottoms, I notice a figure running away from the light. Being a zombie expert now, I know they can't run. It requires too much coordination and concentration. Wayland. I take off after him dodging both headstones and corpses. Have I ever mentioned how much I hate running? I'm winded after ten seconds, but he's in even worse shape than I am, so I'm gaining on him. He's less of a black blob now, and I can make out a definitely male figure.

Headstones vanish and after a large strip of grass, the figure runs through a high metal fence with nothing but crypts and other small stone buildings on the other side. The small white and gray buildings seem connected, with a foot or two between them and paths to every grouping. Some are crumbling, with huge chunks missing, and others have serious water damage. The ground is uneven with cracks in the concrete and sections raised. I have to look both up and down so I don't trip or walk into someone's final resting place. The figure runs behind one of the more intact crypts, and I follow. But when I get to the other side, he's gone. I look but don't see anyone. I've lost him! I pull off my walkie. "This is Alexander, come in."

A second later, "Alexander, this is Price."

"I think I've tracked Wayland to the back of the cemetery. It's full of mausoleums. I've lost sight of him, but he has to be around here somewhere."

"Alexander, proceed with caution. The person closest to her position rendezvous with her immediately."

"On my way," Oliver says through the walkie.

I scan the area again, but there is no movement. I replace Bette with my gun; all the corpses in this area are either locked in or too decayed to move around so I won't need her. Crud. Wrong. The second the gun is in my hand, shuffling starts nearby. I shine the flashlight in a circle but see nothing.

"Pretty," a gravelly voice says behind me. I spin around just as a blur of blue leaps from the top of a crypt onto me. Me and Boy Blue land on the ground, my head narrowly missing an edge of concrete. The jumper quickly pins my body, holding my wrists down. The flashlight clatters beside us, the beam still shining on us. The stink from this guy is as intolerable as his face—yellow and brown with only one eye. His skin feels loose and dry around my wrists. I'm going to barf. "Too old for my taste though."

"Fucking kiddy raper," another man says. He steps toward us. He's not in any better shape than his buddy—his skin is more sunken and yellow, but he has both his eyes, though they're clouded by milky cataracts. He has a mullet too. "You wouldn't know what to do with her. Let a big boy show you how."

Oh no, these aren't zombies. They're ghouls! They can think for themselves.

"You should be watching the other one," one-eye says. "She called for backup."

"I say we kill 'em both now. We're missing out on all the fun. Hey, boss!"

233

Footsteps move toward us until he's in view. Wayland. I quickly rule out killing him there because the Gruesome Two-some might do the same to me and then Andrew, who must be around here somewhere.

"Good job, Jay," Wayland says. "I knew she'd follow you." He walks closer toward me, looking down. From this angle, he has a triple chin. "Now where the hell is my daughter?"

"Stop the zombies and I'll tell you."

"No deal. Kill her and the blind one, and then get another one to talk."

"You dug us up, boss," Mullet says.

"Just make it quick," Wayland says walking away, "we have things to do."

The ghouls seem disappointed. Too bad for them. I don't wait for them to carry out their orders. I push Boy Blue off me with my mind, only he doesn't let go of my wrists. We fly, then his head bumps into the crypt behind him and I fall on top, doubling the impact. He releases my wrists, and I roll off him like a log. Mullet lunges but only reaches my foot as I kick him in the groin. Dead or alive, that still smarts. He doubles over with a howl of pain. But Boy Blue jumps me again and a wrestling match ensues. We roll around with me kicking his legs and holding his head away from my neck as he chomps at it with yellow teeth. I keep ending up on the bottom.

Still holding his crotch, Mullet finally stands but not before taking my gun from the ground. Well, I'd rather be shot than eaten any day of the week. He stumbles toward our match, gun raised. Oh, crap! I push down on the ground and roll us again just as the gun goes off. The bullet hits right where we were. Too freaking close. And I've moved us right against another crypt so we have nowhere else to roll. Oh, fudge. New plan. I fling Mullet as hard as I can sideways into a crypt with my mind, which darn near explodes into huge chunks on impact. Should have done that sooner.

"Impressive again."

Both the ghoul and I look sideways just as Oliver's fist smashes into my attacker's face. Boy Blue's head leaves a dent in the wall. The ghoul releases me, and I stand up. Bette the Machete unsheathes and off goes his head. That does the trick. The rest of his body stops moving. No need for dismemberment. Well, that's refreshing.

"Took you long enough to get here," I pant.

"A thousand pardons." Mullet stands from the rubble, no longer stunned. "Allow me," Oliver says. He disappears then reappears next to the peeved off animate corpse and instantly rips its head off, yellow fluid dripping to the cement. The body falls and Oliver drops the head next to the rest of it. "I prefer ghouls, do you not? So much easier to dispatch."

"Yeah, love 'em." I pick up my flashlight from the ground. "I think Andrew's around here somewhere. Wayland too."

Oliver rips my gun out of the ghoul's hand. "Then we shall find them." He appears beside me and hands me the gun. Guess I'm getting used to the disappearing and reappearing act of his. I only had a slight urge to pee my pants. "Stay close. You appear to be a magnet for danger. Never a dull moment with you, is there?"

I put the gun in my holster. "Stop flirting." I follow him, Bette at my side, through the crypts. He stops at a random crypt and puts his ear against it. When satisfied he moves onto another.

This is a plan? "This is going to take forever," I mutter. "Andrew!" I shout. "Make some noise so we can find you!"

"That works as well."

I listen but hear nothing. "Maybe he's unconscious." Spoke too soon. Oliver grabs my hand and near drags me farther into the crypts. I start to hear the pounding. He stops pulling when we reach one of the larger mausoleums, the source of the noise.

"Andrew?" Oliver asks.

"I'm here," he shouts from inside the onyx polished marble mausoleum with an iron door.

"Move from the door, I will try to break it down." I move out of the way as Oliver starts kicking the iron door. It shimmies but doesn't open. He kicks again. "This iron is too strong. Perhaps the combined strength of Will and me … "

I pull off my walkie. "Will, come in."

"Alexander? Did backup arrive?"

"Yeah, but we need you. We found Andrew, but we can't get into the mausoleum."

"On my way. Out."

I replace the walkie. "Let's keep trying. Maybe if you kick and I push?"

"I suppose it is worth a try. On three." I concentrate on the door. Push at the center. "One … two … three!"

He kicks and I push with my mind. Hard. The door dents in the middle like a crushed can and jets into the mausoleum like a projectile missile, smashing to the back wall, shaking the whole structure. Lord, did I do that? Oliver turns to me and if I didn't know better, I'd think he was afraid of me for a second. Something about the way his mouth hangs.

Andrew steps out of the crypt, feeling the wall for guidance. Dried blood covers his left forehead. Without the sunglasses, his eyes look as white as a zombie's. Ugh, bad comparison. "I think I'm deaf."

"Well, at least you're not locked up anymore." I take his arm to help him out. We all start walking toward the entrance. "Are you okay?"

"My head is killing me. I don't know what happened. Someone knocked on the door, and when I opened it there was a gun to my side. He took me to his car and clubbed me. I woke up here. I did, however, have a lovely conversation with the inhabitant of the mausoleum."

"Well, at least it wasn't all bad," I say. He almost walks into a crypt, but I lead him away.

"Stop," Oliver says. We do. I glance around but only see stone monuments. "Andrew, do you feel that?"

"Oh, yes. He's close."

"Wayland?" I ask. "Where is he? I don't see anything. Oliver, do you?"

He has the strangest expression on his face, darn near vacant. He doesn't blink. "Oliver?"

"Get away from me," he whispers. "Something … "

"Oliver? What's the matter?"

He walks in a trance away from us. His head cocks to the left, listening to something only he can hear. "You need to leave! Now!"

Andrew tugs on my arm. "I think we should do what he says."

I can't leave him here like this. His eyes have doubled in size. "Oliver—"

Oliver grabs my shoulders so hard I think I hear a crack. Oh God, his eyes are black but it's the fanged snarl with saliva dripping that makes my heart beat triple time. He's vamping out. His trembling hands dig into my arm so hard I cry out. "RUN!" Oliver bellows. He shoves me against Andrew and disappears. What the heck was that? I don't think I want to find out. Time to run.

I take Andrew's hand and start moving. The old man slows me down, as does the maze of crypts. This is a bad plan and I know it. I can't outrun Oliver. New plan. Hide. Andrew's prison is still in sight. That'll have to do. Eyes roving for movement, I walk the strangely calm man back. I lead Andrew inside, helping him around the two stone sarcophagi to the back wall. Using every bit of concentration I can, I lift the door I just smashed and move it back to its home, filling the empty space. There but for the grace of God, it doesn't fall.

"We should be safe here," I whisper, not sounding convincing.

"He's following us," Andrew says. "I can hear him. You need to leave me behind."

"Not an option. We can't outrun him anyway. When he wants us, he'll come." I start pacing. "What happened to him? He completely vamped."

"He must be under the control of the necromancer."

Super. "They can control vampires?"

"Only the most powerful ones."

"Of course," I mutter.

Okay, we need a plan. We'll just need to keep him busy until Will arrives. Plan, plan. Um … we can't outrun him, don't have stakes or holy anything. Putting Bette down, I release the clip of the gun. Three bullets, not good. Who knows how long it will take Will to get here with an army of corpses between us. I have to do something. He can hear us in here. "We're sitting ducks. I think I'm going to have to leave you here. I'll, uh, lure him away and keep him busy for as long as I can." I put Bette in his hands, wrapping his fingers around her. "Take this, it's a machete. If that door opens and you don't hear a familiar voice, just keep swinging.

You're bound to hit something. Just keep quiet, okay? I'll come back with help."

He nods his head. "Okay."

Gun at the ready, I stare at the door. *Pull.* I open the slab enough for me to squeeze out and then push it closed behind me. So far, so good. No vampires lying in wait. I feel him, though. His eyes. Stalking me. I scan and listen but it's as quiet as a grave—pun intended. The crypts block my view. Anything can be hiding behind them. Just get this over with. Leading with gun and flashlight, I cautiously walk toward what I hope is the exit. Running would provoke him, so I stroll. Lovely night for a walk through a cemetery. For the first time tonight, I notice that I'm freezing, but the gooseflesh covering every centimeter of my skin is from his eyes on me, not the cold. Just get to the clearing, Bea. Cool, calm, collected. I see the entrance, the rusted fence. There's a flash of movement to my left. I spin and it's gone. He's toying with me.

I make it out of the crypts but not by much. I feel him right beside me. There isn't even time for me to look. Before he can touch me, I toss him to the right, and I take off running. I don't dare look back. "Help! Hel—" Cold hands grab my waist and lift me off the ground. My turn to soar. I hit about ten feet away, landing feet first, rolling to a stop on my back. The gun escapes my hand, and I have no idea where it goes.

Oliver is on top of me the moment I stop, pinning my wrists to the grass. Fangs enter the flesh of my neck. Often found sexy and romantic in movies, I can attest that being bitten by a vampire is not so great in reality. It feels like two huge, dull needles plunging in, invading my body. I scream so loud I hurt my own ears. The fangs come out as fast as they came in, and his hot mouth suckles the wounds like a newborn, catching as much of the warm flowing blood as he can. He moans in ecstasy as his tongue laps against the raw openings. Oh God. The bulge in his jeans grows against my thigh. As I squirm under him, I swear it doubles in size.

He's getting off on my pain. Rage fills me, hot like summer in the valleys of Arizona. I turn my head and bite the piece of him closest, his ear. His mouth leaves my neck to cry out in torment. More important, he releases my wrists. *Lift!* Oliver floats off my body like that girl in *The Exorcist*. He snarls with bloody teeth barred, long white fingers grasping for me. He rises six feet off the ground. I manage to sit up, my breath escaping in spurts. He attempts once last grab, almost reaching my hair. He weighs nothing. Perfect for flying. I watch as he soars ten, twenty feet away, slamming into a tree with the force of a train. The tree snaps in two, splinters flying everywhere. Oliver falls motionless to the ground. The top of the tree crackles like lightning then falls over, crashing into the metal fence and onto some crypts, which crumble like gingerbread houses. Wow.

I spit out Oliver's blood and wipe my chin. I so need Scope right now. Or vodka. It takes me two tries but I manage to stand up. My neck throbs something awful. Normally vamps enter your mind and make the experience pleasurable, then lick the wound to close it. They have a thin coating of an enzyme on their tongue that reacts to blood and clots it. Of course there is no way Oliver's getting near my neck again, so I'll just bleed. I put pressure on the holes, but blood pours between my fingers. I better not get a scar. At least he missed an artery. Count my blessings there. Gosh, the world spins a lot.

Even with my brain on a Tilt-a-Whirl, I make it to my attacker. Oliver doesn't move at all. I can see why. The back of his head is a bloody mess, almost fully caved in. All but one of his limbs is twisted at a grotesque angle. I think I've killed him. Oh, no. Kneeling down beside him, I flip him on his back. His white face is almost totally covered in blood. Relief washes over me when he groans a little. He'll heal and be peachy by tomorrow. I really have to stop almost killing my co-workers, even if they deserve it.

"Alexander?"

What? Oh. Well, it's about time. What did he do, take a detour to Mexico? "Over here," I shout and stand at the same time. This spinning is making me a little light headed. Will, who is plastered with blood and gore almost as much as I am, stops a few feet short of us, assessing the situation. First, his eyes dart to the crypts and tree, then the unconscious Oliver, finally to me. His nostrils flare and I'm hit with his overwhelming fury.

"He did that to you?" he asks in a low voice through gritted teeth.

"Yeah, but—"

Before I finish Will bridges the gap between us. He kneels beside the vampire, studying him. "You didn't kill him."

"Of course not! He didn't mean to—" Obviously not wanting to hear me out, Will picks up a fallen branch and raises it over Oliver's body. Oh, crud. "Stop!"

"He attacked a human. That's an automatic death sentence." He raises the makeshift stake above his head. It flies out of his hand and as far as I can send it. "What the hell are you doing?" he snarls at me. Another wave of fury hits me.

I jump between Will and Oliver. "Get away from him, Will. He can't hurt anyone now. He's knocked out."

"*You* get away from him. It's the law and I have to carry it out."

I step over Oliver's body so a leg is on either side of him. "If you would just listen to me for—"

He picks up the nearest piece of wood. I have no choice. I elevate the angry werewolf up off the ground and send him away. He lands in a grassy area, knocking down a zombie. Almost as soon as he's down he's up and running back toward us, nostrils flaring. I have just enough time to kneel where Will was standing beside Oliver. Just as the peeved werewolf reaches us, I raise my hand like I learned in training to focus my power. Will freezes mid-stride. He tries to move his legs, but I won't let them budge a centimeter. I have control of all his limbs. If I wanted him to do a jig, I could make him. It takes a lot of concentration to control four things at once but focus is key.

"Alexander, let me go."

"No. I'm sorry. Not until you calm down."

"Alexander!" Another fury wave damn near makes me lose concentration but I maintain.

"You obviously have a lot of unresolved anger toward Oliver, but now is not the time to vent it. He didn't mean to attack me. Wayland made him do it. Now, he is unconscious and we can keep him that way, but if you come *near* him hell bent on killing him, you will have to go through me. Do you understand? Can I let you go now or do you want a date with a tree trunk too?"

We stare at each other, neither set of eyes giving an inch. His face is so tight with anger I can see every bone. I really, *really* don't want to hurt him but if I have to … Him or Oliver, he knows which one I'll choose in this scenario. He looks away first, nodding in agreement. I hesitate for a second then let him go. "Thank you," I whisper. "I'm sor—"

"Don't."

I want to say something, but there isn't time. Can't I even have three seconds of peace? Every zombie within sight has heard our squabble and is looking to take advantage. At least a dozen, maybe more, stumble toward us. "We need to get him out of here," I say. "Help me pick him up."

"I am getting fed up with this situation," Will says but not about my request. His eyes don't leave our unwanted visitors.

"Earth to Will!" I shout. "Help me!"

He snaps out of limbo and picks up Oliver in a fireman's carry. "Take off my walkie." Backup, good idea. "Is Andrew safe?"

"Yeah, he's in one of the mausoleums."

"Is it strong?"

"Um, I guess so."

He starts toward the crypts and away from the zombies, so I follow. "Call Irie and tell her Plan B. And give the name and location of the mausoleum. We'll rendezvous there."

"Plan B?"

"Just do as I say!"

Can I get a *please*? Jeez! I do what he says. The rest of the team seem to know what he's up to but darned if I do. I just follow him blindly back into the field of stone buildings, the world still spinning like mad. I'm sure I'm walking like a drunk, even having to stop and blink to focus. Will slows down and I take the lead like I actually know where I'm going. We stumble around looking for the name "Perault," which I am ninety percent sure was the name on the mausoleum. "Um, I think it's around here."

"But you're not sure?" Will asks, exasperated.

"No. I didn't really draw a map when I was running for my life. Andrew! It's Bea! Make some noise!"

Even I hear the pounding down the line of crypts. Will reaches it before I do, dumping Oliver's inert form and kicking down the iron door. Damn, he's strong. Andrew stands at the back of the mausoleum, machete raised like a baseball bat.

"It's okay, it's me," I say.

Andrew lowers Bette. "Where's Oliver?"

"Here, but he's unconscious."

Will prods Oliver roughly with his foot, which would hurt if he was awake. "I need to check the structure's integrity." He then proceeds to hit the wall with a fist. Okay, one of the stranger things I've seen today. "Call everyone and inform them we're located in the tenth row, seventh from the left. And tell them to hurry."

I pass the information onto the team. Very little chatting, just an "affirmative" from everyone. Will, finished pounding the inner walls, moves outside to pound out there. I'm sure there is a point to this, but what it is I have no idea. I'm just glad he's pounding the walls and not Oliver's face.

I sit between Andrew and Oliver's head while the pounding continues. A nice rest, that's exactly what I need. Oliver groans beside me. Except for all the blood covering his face, he looks almost peaceful. I shouldn't have tossed him so hard. It's odd, not twenty-four hours ago we were hugging, now we almost killed each other. What a strange life this is. I pick up his damp head and put it in my lap. I just can't help myself. He'd do the same for me.

"I smell blood, are you okay?" Andrew asks.

"Yeah. He missed the artery and vein."

"Will he be okay? It takes a lot to knock out a vampire."

"The back of his head is already healing. We just have to keep him unconscious until Wayland's dead."

"What about broken bones? Does he have any?"

"Yeah. Why?"

"You'll have to set them or they'll regenerate as is."

Eww. "I'll let Will handle that when he's done." He'll probably get a kick out of it. "What is he doing?"

"Seeing how strong this place is."

"Why?"

Will steps back in. Without a word, he grabs Bette from beside Andrew. His eyes briefly stop on Oliver and me but leave us just as quickly. "I'm going to help the others. When everyone but Irie is here, radio me, okay?" He runs out, not bothering to close the door. What's the hurry?

"So that's Plan B? Have everyone but Irie hole up in here until the zombies go away? Great plan."

"Everyone but Irie? Oh my. Is it really that bad out there?"

"What—" I gasp instead of finishing.

Nancy flashes in, sweating like she just got out of a sauna. The flamethrower is conspicuously missing. "Sorry," she says wiping her brow. "Didn't mean to scare you." Her eyes go down to Oliver. "Ohmigod, what happened to him?! Is he okay? Why is your neck bleeding? Are you okay? Did he do that to you? Did you, like, kill him?"

"Nancy! He's fine, I'm fine."

"He bit you? And he's still alive? Will didn't kill him?"

"Wayland made him do it, okay?"

Agent Rushmore, dressed in black fatigues, runs as best he can with a limp into the mausoleum. "They're going to be here any minute," he pants. "Fuck, there are so many of them. I barely got through. Is this place strong enough?"

"For what? What is going on?" I ask.

"Will apparently thinks so," Andrew says.

"Hello? What's happening?"

"It's bar-be-que time," Nancy says, looking out the door. "Flash fire, like everything out there incinerated. But we should be safe here if Will says so."

I don't share her confidence. If Irie is powerful enough to burn down her whole school, then I doubt a few stone walls will protect us. *This* is the brilliant plan? Jesus Christ, a two-year-old could come up with something better. We're all going to die.

Oliver shifts and moans on top of me, my whole body freezing. All eyes, even Andrew's, turn as I lift up his head. The skull, though still bloody, is almost back to its original shape. I gently put his head on the floor and stand. Andrew does the same but takes a step away from him. "We need to keep him unconscious," I say. "He could still attack."

Without warning, Agent Rushmore takes out his gun, firing two rounds into Oliver's head. Everyone has enough time to cover their ears but still the ringing starts. Oliver isn't moving anymore. Like a tear, a trickle of blood falls from the pulp where his eye was. I think I'm going to be sick. "What the hell?" I'm pretty sure I scream, but can't hear myself.

He shot him. He shot him! These people … Agent Rushmore's lips move but all I can make out are the words "regular bullets." So they won't kill him, thank God. Still, there had to be a better way. The guy was just slammed into a tree, he didn't need two bullets to the head too. Nancy's lips move, and she points down to Oliver. Agent Rushmore nods and bends beside Oliver's broken leg. He grabs the parts above and below the fracture. I turn around before he snaps the bone into place.

I shouldn't be here. This isn't happening. This *can't* be happening. The spinning and nausea damn near drop me.

Something happens to me. The room, the people, everything zooms away miles from me. I feel like I'm floating above myself in the ether. Even the pain disappears. I know there are people and walls but I don't *feel* them here, it's like they're ghosts or unreal. Far away. It's wonderful. Freeing. I start walking.

It's as cold outside the mausoleum as it is inside, but at least I can breathe out here. Off in the distance I can make out people walking toward us. Strangely, the fact that a zombie army is creeping closer does not scare me. I just feel … nothing. No fear, happiness, or even anger. Nothing. Numb. They could chomp on my liver and I wouldn't care. Death? Bring it on. I could use the rest. A zombie steps close enough for me to make out its skeletal features but disappears in a cloud of dust. Huh. That's better. All the black blobs getting closer vanish into the night. More dust flies into my face. It's actually quite beautiful. Swirls of gray dancing and twirling in the wind. So much better than blobs. No more blobs. Oh, there are more. Oop, they're gone too. So much better.

Someone moves beside me, but I don't look to see who. Another blob goes poof. Poof, poof, poof. Everyone here goes poof. The person next to me puts his hands on my shoulders, moving me back into the mausoleum. I'm pushed to the back wall and helped down on the floor next to Oliver. Nancy stands above me, concern all over her face. Why is she so worried? She's too young to be so serious. She should be out with friends, not holed up in a mausoleum about to die. She walks over to Andrew and starts talking, occasionally glancing at me with worry. I can't hear her and don't care. I am dust. We are all dust. I put Oliver's head in my lap but don't look at it. Instead, I just stroke his hair like he did for me last night. When he convinced me to stay.

I don't know how much time passes, maybe minutes. The others pace around the mausoleum, sometimes saying things I still can't hear. Nancy drums her fingers on one of the stone slabs, glancing at the open door. Agent Rushmore stands guard at the hole. I just keep stroking my attacker's hair as first Agent Chandler and then Carl find us. Both are covered with sweat, blood, and bits of gore. Carl actually bends down next to me and waves his hand in front of my face, his lips moving but no sound is coming out. He looks concerned, just like Nancy. Everyone is so serious. I just keep stroking.

I wonder what Nana's doing right this moment. Probably in her coral bed watching a horrible Lifetime movie about a stalker, sipping a cup of chamomile tea. April's sitting in her mother's old rocking chair singing her son, Carlos, to sleep as he sucks his thumb. I hope he stops doing that soon. I bet my brother, Brian, is still at his office under stacks of legal briefs and law books. I can even imagine little Randy Dodson, fully recovered from almost becoming road kill, playing a video game with his older brother. So strange, I save his life and mine ends months later in a cold mausoleum hundreds of miles away. That kid had better grow up to cure the common cold.

Will walks in carrying Agent Wolfe over his shoulders. The agent's shoe is off and the foot is covered in blood. Something took a chunk out of his Achilles tendon. Will sets him down in the far corner, his mouth moving the whole time. Barking orders, no doubt. What a control freak. He sure is cute, though. Carl says something then gestures toward me. Will's gaze whips toward me. Pissed-off look turns to familiar concern on the trip. His lips move, Carl shrugs. Now they're all looking at me. I should care but I don't. Let them stare at the freak, nothing new to me. It's Will's turn to wave his hand in my face. But unlike the others, he reaches down and takes my still stroking hand in his own. His lips move to say "Beatrice" as he squeezes my hand. I don't squeeze back. I pull my hand away and keep stroking Oliver.

Shaking his head, Will stands, mouth moving. He unclips the walkie and starts talking into it. Nancy sits next to Andrew and takes his hand. The rest sit down against the wall. The nervous energy in this place is making me even more ill. The men have no expression on their faces, but their feet and hands jitter in rapid fire. Something bad is about to happen. Will picks up the iron door, putting it back in place. He holds it in position with his back, his legs, and arms acting as anchors. Like that will hold it. Me, I pull Oliver toward me so his body covers mine and his head rests on my shoulder. I wrap my arms around his chest, squeezing tight. If I had a teddy bear I'd use it, but the bloody vampire will have to do. Even unconscious, he comforts me.

I feel it when Irie lets loose. My skin doesn't prickle, but for a split second something is sucked out of me—the air, my soul, I don't know what. This is bad. As sure as I know two plus two makes four, I know this place will crumble around us. But it's too late. There's a whooshing sound like an airplane taking off and just as fast. Almost the moment I hear it, the mausoleum rocks like it was made of Popsicle sticks, and the door Will holds knocks him in toward us. The orange glow outside shoots in. The world slows down almost to a standstill.

Will floats just inches from the slab, arms and legs straight out. He'll hit the back wall, and then the door will slam into him, probably knocking him right through it. He'll be incinerated. So will we. The flames from outside shoot in with us and there is nothing stopping us from frying. I don't want to die like this, burnt to a crisp. I just don't want to die. Not here. Not now. I haven't fallen in love. I haven't had babies. I haven't even seen Egypt. I'm not going out like this. That orange heat pushes out whatever fog enveloped my brain.

Focus.

Know the structure. Hold it together.

Just ten seconds.

I raise my hand to focus the energy. I push Will to the side so he falls at Agent Wolfe's feet. The slab floats in the air for a moment then rockets back to its original place, pushing the flames back outside. *Push.* The cracks in the front wall that grow with each millisecond stop when my mind touches them. They close. My kung fu is greater than yours. People are shouting from far away, though I am sure they are just beside me. *Keep your focus.* I feel the blood trickle out from both my nostrils. *Keep your focus.* The force outside is so huge, my brain actually hurts. I feel it pulsating like a runner's heart. I can't hold it much longer. I think I scream.

Then it stops. The force outside stops pushing in. I can't stop pushing out.

The door, the front wall, even the roof explodes outward, turning the stone into nothing but particles of powder. I pull back whatever I unleashed, still hearing nothing. The second my power hits me, so does the darkness.

This is a better way to die.

FOURTEEN

THE UPPER HAND

"BEATRICE? BEATRICE ALEXANDER? CAN you hear me?"

I'd answer but the blinding white light flashing in my eyes seems more important. I push it away. Weird, it's attached to a warm hand. With the light gone I can open my eyes, though my focus stinks. I blink a few times and it becomes less fuzzy. Dr. Neill and Will are no longer blurry blobs, just concerned co-workers. I'm in the back seat of a car again. God, my head kills. And what... there's a tube in my arm attached to a hanging bag with blood in it. The scene from the mausoleum comes rushing back to me. From the pain I'm feeling, I figure I must still be alive.

"How do you feel?" God, does he need to yell?

"I have a bitchin' headache and don't shout at me."

"She's fine," Dr. Neill says. "I don't think there's any permanent neurological damage, but we'll do a scan later. The headache should fade in a few days." She looks at me. "What was the last thing you remember?"

"I guess fainting. Again. Can I please get something for my head?"

"Sorry. Not until your blood volume is higher. You lost a lot."

"But she'll be fine?" Will asks, jittering next to me like an expectant father during delivery.

"Few days, good as new. I need to check on the others. Excuse me." She picks up what looks like a giant tackle box and leaves. Will doesn't follow. He just looks at me, waiting for something.

"What? I'll be okay. Just blood loss, possible brain damage, it's nothing. Did we get Wayland?"

"I don't know. His body would have disintegrated with the rest. He was in the cemetery, and the blast took out everything in a quarter-mile radius."

"We could wake Oliver and find out. If he attacks..."

"No, he stays as is."

"Is everyone else okay?"

He sighs. "Irie's in a coma, which we expected. She should come out of it in a few days with no damage. Everyone else is fine, thanks to you. Doc's staying around to fix them up. Carl's going to drive you, Irie, Wolfe, and Oliver to mobile command for tests and further treatment. You might need another transfusion. And please don't fight me on this," he says in a soft voice. "There is nothing more you can do here. You've done enough."

"No argument here. I'm a crappy liar anyway. What's the story, cult lets off bomb in cemetery?"

"That's actually not a bad idea," he mumbles.

I close my eyes and lay my head against the headrest. "Glad to be of assistance."

Will misses his cue to leave. "You saved us tonight. I don't know how, but you did."

"Then give me a raise." And leave me to suffer in peace.

"This is serious," he says. I open my eyes to his somber face. "You saved our lives."

A smile crosses my face. God, even that hurts. "That's my job."

"You're good at it. Born to it." He pauses. "And I am so sorry for earlier. For Oliver, for the kid. I handled it badly. I should have listened to you, and I sure as hell shouldn't have lost my temper. I just saw what he did to you, and I ... " He runs his hand through his hair. "I'm sorry."

"I forgive you."

We stare at each other for a moment, both smiling and neither wanting to look away. I doubt the butterflies in my stomach are from the nausea. I'm such a softie. It takes all of two hours for us to forgive each other with a simple gaze. I'm nuts, I know. I was ready to kill him an hour ago, and now I'm making goo goo eyes. If he kissed me, I'd probably forgive him for anything, even if he killed my cat. I may not be an actual mind reader or have much experience with men, but the sparks between us rival those on the Fourth of July. I am *not* imagining this. He looks away first. "I, um, have a lot to do. I'll let you get some rest. If you need anything ... "

"I'll scream."

Will opens his mouth to say something but closes it. He just nods his head and walks quickly away. Time to test a golden rule. "Okay, if he looks back, he so likes me," I whisper. He takes a few more steps then his head turns back for just a second, a private smile on his face. "Yes!" I flop back in the seat, my face hurting from the huge grin stretched across it. Is it too soon to pick out china patterns?

Not even the stretcher with the comatose Oliver coming toward the car breaks the smile. "What are you grinning about?" Agent Chandler asks.

"Nothing," I say, still smiling.

Agent Chandler opens the trunk. "Wish nothing would make me smile." He clears a space big enough for the body, steps inside the trunk, and pulls the unconscious Oliver into it. The two bullet wounds, along with his other injuries, are now nothing but deep bruises and some dried blood. I doubt even a chain saw could ruin his perfect face. My hand moves to my neck. It's bandaged but still sticky. Hope they stitched it up when I was out.

"You have to get into the front," he says, closing the trunk door. "We need to lay Irie back there."

"Okay." I unhook my blood bag and step out of the car. The moment I'm upright the spinning starts and my knees buckle. Agent Chandler catches me in time and helps me walk to the passenger's side door. I look up. Dear Lord, what a sight. This must be what hell looks like.

For as far as I can see, there is nothing but patches of bright orange flame on top of smoking black ground. Nothing stands. No headstones, no trees, nothing living or undead. Fire trucks, red and white lights flashing, litter the scene with men in yellow suits doing their best to extinguish the roaring flames. A helicopter hovers above, using its spotlight to help the men see. I think maybe I'll avoid Irie from now on.

Agent Chandler pretty much lifts me into the seat and hangs my bag on the dry cleaning hook. He does this without saying a word, and slams the door shut when he leaves. Fine with me, I could use the silence. I close my eyes and rest my head. I don't care if the Creature from the Black Lagoon takes over Chicago, I am so taking tomorrow off. I've been chomped on by zombies, hunted by a werewolf, fought off more zombies, bitten by a vampire, and held off a nuclear blast. Huh, maybe I'll take a *week* off.

The driver's side door opens and closes. I open my eyes to the sight of a gun an inch away from my nose. My eyes leave the barrel and move to its wielder. Fat, sweaty, incredibly peeved-off Walter Wayland. "Oh, come on!"

"Take me to my daughter, bitch!"

"How did—"

He cocks the gun. "Shut up and do as I say, and if you try anything I shoot you and dump your dead friend by the side of the road to burn."

"Okay, just don't hurt us. We'll go get your daughter."

Still pointing the gun, he starts the car. We pull away slowly past the fire trucks and the pile of fiery metal of what used to be our SUV. We aren't stopped or even glanced at. Please let them figure out I'm gone soon. Please.

Wayland drives like an old lady until the fires fade, past the reporters shouting questions, and then guns it down the little road, pistol never leaving my chest. This is not good. I'm in no shape to handle this. When we reach the main road, he stops. "Which way?"

"Uh, left."

He turns the wheel and off we go.

Okay, Bea, think. He's driving, so if I do something we could get into a wreck and there's no guarantee he'll be knocked out. The gun could go off. The gun, the gun ... ugh! I can't think. My head is literally pounding. I couldn't lift a feather let alone slow a bullet. Think. What did Steven say to do in a kidnap situation? Yes, my ex and I had weird conversations like this but never ones about important stuff like our future. My fault for dating a cop. What did he say to do? Um ... make the assailant see me as a real person and he might hesitate to kill me. Worth a shot. "Do you by any chance have an aspirin? I have a real bad headache."

"What? No."

"Damn, I mean darn. Lord, I think I owe my Nana a buck fifty with all the swearing I've been doing. A nickel a curse word."

"I don't care. Shut up."

"I'm nervous, okay? I talk when I'm nervous. My talking isn't going to hurt anything. I can't kill you with words."

"I don't know what you people are capable of. That's a vampire back there, right? I thought they were made up."

"Dude, you raise the dead."

He scoffs. "I knew there were other psychics out there. My grandpa could raise the dead too. I just thought the other stuff was impossible."

"Did your grandpa train you?"

"Yeah, for five summers. Never used it really, until now."

"Me neither; well, not consciously. If I had a nightmare, the bed would float. Couldn't control it though. I never thought there were others like me. Did your wife know?"

He doesn't answer for a few seconds, probably debating if I'm worth the trouble. "Not until the end," he finally says. "Emma knew. Her bird died a while ago and I brought him back."

"That was nice of you."

"He started rotting and I had to kill him again. She was devastated."

"Oh." This conversation is about to take a wrong turn. No death talk. "Well, I'm amazed your wife or anybody else never found out. You're very powerful."

He glances at me. "I am?"

"Oh, yeah. Most necromancers can only raise a couple zombies in a night, and they need rituals. And having power over a vampire is very rare too. You're probably the most powerful necromancer on earth." Ego stroking, the best defense.

"Good for me," he says, not at all impressed.

We ride in silence for a few uncomfortable seconds. The other cars zoom past, oblivious to what's going on. "May I ask you a question?" I finally say. "It's been really bothering me."

"What?"

"Why did you kill your wife?"

"None of your fucking business. Jesus, do you ever shut up?"

"Please. I've been bitten, chased, and nearly fried. You're going to get your daughter. You're probably going to kill me anyways, I just want to know *why*. Was it just the affair?"

He doesn't answer right away. "I didn't find out about that until she died. That son of a bitch Wynn came over all buddy-buddy, and I caught him holding one of her shirts, smelling it."

"So why kill her?"

"Val found Emma. She freaked out. That bitch actually demanded I put her back in the ground. It was my daughter or my wife. Easy choice."

"And Wynn?"

"Thought maybe she told him … and yes, I was pissed he'd been sleeping with my wife. And I knew that if someone came looking, that slut Carrie would be the prime suspect, what with her record and all."

"Good plan; it worked for the most part."

"Yeah, well, you people, or whatever you are, got too close. Had to take you out." He says this so matter-of-factly that I get a chill. Another night of firsts. I've never met a sociopath before.

"And you nearly did. Twice. We thought for sure you were dead from the blast."

"I had another car parked near the back of the cemetery. Just floored it."

"Very smart."

My cell phone rings, startling us both. Wayland thrusts the gun into my stomach. "Toss it out the window. Now!"

I unclip the ringing phone and chuck it. "It's gone, it's gone. Could you please move the gun back a little, you're hurting me." Surprisingly he brings it back to its original position. He's nervous now. I can feel it. I don't know if that's a good or a bad thing. "Thank you. Now look, if they're calling me, then they know I'm gone and they probably know who I'm with. If you kill me, there is going to be a very pissed-off werewolf and a pyrokinetic after you."

"Shut up."

"I'm trying to save us both here. Now, I will take you to your daughter. You can leave with her. I promise I won't stop you. You can disappear into Canada or wherever, but if you kill a federal agent, there will be a worldwide manhunt for you. You won't be able to hide anywhere, let alone if you have a child . . . in her condition." Except he already killed an agent. Please don't know about Agent Konrad's death, please!

"Shut up!" he yells through clenched teeth.

"And if they catch you, you'll either be killed or turned into a science project. And Emma will be incinerated."

He pokes the gun into my stomach again. "I said shut the fuck up."

I guess Q&A is over and I've failed miserably. He's angrier now than before. The second he gets Emma it's a bullet to the brain. I'm too light-headed to run and my power is on the fritz. I can't hold them in anymore, tears roll down my face and all I can do is wipe them away and try not to sob.

"We're here."

We pull up to the trailer and he stops the car.

"My daughter is in there?"

"Yes, but you'll need the codes to get in."

"You know them?"

"Yes."

He raises the gun to my head. "Then give them to me."

Oh crud, I've lost my usefulness. *Think!* "You'll also need my fingerprint to open her door."

He glares at me, gauging if I'm telling the truth. "Fine." He closes his eyes and the prickling starts again. "Arise." In the rear-view mirror, I see Oliver sit up. His eyes are black and dead like a shark's. My dried blood still covers his chin. "Get out of the trunk and come get her."

Like a good puppet, Oliver smashes the glass window of the trunk, making it darn near disintegrate. Just as his feet reach the ground, my door flies off its hinges with metal twisted on metal. Cold hands grab my arm, pulling me out. The needle in my arm rips out and I scream in pain. The blood they just put in rushes back out down my arm in a small stream. The world goes black and I fall down to the grass, clutching my new wound. I can open my eyes but the world is gyrating.

"Pick her up and carry her inside."

Arms wrap around my chest and jerk me from the ground. Oliver has me in a bear hug so tight I can barely breathe. My feet dangle inches from the grass as he carries me toward the trailer. The world keeps spinning.

Wayland opens the unlocked front door and steps in first. "Which way?"

"Left," I say. I'm jiggled up the stairs and into the hallway toward medical.

"Punch in the code."

I have to blink a few times to focus, but I get the code right and the door opens. I'm led in first. "She's in the freezer over there."

Gun still aimed, Wayland walks toward the freezer, examining it. "Where's the fingerprint panel?"

"I lied. You can just open the door."

He doesn't seem to care about the lie. The door opens and a blast of cold air hits us. "Hold her tighter."

Oliver squeezes so tight my ribs make small pops. There's no pain but even less air can pass. The trailer spins even faster. I'm going to pass out.

"Emma?"

She must have been waiting by the door for him. Her daddy. The little girl walks out of the dark freezer into her father's awaiting arms. Her tiny arms encircle his neck and his around her torso. He clutches onto her like a life preserver. "Oh, my baby," he says into her hair. His eyes well up as he kisses her hair. "I love you. I love you so much." There isn't a doubt in my mind those words are true. She grunts, probably trying to say the same thing. This is what I understand. The reason for all of this. Failing the person you love the most and doing everything in your power to make it better.

"I'll never leave you again. Never again. My pretty, pretty girl."

The spinning stops and the whole world becomes crystal clear. I know how to stop him.

I know what I have to do.

There are moments in life that a person can never escape. That change who they are and what they'll become. Mine happened when I was eight. My mom was in love. His name was Leonard, he owned a car wash, and I wanted him for my daddy. He gave us our first home that wasn't on wheels. He'd give me baths. I guess I loved him too. Then I killed him.

One night he came into my room when Mommy was working at the bar. Leonard lay next to me under the covers, kissing and touching me like he did with Mommy. His calloused hands moved from my chest down. I didn't like it. It was wrong. He was only supposed to do that with Mommy. I wouldn't open my legs like he whispered for me to do. I said no, and he slapped my face hard. I whimpered, but I wouldn't let him push my legs apart. I screamed, I cried, I clawed, but he wouldn't stop trying. He almost had my legs open.

A picture flashed into my mind, something from Brian's school book. A red heart, Leonard's, pumping. Something like a jolt of electricity shot through me and passed into him. In my mind I imagined his heart twisting and bulging like that frog Brian put in a vice. Leonard gasped for air, clutching his chest and clawing at it. The picture returned, still twisted and struggling to pump. I didn't see anything but that heart, so I barely noticed Leonard falling to the ground beside my bed. Dead. The heart disappeared when he landed. I blinked the tears away, focusing my eyes. His red, swollen tongue poked out like a dead slug. I didn't scream or cry, I just moved to the corner staring at the dead man, my whole body violently shaking, clutching my knees.

This is how Mommy found me.

She stuck her head in our gas stove a month later.

No.

261

I won't do it. I *can't* do it. Anything but that. *"It's the only way,"* someone replies in my head. He'll shoot me, maybe keep coming after everyone who knows what he is. He will kill again as sure as the earth moves around the sun. Innocent people will die. They already have. I have to.

He just wanted his daughter back.

Walter Wayland picks up his daughter, her head resting on his shoulder. They both look so happy together. So safe. "Isn't she beautiful?" he asks, almost breathless, wet face full of pride.

"Yes," I whisper, meaning it from the bottom of my heart.

"Best girl in the world. How could I let them keep her in the ground?" He pets her hair and kisses her forehead's sloughing skin. Ugh. "My baby girl."

Emma flips her head to look at me. She smiles cheek to cheek. "You have no idea how lucky you are to have her."

"I do know." Wayland looks toward me, his expression turning from pure joy to regret. He sighs heavily, raising the gun to my head. "I am sorry for this."

"Me too."

I close my eyes. God, forgive me.

The human heart has one entry and one exit point for blood, the vena cava and aorta. Just two thin tubes that keep us alive. If you put even a little pressure on either one, the blood can't flow and the heart stops. I put pressure on both.

I open my eyes.

Emma and the gun drop to the floor as Wayland clutches his chest, gasping for air. He falls next to his daughter writhing in pain, small grunts escaping him. His body contorts and convulses. Emma wails, shaking her father's body. The child looks up at me, groaning for me to do something. She's so scared. It breaks my heart. But I can't stop breaking his.

"I am so sorry," I cry.

She looks back at her father, the most powerful necromancer on the planet who just wanted to be with his little girl. He's gone red as roses and has stopped grunting. His fingers fan open when there is nobody left to control them. The eyes close. His swollen tongue lolls out of his mouth to the side. His little girl slumps on top of him, resting on his chest where his now-still heart lies. They're dead. I release the pressure.

The arms clutching me vanish, and I crash onto the ground. Pain shoots through my ankles. Oliver slumps on top of me like a marionette without strings. With my shaking arms, I roll him off me, whimpering the whole time. I can't stand anything touching me right now. My breath ragged, I scoot back until I hit the corner of the room. Walls squeeze my sides as I push my back into the corner, hard. Safe. My whole body shakes violently, and I can't stop it. The sobbing starts as I pull my legs to my chest, holding them to stop the shaking.

This is how they find me.

FIFTEEN

A NEW DAWN, A NEW DAY

To LEAVE OR NOT to leave, that is the question I must answer. It's odd. I labored over the same question over two months ago in George's hotel room. Look where I ended up. The holes in my neck and the one where the needle ripped out both needed stitches, and Doc thinks the bite will scar. My arm with the quarter-size chunk missing will definitely scar. At this rate, if I stay, I'll look like the Phantom of the Opera after a year.

Most of my bags are still packed. A sign. They're sitting open at the edge of the bed just waiting for the rest of my things. Almost every fiber of my being screams at me to pick up and run, not walk, to the airport. I ponder the same old options. Maybe I can get my old job back. Maybe Nana will let me stay in my old room again until I find another apartment. Maybe April will give me my goldfish Scarlett back. I really should go ... but there's a part of me that just won't let me do it. So I've been lying on my cloud bed at the mansion all day locked in battle with myself, neither side giving in.

I was one of the lucky ones who got to fly back to Kansas last night along with Nancy, Andrew, Carl, and the still unconscious Oliver and Irie. Doc came with us to make sure those two didn't die on the way home. She seemed as relieved as we were to get out of Colorado. Patched me up on the plane too. Stitches and a blood transfusion at thirty-five thousand feet. The rest stayed behind for damage control and to deal with the soon-to-be-declared missing Walter Wayland. Nobody spoke to me; nobody has bothered me all day. Nancy chattered on the plane about organizing a memorial for Agent Konrad, so they're probably busy planning that. Me, I hate funerals for obvious reasons. Burying your mother at eight will do that. Agent Konrad's memorial will probably happen after I leave; well, *if* I leave.

My body aches down to every cell, as does my brain. Doc wouldn't give me a Vicodin, claiming I still wasn't strong enough. The aspirin I was allowed did exactly nothing. At least the light-headedness is gone. I haven't moved from this bed since we arrived back late last night. I just can't move. It hurts too much. I haven't even turned on the television, finding the silence comforting. Eating requires too much energy. I just want to go home. So why can't I, darn it?

I watch for over an hour as the light behind the gauzy curtains fades. It's dark now. It's been close to twenty-four hours and I still can't decide. What the hell am I waiting for? A sign? God has better things to do than deal with me.

Someone knocks lightly on my door. The sound filling the silence after so long jars me. I groan. Why are they bugging me now? I don't want to see anyone, but I don't want them to break in from worry. Play the tired weakling and whoever it is will leave quick enough. "Come in."

The light from the hallway spills in first, assaulting my sensitive eyes. I have to squint so I can't make out the features of my guest, only his silhouette. I still know who it is. The expensive cologne gives him away. I should be scared and my heart does skip for a second, but I just can't muster any real fear. He won't hurt me now. Don't ask me how I know, I just do.

"Trixie?" He steps in holding something in his hand. "Would you like me to turn on the light?"

Reflexively, I smooth my braided hair trying to tame the frizzes. "I guess." Before it turns on, I pull the covers up to my chest hiding my blue Oreo pajamas as best I can. He flicks on the light but stays at the open door staring at me. Judging by the way his mouth drops open, he isn't thrilled by the sight. I haven't looked in a mirror but I can imagine what I must look like. Pale, bruises all over, bloodshot eyes. He, on the other hand, looks normal—normal as in gorgeous. No sign of bullet or tree wounds, not a single scratch on him. Heck, even his hair shines like a shampoo model's. Life is so unfair.

"What do you want?" I ask.

He blinks away the gawk, replacing it with a small smile. "I wanted to check on you. And to bring you these." He holds up the plate in his hand. A huge piece of cake, pink frosting rose included. "I can leave it by the door if you like." He brought me cake. My empty stomach suddenly returns from its twenty-four-hour strike. I didn't think it possible today, but I smile. "I will just … ," he says, bending down to put the cake on the ground.

"Oliver." He looks up. "Can you … bring it to me? I'm still kind of weak."

It's his turn to smile. It quickly turns into a smirk. "As milady wishes."

I scoot over a few inches so he can sit next to me. I feel his nervousness now. Him scared of me. That's a laugh. I take the plate, which has an added surprise: a white pill. "What's that?"

"I believe it is called a Vicodin."

My mouth gapes open, and I darn near tear up. "You brought me cake *and* drugs? If you included *Casablanca,* I'd have to marry you." I take a bite of the cake. Dear God in heaven but that is delicious. I haven't had anything to eat in over a day so this just bursts in my mouth like a sugary bomb. I moan, it's so good.

"If that is how you react to food, I hope to see one day how you react to real pleasure."

"Keep bringing me drugs and cake and you may," I say with a full mouth. I take a couple more huge bites. The whole time Oliver watches me with a smile so wide he could double for Julia Roberts. "Quit staring at me, you're making me feel weird."

"I apologize, it is just very hard to take my eyes away," he says seriously.

"Yeah, right. I look terrible," I say, wiping the frosting from my mouth.

"Not possible."

My cheeks go hot with a blush. "Did you just come up here to embarrass me?"

"I came to see with my own eyes that you are in good health."

"I'm—I'll live." I take the pill. "I'll feel much better when this takes effect."

"You are in much pain."

"Yeah, well…" I shrug. "Part of the job, right?"

"Only occasionally. What happened was not a common occurrence, I assure you."

I meet his sincere gray eyes. "I know. And really, I'm okay. I know you wouldn't deliberately hurt me. And besides, now we know I can kick your butt."

"This is true," he says with a small smile. "Regardless … " His eyes dart to my bandaged neck. "You still saved my life."

"What?"

"Andrew told me. I—and you—"

"It wasn't your fault."

"Even so. You showed great strength and compassion. More than I deserved."

"You need to stop always complimenting me. It'll go to my head."

"I am being serious." My smile drops. "You kept me safe after I took your blood in a most vicious manner. You should fear me and instead you invite me into your room without a moment's hesitation."

"You're … my friend. You help me out, I help you out. It's what we do."

He considers this for a moment. "Friend. I suppose I can live with that for the moment." His devilish grin returns. "I hope this reciprocity can continue in other areas."

I pat his hand and, meeting his eyes, I say, "Not now, not ever." I fall back into my pillows. "Besides, I probably won't be around by tomorrow."

"I thought we put that nonsense behind us."

"That was before," I shake my head. "Look, I'm just not cut out for this. My eyelashes hurt. I'm literally scarred for life. And hacking up zombies and fending off vampires is not my idea of fun. No offense."

"None taken, my dear."

"I'm just not strong enough. I'm not ... *brave* enough."

"That is nonsense and you know it. Give me a real reason and I will personally drive you to the airport."

I don't say anything for a few seconds. Admitting is the hardest step. I can't look at Oliver. "I killed someone and I'm scared because ... honestly ... I don't even feel bad about it. I squeezed his heart until it stopped, I watched him die in agony, and I hate to admit it because I know I'm not this kind of person, but I have no guilt. I should feel guilty, and if I don't ... my brother was right. I am a monster."

It's Oliver's turn to remain silent. I still can't look at him; I don't want to read his face. "Look at me, my dear." His cold hand on my chin moves my gaze to his. There is no emotion in those gray eyes. "I have lived a long time. I have traveled this world three times over and seen things done to others that would drive people to madness. I know monsters, and I can say as sure as night will turn into day, *you* are no monster. In the short time I have had the privilege to know you, you have displayed more compassion, more bravery, and more strength of character than I have seen from a human being in close to a century, if not ever. You are a good person. You killed a madman who surely would have done the same to you. There is no cause for guilt, so do not be ashamed."

I look away. "But—"

Oliver moves my head back. "Look at me. I know you are frightened, and I would love to tell you it will never be that awful again, but I cannot. This is a dangerous job, and you will be called upon to take lives in order to save others. But because of you, countless lives will be saved, including those of the people inside this house who care for you and respect you. But I can promise you this: never again will you feel like an outsider. Never again will you be called a freak, because you, my dear, are no freak. *You are a goddess.* And if anyone ever makes you feel any less than that, I will rip their spine out," he says, so seriously that I suppress a chill. He cups my hand. "You belong here. With us. And I believe that you know it."

I let out the breath I've been holding. Tears join it. I wipe them away. He's right. I haven't wanted to admit it, especially not to myself, but … I've never felt so alive. So free. Except for those few moments with Walter Wayland, I've loved being here. I've faced monsters and won. I can be myself, warts and all. I need that. Never realized how much until now. I'm not alone anymore. "If I die, I am so coming back to haunt you."

"You can even watch me shower."

A huge laugh bellows from me, releasing all the tension bottled up. I can't stop laughing! I laugh for seconds, barely able to breathe, my body wracked, all the while Oliver stares at me. "Oh! That wasn't even funny!" It takes several more seconds but the laughs lessen so I can actually breathe. I'm such a loony toon!

"Do you feel better now?"

"I think the Vicodin's taking effect," I chuckle.

"It would appear so."

I finally stop chuckling. Oliver still smiles, watching me. I just can't help myself. Blame the drugs later. I grab his white shirt by the collar, pulling him down to me, wrapping my arms around his neck, and squeezing tight. He's stunned for a moment, stiff, but quickly lifts me off the bed and hugs me back. His neck smells wonderful, like cologne with just a hint of that man smell. "Thank you," I whisper.

He releases me enough for us to face each other, our eyes locking. His eyes seem hungry, but in a way that sends electricity and heat to my nether regions. I forgot how much I missed that feeling. The butterflies flutter too. He is so beautiful, like something out of a dream. Radiant. We stay locked like this for a second until his lips move toward me. Mine plump in anticipation. He's going to kiss me, and I don't even mind. I want him too. More than anything.

But his lips meet my forehead in a tender kiss. Huh? A strange mix of relief and regret wash over me. More regret than relief though. "You are welcome," he whispers into my forehead. His arms leave my body, and I fall back into my pillows. My heart still goes a mile a minute. Hope he can't tell. It's the drugs. Yep, I'll stick to that.

"We are about to have a visitor," he says.

Sure enough, someone knocks on the door. I have the strongest urge to push the door down on them. I resist it. "Come in," I say pulling the sheets up again.

My face grows hot the moment Will steps in. The butterflies flap even more in my stomach. I really need to get my hormones in check. "Hi, Will," I say in an overly high voice.

His eyes move to Oliver. "I hope I'm not interrupting anything."

"Not a thing," Oliver says. "Trixie here was just throwing herself at me. I had to fend her off."

Now my face is on fire.

Will just scoffs. "Right."

Oliver pats my hand and stands. "I will leave you two alone, unless William does not think he can defend himself against our goddess here."

"Goodnight, Oliver," I say through clenched teeth.

With that smirk, he walks to the door. "Remember, William, she is yours … for now." He bows to us both and shuts the door.

I roll my eyes. To think I almost let him kiss me. This Vicodin is dangerous stuff.

"Was he bothering you?" Will asks. He doesn't move from the door.

"No more than usual. When did you get back?"

"Just a minute ago."

Which means he came straight up to check on me. My ego swells to double its size. "Everything okay?"

"Yes, coverup in place. They believed us as much as they can. How are you doing?"

"Better. Much better, thank you. A little sore. A little hungry."

He steps toward me. "You haven't eaten?"

"Just cake."

"Well, um, dinner's ready downstairs. Everyone's down there. I know they'd love to have you. We didn't get to have your welcome dinner."

"No, we didn't, did we? Seems ages ago. I mean, I'd love to but I don't think I can walk all that way. I just took a pill and I'm a little—"

"I'll carry you," he says eagerly.

I bite my lip to stop my smile, but I don't think it works. "Okay. Grab my robe." I toss the covers off.

He picks up my fuzzy pink robe off the chair and hands it to me. I put it on and the moment the knot is tied, he wraps his warm arms around my back and legs, lifting me as if I weigh nothing. I feel like Scarlett O'Hara when Rhett carries her up the stairs, except I have a small smile on my face the whole time I'm in his strong arms. He smiles down at me and I up at him, savoring the feel of his warm chest. A girl could get used to this. One gorgeous man bringing me cake in bed, another carrying me to dinner.

This job certainly has its perks.

THE END

Coming Fall 2012 from Midnight Ink

BROTHERLY LOVE

FOR THE PAST TWO MONTHS—God, has it only been that long?—I've been fighting the good fight against creatures of the night, and you know what? Sitting in this Starbucks, drinking an overpriced coffee, surrounded by people chatting with friends or working on their novel, it dawns on me: There isn't one normal thing about my life anymore. I don't feel a part of this world anymore. I live in a mansion in the middle of Kansas with psychics and monsters, jetting to places like Butte, Montana, and Trenton, New Jersey, in order to stop homicidal, preternatural nasties. Now, I drink my stale coffee in diners, sitting across from either a werewolf eating more meat than a pack of lions or a vampire grinning at me with bloody teeth. Meeting for coffee with my brother—who I almost accidently killed not too long ago—is the first ordinary thing I've done in a while. How sad.

To say Brian hates me is an understatement. He blames me for killing our mother eighteen years ago. On a bad day, I blame me too, but I didn't force her head into our gas oven, but try telling Brian that. As if the "you ruined my life" thing wasn't bad enough, he's also deathly afraid people will judge him for associating with me. To a man who models everything—including what brand of socks he buys—on other people's reactions, having a sister who can pick up a Buick without lifting a finger doesn't exactly seem normal. When he was living just a couple of hours from me, he never spoke to me or bothered to call. Yet, when I'm three states away, I get a call to meet for coffee. Is it any wonder my imagination is running overtime? He can't stand to be in the same room as me, and now he's volunteered to do it. Therefore, our Nana must be dying.

I've been waiting ten minutes, growing more apprehensive with each passing second. I don't know what to expect. The last time I saw him, I almost killed him. Before judging me too harshly, just know I couldn't help myself. Really. I had no control over my curs—sorry, I mean gift. He was calling me nasty names and I blew my top, and came close to literally blowing his off too. No excuse, I know, for almost giving someone a brain aneurysm, but it was bad. Really bad. Thank God there was no permanent damage, at least to his physical self.

I pull down the sleeves of my turtleneck and make sure the high neck covers the two circular scars the size of pencil erasers. The long sleeves cover the chunk of skin missing from my arm. I feel like a walking hot dog in the July heat, but it'd be just too hard to explain what happened. As far as my family knows, I'm running a daycare center for a national company and living alone in a crummy apartment. I wish the government could have come up with a more glamorous cover story. I could have driven Oliver's Jaguar convertible to this meeting instead of a seven-year-old Camry. At least then I could console myself with the fact my materialistic brother would turn green with envy.

I see him before he sees me. I tense as he walks up to the door, cell phone stapled to his ear. The person on the other end says something very amusing judging from the smile on Brian's face. Smiling, a good sign. He closes the phone a moment later, and walks in. He catches sight of me, and the smile disappears. Bad sign. This is going to be rough.

Avoiding my gaze, he walks around the other tables to my booth. He's out of place here in his gray suit and red tie, surrounded by people in jeans and tank tops. They probably think he's here for a business meeting. It'd never cross their minds that we're brother and sister. Well, technically we're half brother and sister. Different fathers. Brian's was some musician who dumped our mother when she was five months pregnant. All she told me about mine was that he was British and "the one night we shared together was the most magical of her life." In other words, I am the product of a one-night stand with a man whose name she never bothered to get. Both Brian and I inherited her brown eyes and thin lips, but the similarities stop there. He has straight medium brown hair cut short and is a thin six feet tall. I am stuck with frizzy, wavy auburn hair and a sturdy peasant build that no amount of time on the treadmill can alter. I should be the one who hates him.

As he slips into the chair across from me, I smile. It isn't returned. "I didn't order for you," I say.

"It's okay," he says, "I can't stay long."

"Oh. Why?"

"I'm just here to get some contracts signed. Hugh Jackman is filming a movie here." Brian's in entertainment law. He can name drop with the best of them.

"So … Nana's not dying?"

He scoffs. "Of course not. Why would you even think that?"

"I ..." I shake my head. "I don't know."

"She wanted me to check on you."

"Oh."

"You look ... well. Lost weight?"

"Yeah, a little."

He glances at his watch. "Good. Good."

"You look good, too. How's the job going?"

"Fine. Yours?"

"Fine. Interesting."

"Oh."

We sit in silence, neither looking at the other. The elephant in the room practically trumpets. It's my elephant, I'll put it down. "I was surprised to hear from you. Glad, but surprised. I thought—"

"Look, whatever you thought, you thought wrong. I am here simply because Nana asked me to come. Nothing else." His phone chirps. When he reaches for it, the gold ring on his left hand catches my eye. "And now I can tell her you're alive with all limbs intact." He opens the phone, scanning the message. "Damn it!"

Brian stands, flipping the phone closed. He doesn't give me so much as a glance as he walks out of the shop. I'm not even worth a good-bye.

I sit glued to my seat, my mouth slack. That's it? I drove an hour to have my brother take one look at me and leave? Now, old Bea would hang her head, slink back to her car, and cry her eyes out. She'd make excuses for him. She'd let him get away with this. But the new and improved Bea picks up her purse, and follows the jerk out.

I catch sight of him right away in the parking lot. "Brian!" He glances back but continues walking. I run after him, but he refuses to stop walking.

"Leave me alone," he says, still walking.

"No. We need to talk. I'll follow you to your hotel if I have to!" This stops him. I've hit his Achilles heel, introducing his oddball sister to his colleagues.

He spins around. "I have nothing to say to you."

"Well, I do!"

He folds his arms. His anger rolls into me like a tapeworm. I hate when emotions hit so unexpectedly that my stomach doesn't have time to prepare. "Then speak!"

"Please don't yell at me! God! I'm trying to apologize here!"

"Right," he scoffs. "Well, I don't want your fucking apology. You tried to kill me."

"That was an accident."

"I could give a shit! I had to miss two days of work because I was in the fucking hospital being poked and tested! I still get migraines, and will for the rest of my life. You scared the hell out of Nana. So, your apology means shit to me." He starts playing with his wedding ring. "The only consolation out of the whole fucking debacle is you moved a thousand fucking miles away from everyone I care about so you don't almost kill them too. And if you give a damn about any of us, you'll stay there and never come back. We don't want you back."

"Does that include your wife?"

His righteous anger disappears, replaced with the look of a young boy caught looking at Daddy's secret magazines. "Nana told you?"

"Your wedding ring did." He stops playing with it. "You got married and weren't even going to tell me about it?"

He clears his throat, refusing to look at me. I've learned through two months of investigating that this is a sign of a guilty man. He squares his shoulders to regain some dignity. "I didn't want you there."

"Is it Rennie?"

"Of course." He'd been dating Renata Goldman, daughter of Hollywood producer James Goldman, for almost two years. She's the one who got him the entertainment lawyer gig at Sunrise Studios. That's one other thing Brian and I have in common, our love of old movies. Nana's influence. I've only met Rennie a few times in passing. Skinny, rich, but Nana says she's sweet. It's just typical, my brother marries into the movie world, and I don't even have time to watch them anymore. Life stinks.

"And you're going to find out eventually, so I might as well tell you now. She's pregnant."

This time I'm the one with the surprised look. "Really?"

"Yeah. She wants to have it. I couldn't convince her otherwise."

I'm taken aback. "Why would you?"

He scoffs again. "Why the fuck do you think? It could be like you. Some … freak. Just what I need in my life, another you." He sneers. "Just stay away from us, okay?" He glances at his watch. "Shit, I'm going to be late now. Don't follow me." He turns his back and walks away. I don't move until the car, a Mustang convertible, pulls away. He doesn't look back once. Good. He doesn't see me wiping away stupid tears.